Mind Games

A HARP SECURITY NOVEL

Laura K. Curtis

BY LAURA K. CURTIS

THE HARP SECURITY SERIES
Twisted
Lost
Echoes
Mind Games

THE GOODY'S GOODIES SERIES
Toying with His Affections
Gaming the System

For Elina, for all the dinners past and those yet to come

CHAPTER 1

MAYBE IT WAS just an attack of paranoia. The excitement of inching closer to a personal goal combined with the worry she wouldn't complete it in time for it to be truly useful wore on her day by day. She ducked her head, sipping her coffee, and glanced around but couldn't spot anyone on the busy street paying her unusual attention. The hot dog vendor to her left tipped his cap when she accidentally caught his eye, and she smiled back at him as she passed, but the creepy feeling at the back of her neck persisted, and she shivered beneath her wool peacoat. Maybe she should tell Clive about it. Her boss believed strongly in intuition. He wouldn't blow her off. Or call her crazy.

Unless, of course, she was. Twenty-eight was a little late for the onset of schizophrenia, but nothing was outside the realm of possibility. She didn't hear voices, didn't feel crazy. But would she know? She stopped at the light, waiting to cross, and scanned the crowd of New Yorkers around her. Maybe at home in Larchmont, her quiet little town in Westchester County, she might notice a new face suddenly popping up around her regular haunts, but here . . . every face looked both strange and familiar. She knew none by name, but all by type: the messenger, the thirtysomething businesswoman, the homeless man—they all wore uniforms.

She crossed the street and turned up the block toward her lab. Two guys unloading a delivery van blocked the sidewalk. More uniforms—navy blue chinos, heavy, puffy jackets over white shirts, baseball caps. She started to detour around them, but the one standing by the back doors grabbed her. He slapped a rag across her nose and mouth, and the reflexive breath she sucked in tasted of chemicals. She threw her coffee in his face, but she was dizzy and he jerked out of the way. At least the movement gave her a chance for fresh air. She sucked in a huge lungful and screamed, but his hand clapped over her mouth and he hefted her toward the back doors of the van. She slammed her foot down onto his instep, and he grunted but didn't budge.

"Get her in!" his companion shouted. Jane braced her feet on the rear bumper of the van and pushed backward as hard as she could, biting at the fingers over her mouth. She toppled to the pavement atop her attacker, but a second later he was back on his feet.

And then he was gone. A huge, blond figure dressed all in black had him in a choke hold. Her savior sported aviator-style sunglasses that hid his eyes, and wild, long hair coming loose from a ponytail. Enough scruff to qualify as a beard and mustache hid his chin and lips, but she could see his snarl nonetheless.

"Run!" he yelled, and she took off, her legs wobbly and her head spinning. A hundred feet down the sidewalk, she ducked into the lobby of the building that housed her lab at Applied Human Intelligence and slid down the wall until she was sitting on the marble floor, her heart slamming against her ribs and her blood buzzing through her veins.

Breathe, Jane. Breathe.

"Dr. Evans, are you all right?" The security guard squatted down next to her, his hand resting on the butt of his gun. "What happened?"

"I'm okay, Roy. A couple of guys tried to mug me." Or something. What had that been, anyway?

"Should I call the police for you?"

She was considering the question when a noise from the door had the guard rising to his feet.

"Yes, you should call the cops." The blond giant stood framed in the doorway, his massive shoulders seeming even more overwhelming than they had outside. The light formed a halo around him, obscuring his features, and Roy's hand went again to the gun at his hip.

"It's okay," Jane said. "He helped me." But again, she shivered.

"That's all well and good, but I'd prefer if he kept his distance until the police get here."

"Not a problem." The man raised his hands. "But you should call Mr. Handler and tell him his nine a.m. is going to be delayed if I have to stay down here that long."

Roy hesitated, so Jane forced herself to her feet and walked over to the security desk with him. The blond took a single step farther into the lobby, and she finally got a look at his face. He'd taken the sunglasses off, and something about the shape of his face, despite the beard, despite the hair, knocked at doors in her mind.

"Hello, Jane."

He smiled, and she knew. Oh, holy hell. He'd been beautiful in college, the way young men could be beautiful, but now . . . she didn't think there was a word for what he was now. Overwhelming.

"You've changed, Eric."

"You haven't," he said, but there was humor in his words.

"You two know each other?" Roy asked.

"We did. A very long time ago." What on earth was he doing here? And meeting with Clive?

"Dr. Evans was my tutor in college," Eric said with that wry half smile that still tilted his eyes down at the corners and put an extra beat in her heart.

"And Eric was our star baseball player."

"Hardly. That was Wayne. I hear he's playing in Chicago these days. I was nothing more than a halfway decent catcher and a power hitter."

False modesty? He'd been a phenomenal ballplayer. Even she, the consummate nerd, could see that much. But this was not the time to argue. "And now? What brings you here?"

"Now I work for a company called Harp Security. And I have an appointment with your boss to talk about providing you with a personal security detail. Past due, if what I saw this morning was any indication."

"Why don't you two go on up," Roy suggested. "I'll send the police when they get here."

"Sounds good," Eric said, and Jane nodded.

She led him to the elevators and up to the second floor, which housed the conference room, Clive's office, and several smaller meeting rooms. Ruth, Clive's assistant, hurried forward when she saw them.

"Oh, my," she said, holding out her hands to Jane. "Roy just called up and said you'd been mugged!"

"Yes, but I'm okay. I swear, Ruth."

The older woman cast a long, assessing glance at Eric, taking in his shaggy hair, bearded face, black leather jacket, T-shirt, and black cargo pants.

"You're Eric Sorensen?"

Eric inclined his head, ever a man of few words. But Jane watched his eyes, which never stopped moving, surveying the space the way she'd watched him survey a baseball field in his youth.

The door to Clive's inner office opened, and the man

himself stepped out. "Jane! Do come in and sit. What a terrible start to the week. Can Ruth get you anything to calm your nerves?"

"No, honestly, I'm fine." Her hands shook, but she kept them clasped together. "I just need to clean up. But then I want to talk to you about what made you think I needed security."

⌒

YEAH. ERIC WANTED to talk about that, too, though he suspected he had different questions. Jane would ask how her boss had come to hire security at just the right moment, whereas Eric wondered why the guy had waited so damned long. If Jane hadn't been, well, *Jane*, he'd have shown up on time for his meeting with Clive Handler, only to be too late to prevent Jane's abduction.

Jane hung her jacket on a coat tree in the corner and disappeared through a small side door he assumed led to a restroom, and Clive ushered him into a large office decorated in brass and mahogany. *Swank.* Not showy, but expensive as hell. Built and decorated to impress, possibly even intimidate. But working for Nash Harper, Eric had come into contact with fancier. He stood at parade rest and allowed Handler to see his appraisal.

"We've developed a couple of very nice patents," Handler said. "One of them paid for this building. Our work is used worldwide."

"I guess so," Eric said, lowering himself into the seat Handler indicated as the other man sat behind his desk. The position put his back to the door, which made his spine itch, but it couldn't be helped.

"And we're hoping that Dr. Evans's research will result in at least one more."

The bathroom door opened and Jane appeared. She'd cleaned the smudges of dirt off her face and put her streaky red-blond hair—which he remembered as being carrot orange when they were younger—back up into a sloppy knot, a loose approximation of the classically perfect one he'd followed that morning. Her hands—and knees—had steadied, but the flush of adrenaline still rode high in her pretty cheeks. Eric rose and pulled out the second chair, then rested a hand briefly on her shoulder as she sat before returning to his own seat.

"What happened this morning?" Clive asked.

Jane started to speak, but Eric covered her hand with his own, feeling the tremors she tried to hide shudder through fine-boned fingers. "If I know cops, and I do, Jane's going to have to tell her story all morning. You can get it then. I am more interested in *your* story. Why did you hire us? And why wait until yesterday to call HSE?"

Handler's eyes flicked to Jane, then back. "As I explained to Mr. Harper, I became concerned about Dr. Evans's safety when her research assistant disappeared."

"Dani?" Jane leaned forward. "You told me Dani had gone back to Argentina for a family emergency!"

"That's what I believed at the time. But on Saturday night I called her mother to ask how everything was going and found out Daniela hadn't gone home at all. There *was* no emergency. I considered that she might just have run off, but she's very responsible."

"And you thought she was in Argentina because of an e-mail, is that correct?" Eric asked.

"Yes. I got an e-mail from her last Sunday saying she

wouldn't be in Monday because she had to fly to Argentina, that she wasn't sure when she'd have Internet access and she would get back in touch when she could. But on Saturday evening, I was sitting at home looking at our schedule and I realized that in the five days she'd been gone, we'd already fallen behind. I either had to have her back or I had to fill her shoes pretty damned quick. So I called her mother. You know the rest."

"Oh, my God." Jane wrapped her arms around her body. Eric stood, shrugged out of his jacket, and placed it around her shoulders before returning to his seat. Her cheeks were pale, the freckles standing out starkly against her too-white skin, and he caught a flash of tears in her eyes.

"You called the police," Eric said. There would be time later to assess Jane's response. First, he had to get all the facts. "What was their response?"

"They didn't take me seriously. Dani's young. Twenty-five. They figured she wanted to get away from her responsibilities for a while."

"She wouldn't," Jane said. "She wasn't depressed or overwhelmed by the pressure here. She could have taken a vacation if she wanted one."

"I know," said Handler. "But the police were also concerned that we work with a lot of psychoactive chemicals. They insisted on a full inventory of our drugs."

"She would never steal."

"And she didn't. I came in yesterday and did the inventory myself. But if she didn't go to Argentina, and she didn't, and she didn't run off with hundreds of thousands of dollars' worth of drugs, and she wasn't the victim of random violence — which the e-mail indicates she wasn't — then what *did* happen to her?"

"You believe it has to do with your company, not with her personally." Eric had found the idea highly unlikely when Nash explained the situation, but if a single drug patent could pay for an entire building in Manhattan, maybe the idea wasn't so far-fetched after all.

"It's the only explanation left. Dani's a responsible girl. She wouldn't voluntarily leave Project Calm in the lurch."

"Project Calm? That's what you call the work?"

Clive nodded. "It's not very exciting, I know, but every project needs a name."

"Okay. But you didn't hire Harp to get Dani back."

Handler cocked his head. "There's no ransom demand. No clue who took her. I didn't think there was much point. I . . . brought some influence to bear . . . and the police will do whatever they can to find her. Right now, my concern is for Jane."

"And why is that?"

"Because we're set to sell the Project Calm patent—the patent for the schizophrenia medication we've been develop-ing—to a major pharmaceutical company next Wednesday. We just have one last bug we have to work out first. I shouldn't have contracted before we had definite results, but things looked promising, so I went forward. And then we hit the snag. We *need* Jane. As I said, we needed Dani, too. We're all working a lot of overtime because she's not here. I can pull researchers off other projects to do the actual testing, to per-form the experiments, but the interpretation—only Jane can do that. Dani was preparing it all for her. If someone wants to stop me from selling this drug—if they have another one they're close to bringing to market, for example—this is the way to do it."

"Your buyer won't wait?"

"My buyer will give me substantially less if I can't meet my date. And if someone else *can*, I might get nothing. So, yes, I called HSE to protect Jane."

And Nash had given the file to Eric because Nash knew everything, and remembered, when he saw Jane's information, that Eric had gone to Duke at approximately the same time. Beneath half-shut lids, Eric examined her. He'd lied when he told her she hadn't changed. That wild, carroty hair had been tamed to a fiery elegance, and she seemed . . . smaller. Of course, he'd grown. And, too, she'd been so forthright and almost, well, pushy, when he'd studied with her that somehow, over the years, she'd become a larger physical presence in his memory.

And then she spoke, and he realized that whatever else had happened to her, she hadn't lost any of her pushiness.

⌒

"So you hired me a bodyguard? And it didn't occur to you to call me and tell me about it?" Jane couldn't decide which was worse.

"It's just a couple of weeks," said Clive. "I planned to bring you in this morning after I met with Mr. Sorensen. Once we work out the kink in the new drug and sell the patent, everything will go back to normal."

"And until then?" She glanced over at Eric, sitting impassively, his big frame dwarfing the chair. In college he'd been neat, clean-cut, presentable. Manageable. Now he was anything but. Enormous. Ragged. Rugged. He hadn't bothered to pull back the hair that had come loose from his ponytail, and a few strands lay along his cheek, caught in his beard.

She squeezed her fingers together to stop herself from reaching out to brush them away. Would his hair feel as silky as it looked? And that little pirate's beard . . . She'd never found facial hair appealing, but on him it totally worked.

She dragged her attention back to Clive. "How is this supposed to work? Eric comes to work with me every day, then escorts me back up to Westchester every night? What's he supposed to do the rest of the time? Surely you don't think I am in danger while I'm in the lab."

"No, of course not. Mr. Sorensen won't have to shadow you while you're here, but you're too vulnerable in the rest of your life. The subway, the train—you don't even live in a doorman building."

Clive's befuddlement over her preference for living in a tiny house in the suburbs, where one could not have hot and cold running Thai food delivered 24/7, usually amused her, but now she found it irksome.

"You don't expect him to move in with me, for God's sake, do you?"

"That's the way personal protection usually works, yes," Eric said. Jane noted his relaxed posture and the tiny smile playing on his lips. That sexy mustache did nothing to hide his expression, especially when his eyes lit like lightning in a clear blue sky. Confidence practically oozed from his pores— regardless of her protests, he would get his way. Clive signed both of their paychecks, and once he decided on something, he was immovable.

"I'm good at my job, Jane. Nothing about your life has to change all that much. You'll hardly even know I'm here."

Right. Like she could miss six feet, two inches of overwhelming male suddenly invading her space.

"It's not even two weeks," Clive said again.

"Yeah, okay." It wasn't gracious, she knew, but not even Clive understood how much of her free time she devoted to her studies. The research was her life, and Eric would interrupt it.

He turned those piercing blue eyes on her. "I won't be any trouble, I promise. I even cook. You can think of me like a live-in chef."

"Well, that wouldn't be so bad," she conceded. "I pretty much exist on takeout."

"See, it will all work out." He grinned, and she could almost believe him. At least with Eric, she could ask what he'd done in the years since she'd last seen him, then let him do the talking. She didn't have to worry about watching his eyes glaze over with boredom when she rambled on about her research.

"I want to check out the building," Eric said. "Before I agree to leave during the day, I need to be sure you're safe. Roy downstairs doesn't provide much security."

"We're a research facility," Clive said. "We don't normally have to worry about security. Our researchers *do* testify at trials, and we help out with both civil and criminal cases when we're hired to, but we've rarely come in for threats or harassment."

"What, exactly, do you do here?"

"Well, Jane works in our hard-science division. As far as criminal work goes, that means DNA, document aging and typing, chemical analysis, that sort of thing. But of course her primary focus at the moment is drug development, which brings her into a crossover with what you'd probably call our 'soft science' division. We do forensic psychology, handwriting analysis, that sort of thing. Developing a new drug for schizophrenia requires a handle on both chemistry and psychology."

"And you fund all this through . . . ?"

"We have a well-managed endowment. We also sell patents, as we plan to do with this one, raise money from grants, and we charge for our services, although that is on a sliding scale. Law enforcement doesn't pay as much as a wealthy client who wants to, say, bolster a divorce case with analysis of letters from his wife to her lover."

"But that means you have people in and out of the building all day."

Clive considered. "To a certain extent, I suppose that's true. But they don't go to the lab. They wouldn't have access to Jane."

Eric grunted. He was going to be a pain in the ass, she could already tell. Hot as hell, but a pain in the ass nonetheless. He'd been her best student in college, her favorite because he was so eager to learn, willing to do whatever it took to internalize the concepts. That stubborn determination lost a good deal of its appeal when turned on her.

"What about travel?" Eric asked. "How do you get back and forth from home? Clive said the train and the subway? That's far too exposed—no way to control your surroundings."

"Well, we could drive, but the traffic in the city is dreadful. And if you want to talk about lack of control, you haven't seen anything until you've seen the West Side Highway at rush hour. You'd be a sitting duck."

"One of the other HSE agents will drive. As you point out, I don't have enough flexibility if I'm behind the wheel, though I take exception to 'sitting duck.' We're pretty good at getting out of tight spots, even on crowded highways."

"Just like that?" Jane stared at him, then at her boss, then back to Eric. "You don't ask Clive whether he minds paying for two guys? You don't need to call to find out whether anyone else in your organization is available?"

"Let me worry about finding a driver."

"But the cost . . ."

"I can afford it," said Clive, selling her out in a single sentence.

The intercom buzzed and Clive answered it. "The police are here to speak with Dr. Evans and Mr. Sorensen," said Ruth.

Great. Just great. She wasn't going to get anything done today, but her fingers itched to get back to work.

"Don't worry," Eric said, "you can go first. But then I need you to go to the lab and stay there until they're done with me. Deal?"

"Deal."

⌒

THE POLICE ALLOWED Clive to sit in on her interview, though they sent Eric out so his impressions of the incident didn't taint hers. As soon as he left, the room seemed to chill a few degrees, and she pulled his jacket tighter around her, sinking into its warmth and safety. The interrogation seemed to take hours as they went over and over the morning's incident, asking questions for which she had no satisfactory answers. *Who would want you out of the way?* She had no idea except for what Clive had surmised about their work. *Would anyone pay a ransom for you?* No. Though Clive had spoken up at that point and said he most certainly would. *Did you possibly have a stalker?* No. Absolutely not. *What did the men who tried to take you look like?* It had happened fast. So damned fast. The one who had grabbed her had a port-wine birthmark on the left side of his face. But other than that . . . they were average. Like any guys you'd see loading a truck in New York. One wore a Yankees hat. They both wore bulky jackets.

Which, now that she thought about it, was a little odd. It wasn't all that cold. Commuters like her wore coats and jackets, but men lifting heavy items should have been hot. Why hadn't she noticed? *What did the van look like?* Dark colored. *Did it have writing on it?* She didn't remember. *Did you see anything inside?* She didn't remember.

And then she went up to the lab and had to answer the same questions, this time from concerned colleagues, when all she wanted to do was bury herself in work. At least Stella had a couple of samples for her to look at, so Jane could stare through a microscope and ignore the palpable air of curiosity around her.

Rashid and Sam went down to the deli and brought back egg salad for her, but she waited until everyone else had eaten before taking her lunch—and a swath of notes to study—into the break room to eat. Although the wall separating the break room from the main lab had a window running along its full length and even a glass insert in the door—nothing in the lab being developed for privacy—the separation from her colleagues allowed her mind to settle slightly. The notes were a ploy to keep people from disturbing her, but as usual she became absorbed in her work, and she didn't even glance up as people came and went. Science. Her savior.

All good things come to an end, however, and eventually Eric sat himself down opposite her, stealing her attention away from her work.

"I've organized us a ride back to your place. We leave at five."

She checked her watch. It was already almost four. "I never leave at five. Do you know what the traffic will be like? I'm usually here at least until six, six thirty."

"Uh-huh. And you get here, what, eight o'clock, eight thirty?"

"Exactly. Depends on which train I catch."

"Well, from now on your schedule is about to become more varied. Those guys this morning knew when you would be coming to work; it was barely eight fifteen when they grabbed you."

Which was, oddly, the first time it had occurred to her that *he* had been there, too. Very early for a nine o'clock appointment.

"Not that I don't appreciate your help, but if you were supposed to see Clive at nine, what were you doing here so early?"

"I got your file last night. I take my job seriously, so I checked your address and followed you from your house this morning."

"You . . . what?" How could she have missed him? He'd been on her train and her subway and she hadn't seen him? How was it possible? He was so *big*. So *unkempt*. So full of life. Before the fight he would have been neater, more put together, but he still should have stood out, if for no other reason than that wickedly sexy beard, three shades darker than his golden hair. Had she become so isolated, so caught up in her own thoughts that she didn't notice a frankly gorgeous man? She knew Clive and her coworkers considered her more machine than human, but when had she deteriorated to the point she no longer even window-shopped? Dani had been right to push her to get out more, to come have margaritas with her and two women who worked in another lab on Thursday evenings.

"It's easier before the weather gets warm," Eric said, as if trying to make her feel better. "Everyone looks the same in bulky clothes. I can be inconspicuous when I want to."

She studied him as she would a foreign life-form put beneath her scope. He'd neatened the ponytail of wild blond hair and reclaimed the jacket she'd left in Clive's office when the police were finished with her. Maybe, maybe she did remember him from the platform. But he'd been absorbed in a newspaper, just like everyone else, and when he got on the train he didn't sit near her.

"I almost lost you in Grand Central," he continued. "But since I knew where you were going, it wasn't so bad. And I wasn't afraid they'd make an attempt in the station, not with the enormous police and military presence they have there. It's about the safest place in the city."

"So you followed me this morning, but that's not good enough for the next two weeks?"

"It almost wasn't good enough this morning. I barely held off those three guys to give you time to get away. I couldn't hang on to any of them for questioning."

"Three? I only saw two!"

"Yeah. The other one was the driver. He got into the fray just when I was gaining the upper hand."

"But you're okay?"

His eyes crinkled into that heart-melting smile. "I'm fine. Taking on thugs like that is all part of the job. I'm just pissed off I couldn't keep one of them here. If I'd been willing to shoot him, I could have, but pulling a gun in the middle of Manhattan is to be avoided whenever possible. They didn't try to kill me, and they didn't pose a threat to anyone else on the street."

"Oh, my God."

"It's okay. Really. But Trey will be here at five to pick us up, so you should gather what you need before then. I've arranged for him to leave the car with a friend of ours who lives not far from you. Trey will take the train back down, and Jake — the one who lives near you — will drive us for the next ten days."

"Just like that?"

"Just like that."

CHAPTER 2

Trey collected them from the building's back entrance. New York City always posed extra challenges for personal security with local law enforcement's unwillingness to allow drivers to wait for clients and the fact that the average city driver's aggression level was high enough to send up constant warning flags.

But Trey could be aggressive himself, and a single look from his pale, don't-fuck-with-me eyes was usually enough to have others steering clear. He was waiting when Eric escorted Jane from the building, leaning against the SUV, which was parked flagrantly illegally in front of a fire hydrant.

For his part, Eric would have been happier if he could have had his gun at the ready for the three feet of sidewalk between the building and the reinforced steel cage of the SUV, but that was another issue with security in New York: unlike the hellholes of the world where he usually operated, randomly pulling a weapon in the city was apt to create panic. So he kept Jane close to his body, sheltering her as much as possible as he hurried her to the vehicle.

"Trey's a former Army Ranger," he explained to Jane once they were safely on the road and he'd made introductions. "If anything happens and I leave the vehicle, you need to do exactly as he says, okay?"

"You don't really believe I'm in danger in transit, do you?"

God save him from reluctant principals. "After this morning, I believe it's better to be safe."

"Okay." Jane pulled a sheaf of papers from her shoulder bag and settled in for the ride.

In the rearview mirror, Trey caught his eye and raised an eyebrow. Eric could read the question all too easily: *Is this woman for real?* If he didn't know Jane, he'd be asking the same thing. But Jane wasn't stupid. Far from it. So he figured she was deliberately avoiding worrying about the danger by focusing on work. He wanted to tell her that she didn't have anything to fear, that he and Trey and the whole HSE team would make certain she came to no harm, but he couldn't. He had a great deal of confidence in himself and his team, but they all knew that safety was an illusion. A necessary one for most people, a convenient fiction that allowed them to get through the day. Reality was far less palatable: pass the wrong man at the wrong time on the wrong street and you were dead. Simple as that.

Plus, a scared principal was alert, more apt to obey commands. Relaxed principals, those too sure of their own safety or power, were careless.

They arrived at Jane's without incident, and Eric made her remain in the car with Trey while he cleared the house. It didn't take long—the place was small, and he wasn't exploring, just making sure no nasty surprises waited inside. Still, by the time he came out, Jane and Trey were chatting. He held the door and Trey walked her up.

"Pleasure meeting you, Doc," Trey said as he handed her off, as if they were at a fucking dinner party rather than part of a security detail. "You take care, now."

"I will. Thanks."

Eric locked the door once Jane was inside and followed her into the living room. He hadn't taken the time to examine the place in his initial sweep, and when he opened his mind to the house as a residence rather than a battlefield, he found it nothing like what he would have expected. Perhaps it was her analytical, scientific mind, but when he'd waited outside in his car that morning—a car that HSE had neatly retrieved when he realized Jane planned to take the train—he'd pictured clean lines with plenty of high-tech devices. Instead, inside the small, shingled house, plush, comfortable furniture was covered with an abundance of brightly colored throws.

"Southern blood," she said, watching him take it in. "I get cold easily. And crocheting helps me turn off my brain. So I churn out a lot of afghans."

"I like it," he said. And he did. In many ways, it reminded him of his childhood home. Though his mom had bought sale blankets to lay across the backs and seats of their threadbare furniture, the cozy, patchwork effect was similar.

She led him up a narrow set of stairs to where three doors clustered around a landing.

"That's my room," she said, jerking her thumb at the left door. "I have my own bathroom. So the guest bed and bath are all yours." She cracked the center door so he could see the bathroom, then opened the third to reveal a small bedroom. Here, too, he saw the evidence of her handiwork. A multicolored blanket—an afghan, she'd called it, though the homey item was about the last thing the word "Afghan" brought to mind after his stint in the military—covered the bed, and bright, framed posters hung on the smooth, cream-colored walls.

He dropped his duffel at the foot of the bed. He had no intention of sleeping in it, but Jane didn't need to know that yet. If she was at risk—and no one paid Nash's prices without a clear and present danger—he wouldn't be sleeping at night. His examination of AHI that afternoon proved the lab secure enough that he could catch a few hours during the day while she worked once he impressed upon Jane the importance of never leaving without him. She would fuss and insist his vigilance was unnecessary, but she was wrong.

What was Jane's bedroom like? He hadn't examined it in his brief survey beyond making sure it was safe, and now he wished he'd taken longer. Did she surround herself with pillows and blankets? He'd known a couple of guys who claimed they refused to date women who had more than two cats or three pillows, and Eric had always figured they might be onto something. Women like that didn't want a guy who was gone all the time, a guy who'd as soon shoot someone as talk about their relationship. But despite the pillows and needlework, Jane had been plenty independent in college, and that didn't seem to have changed. She had a great job, her boss obviously valued her, and she clearly didn't believe she needed a man for anything.

Did that mean she didn't have one?

No reason she shouldn't. He hadn't paid attention to her looks in school. Not only was she far too young, but also, he'd been too focused on what she could do for him, how much he needed her help to maintain his GPA and thus his athletic scholarship. But she'd grown into a gorgeous woman. Petite, with perfect curves and that wavy flame-colored hair he would bet fell almost to her waist when not wrapped into a complicated knot on top of her head.

"Do I have something in my hair? A dust bunny?" She touched the knot.

Oops. "No, not at all. I was just thinking."

She looked at him a long moment, as if waiting for him to tell her what about—not like that would be happening this century—then turned away and led him back downstairs.

"That's about it. Down here there's this room, the dining room that you see through there, and the kitchen, which has the smallest half bath known to man."

He laughed. "I guess if I am going to be the chef, I'd better see the kitchen."

"I was just kidding about that. Seriously, you don't have to cook for me."

"No worries. I like it. Probably the same as your yarn. It keeps me busy, lets my brain unwind, relaxes me."

"Okay, then. If you're certain." She pushed through the swinging door into the kitchen, and once again a profusion of colors shone out, this time from mismatched dishware behind glass-fronted cabinets.

He must have made a face, because she shrugged. "The lab's all white and steel. I like color."

"I do, too. It's just a side of your personality I didn't expect." He opened the refrigerator and glanced at the contents. "If you have pasta, I can throw that together for tonight. I'll shop tomorrow while you're at work. Is there anything you don't eat?"

"Not much. Organ meat. Ground meats of any kind. Eggs have to be at a minimum cage free. If I am cooking for myself, I prefer local and organic, but I'm not fussy if someone else is willing to do it for me."

"Fair enough. Let me know when you get hungry, and I'll start it up. Won't take long."

"Oh." She twisted her fingers together, and a line formed between her brows. "You're cooking. We can eat on your schedule."

He grinned. "If you say so. But I warn you, I eat all the time." She blushed, and he wondered what she was thinking. "In fact, I'll start dinner now, if that works for you."

"Sure." She showed him the spaghetti, spices, pots and pans, then walked back out to the dining room, where she began clearing papers off half the table. Some she piled onto the already leaning stacks next to her laptop, others she carried up the stairs. Did the woman do nothing but work?

Dinner took no time to prepare, and soon he was serving up plates of spaghetti with garlicky *pomodoro* sauce and freshly shaved parmesan.

"That smells amazing," Jane said, shutting down the computer and moving to one of the places she'd set at the other end of the table. He settled opposite her, and they ate in companionable silence. Occasionally, Jane's eyes would stray to the laptop, and he imagined she spent most of her nights in front of the screen. But when they were done eating, she didn't insist on going back to her work. Instead, she helped with the dishes, then took a seat on the couch and pulled out some kind of lacy yarn project and a crochet hook.

"Seriously?"

She glanced up at him from under her lashes, and it sent a shaft of heat through him. Was she actually flirting with him? *No. Impossible.*

"What do you mean?" she asked.

He shook off the distracting thought. "I mean, you can't possibly expect me to believe you aren't itching to get back to whatever's on that computer."

"It's fine. I can do it in the morning." But her eyes strayed back to the table.

"Uh-huh. Why don't you tell me about it, then?"

"About . . . ?"

"Your work. Unless your personality's undergone a seismic shift, that's what's calling you."

Her lips twisted into a rueful grin. "That's the nicest way of calling someone a nerd I've ever heard."

"Not a nerd. Driven. And damned good at explaining things to people who don't get them. So explain your work to me. And remember I know nothing about medicine."

Her brow wrinkled and she bit her lip. He fought down an utterly inappropriate reaction to the sight. What the hell was the matter with him? He never got distracted on a job.

"Okay, well, I guess that's as good a place to start as any," she said. "When most people hear the word 'medicine,' they think of doctors. Physicians. But physicians don't create drugs; chemists do. The process is long. I'd be here all night even explaining it, all the phases and trials. But to simplify it to the very basics, you start in a lab—chemists, biochemists, cell biologists, people like that—working with tissue and cell cultures, trying to provoke a specific reaction. Sometimes you get what you want, sometimes you get nothing, and sometimes you get a totally unexpected reaction.

"While getting your expected reaction is good, getting the unexpected can be fantastic. That's where breakthroughs happen. You're looking for a cure for one thing and find a cure for something else entirely." She frowned again. "Have you ever heard of a drug called Phenergan?"

"Can't say I have."

"It was developed as an antihistamine. And in the UK, that's still its primary use. Over the counter. But in the US, it's virtually never given for allergies. It's prescribed, often in hospitals, for violent or persistent nausea or to control spasming coughs."

"Huh." He was less interested in the drug than in her mobile face and the fine-boned hands she used to shape her explanation.

"Anyway, once you have a reaction that you want to investigate, you patent your drug. There are a number of different kinds of patents, and I'm not even going to pretend I under-stand patent law. You'd have to ask Clive about that, and he'd probably refer you to the lawyer he keeps on retainer.

"The drug-research-and-development community is a small one. You file a patent application, people will know. But the patent protects you, gives you time to continue your research without fear that another company will steal the compound out from under you. That's the point at which most people begin to publish."

"Most people?"

"Developing a drug is enormously expensive and time con-suming. If you start publishing and speaking at conferences, you can attract investors, get grants, or even find a buyer."

"Wait. A buyer. That's what's going on with the drug you're working on, right?"

"Yes. As I said, all this starts in a lab. And it doesn't even have to be a particularly big lab. But eventually there will be animal trials, human trials, distribution . . . things one small lab cannot handle. Large pharmaceutical companies don't develop all their drugs in-house from the ground up. They buy patents at all phases of development."

"Thus, the deadline."

"Exactly. We meet the deadline or our work, well, it won't be wasted because it's a good, solid drug we're developing, but it may not pay for itself. We may have to sell the patent for less than it cost Clive to develop it. That wouldn't crush AHI, but it would be a serious blow."

"So who would have it in for the company?"

She shook her head. "I can't imagine. Surely you asked Clive that."

"I did. He gave me a short list of companies doing the same sort of work and a couple of personal enemies. I've turned them over to Nash, and he'll investigate them. I want your take."

"No one. Seriously. Clive's a bit abrasive, but I'm surprised that he could come up with even two personal enemies. He's all work and no play, or at least that's been my impression of him." She took a deep breath. "And besides . . . those men this morning, they wanted to kidnap me. It would have been easier just to kill me. And that would have been more effective in stopping the work on Project Calm as well. So why try to take me instead?"

Tremors shook the hands holding the wool and hook. Eric put his arm around her and drew her close. It was unprofessional, but professionalism had gone out the window the moment he'd seen her name on the front of Nash's file. He owed her. The life he lived, the money he sent home to help his family—he'd have none of it without his degree. And he wouldn't have the degree without her help.

Of course, there was more to his behavior than gratitude, too. He hadn't gotten where he was by lying to himself. Jane appealed to him on every level. The way she'd handled herself during and after the attack had impressed the hell out of him. Generally, principals fell into two categories: either they broke down completely when the illusion of safety fragmented, or they expected their safety detail to take care of every little thing. Jane had done neither. She'd fought her attackers, run when he ordered it, and then had gone back to work, scared but determined.

Brains, beauty, guts—the woman had it all. The years had only made her better, stronger, and he would personally rip the lungs out of anyone who tried to hurt her, even if he weren't being paid to do so.

He gave her a little squeeze. "I wish I had an answer for

you. A lot of people—even ruthless ones—draw the line at murder. The only thing we know is that whoever is after you doesn't want to kill you. That's excellent news." But it bothered him. Yes, the guys who'd attacked her had been wearing hats pulled low, and bulky clothes that hid their true shapes, and that was *good*. If they hadn't there would have been no doubt they meant to kill her. But New York City was a city of cameras; there was a chance the disguises were merely precautionary.

"Was Dani working on anything else, or just assisting you?"

"Since we ran up against the issue with the deadline, she's been with me. Maybe six weeks. Before that, she was on a team developing a phobia medication."

"But Handler didn't think she was taken because of that. Phobias aren't profitable?"

"Oh no, that's not it at all. If they can create a compound that works the way Clive hopes, it could be generalized to many other kinds of distress. Imagine if you had a drug that helped patients get over crippling social anxiety. Or reduced PTSD-induced fears. Not a general antianxiety medication that would leave a patient's senses dulled and their reaction times slowed, but one that targeted precise triggers. There's nothing like that on the market. It has the potential to be enormous."

"So how did Handler know, before this morning's events, that they'd come after you?"

"You suspect *Clive*? But he hired you."

"I suspect everyone. No, he's not at the top of my list, but the timing seems strange."

"I guess it was the combination of Dani being on my team for the last six weeks and the looming deadline. Plus, they haven't talked to *anyone* about the phobia drug yet. As I said, the R&D community is a small one. If you don't have a patent yet, you don't want anyone to know what theory you're working on. If they take your theory, they might get to a drug before you. So right now, Project Phobos is completely under wraps while Project Calm is recognized in the community. So it would have to be Calm that attracted someone to her."

Eric grunted. "Indeed."

⌐∾

JANE ROLLED OVER and flipped her pillow for the hundredth time. How could she have imagined having Eric in her space wouldn't disrupt every single part of her life? Of course, the morning's incident wasn't helping her insomnia, either. Whenever she remembered the grip of those hands on her body, cold sweat prickled over her skin. But the memory of Eric's hands . . . That brought a completely different—if just as unsettling—emotion. He'd spend the day entirely focused on her. No one had ever looked at her quite that way. He hadn't lost interest when she talked about her research, even the research that wasn't related to her current predicament.

It had been ten years since they'd seen each other, but instead of crowing over his accomplishments in that time—and from the look of him and the self-confidence that oozed from every pore, there must have been many—he encouraged her to ramble on about what grad school had been like. And then med school. And when she ran out of stories, he'd stroked her hair away from her face and told her to go to bed.

He hadn't come upstairs. She'd left him watching a documentary about World War II in the living room, but when she stepped out of the shower, she could no longer hear the television. She sat up and looked to the crack under the bedroom door and could see the distinctive blue and white flicker of light that indicated the television was still on. So he was sitting down there watching with no sound? Did he plan to sleep at all?

Somewhere, glass broke. Odd. It sounded as if it had come from down the hall. An instant later, an explosion rocked the house, echoing into footsteps pounding up the stairs. Her window broke—the dim light revealing a pipelike canister—just as her door crashed inward.

"Down!" Eric shouted. He landed on her, knocking her flat. She fought back instinctively as he pulled a pillow over her face and yelled at her to hold her breath. And then the world shook a second time, this time the explosion much closer, much louder despite the muffling of the pillow.

"Come on!" Eric grabbed her hand and pulled her from the bed before the sound fully faded. He dragged her down the hall to the guest bedroom, then over to the window, where she saw a chain-sided emergency ladder piled. Using the rungs to clear the broken glass from the window, he peered outside, then tossed the ladder over, hooking it to the sill.

"Let's go," he said, and Jane didn't hesitate. She slipped one foot over the sill and felt for the first rung, then scampered down it as fast as she could while he slid down right on top of her.

They hit the ground almost simultaneously, and Eric pressed her flat up against the wall, his big body between her and any possible danger, while he scouted both directions before hustling her through the low hedge that separated her yard from her neighbor's. They dashed across the Martins' lawn and around the corner of their house. The Atwells across the street had a large weeping willow surrounded on three sides by dense shrubs, and, one hand low on her back, Eric urged her into that corner of the yard, where the shadows and greenery protected them from view. Voices sounded in the street, and she wanted to stick her head up to look, but he held her back.

"Your neighbors, your alarm will have alerted the police. In a minute, those guys will have to take off."

As he predicted, moments later she heard an engine rumble to life and tires squeal away. Still, Eric wouldn't let her up. "Not before the police arrive."

She shivered as the cool night air cut through her pajamas—thank God she wasn't the silk-nightgown type—and rubbed her hands over her arms. Eric wrapped his arms around her, pulling her into his body, and instantly heat surrounded her. How could he be so warm in a T-shirt? He felt like an electric blanket. Or like a generator with his steady, thumping heart beating against her back.

What would he think if she turned and buried her face in his neck? Suddenly, she wanted to know if he smelled as good as he felt. She'd never had the faintest desire to do such a thing in the past, and a hot blush crept over her skin as she imagined doing so now. But, God, he was so warm. So solid. So utterly in control. And she was totally out of control—of her life, and, apparently, her body, which wanted to run from the danger, but only if he came, too.

Sirens sounded in the night, and two police cars screeched to a halt in front of her house.

"Stand up slowly," Eric said, his warm breath tickling her ear and setting off disconcerting and inappropriate fireworks. "And don't move. They'll be on full alert, and you don't need to get shot because you startled them."

Sure enough, as soon as they were visible above the low hedges, the officer standing outside the house talking on his radio called out to them.

"Tell him it's your house, but stay put until he tells you to move."

She did.

"Come over here," said the cop. "Both of you. But slowly, and keep your hands in sight."

The moment Eric stepped away from her, Jane felt his loss like a physical blow as the cold night air bit into her once more. The cop asked them for identification, and she told him hers was inside.

"Wallet's in my back pocket," Eric said, hands hanging loosely at his sides. "You can get it or I can."

"She can," the cop answered. "Slowly, Miss."

Jane twitched. She hated being referred to as "Miss" in that faintly derogatory tone. Not that she insisted on "Doctor," but even "ma'am" showed a fine amount of respect. Or, since they'd obviously checked ownership of the house, he could have gone ahead and called her by name.

Gritting her teeth, she reached into Eric's back pocket and drew out a black leather wallet, warm from his heat and curved by years next to his body.

"Cards on the right will tell you what you need to know," Eric said as she passed the wallet over to the cop.

Another officer came out of the house just then and pointed a flashlight at Jane and Eric while the first guy examined Eric's ID. He pulled out not only Eric's New York State driver's license, but also another card she didn't recognize.

He frowned. "You carrying?"

"Not at the moment," Eric replied.

"Gun in the house?"

"Yes. Upstairs. Duffel bag in the second bedroom."

"Not a real useful place for it," the second cop observed.

Jane bristled, but Eric just shrugged. "Wasn't supposed to be that kind of job. And as you can see, I didn't need it to keep Dr. Evans safe."

"That's your job? Personal security?"

"You saw my ID."

"Harp Security does more than personal security."

"Well, in this case, yes. I am Dr. Evans's bodyguard. And I would appreciate it if we could get inside, out of the street."

"All right, then."

They walked up the three steps to Jane's front door, then into the house, where the other two officers were standing in the living room.

"I still need to see your identification," the first cop told her. Jane grabbed her handbag off the coffee table, took out her license, and handed it over. He examined it carefully, then passed it back to her.

"I don't think there's any need for all of us to stay," said one of the men who'd been inside. "I was just telling Billy you guys can take off. We've got it from here."

Billy — Cop Two, who'd come outside while they were talking to Cop One — muttered something under his breath, but he and his partner took their leave.

"Shall we sit?" asked the one who'd dismissed Cop One and Cop Two. "The detectives will be here shortly, and I know it's frustrating because they'll want you to go over everything again, but I need to get some information for the initial report."

"I don't want to sit in here," Eric said. "Too many windows. How about the dining room?"

"Sure thing." The cop led the way, and Jane took three

whole steps before she realized her computer was missing from the table.

"My computer!"

"You had a computer here?"

"Yes. A laptop. With attached hard drives. Oh, fuck, *everything's* on there." Her stomach roiled. Sure, all her data was at work, too, and the computer backed up to the cloud constantly so she wouldn't lose anything, but she had no idea how to actually set up a new computer from her cloud backup or how long such an operation would take. Eric settled his hands on her shoulders, and she leaned back against the solid bulwark of his chest. How had her life gone so wrong so quickly?

"Financial data? You need to change passwords or anything? We can wait while you do that on a smartphone or something if you need."

"No, it's nothing like that." She looked at Eric. "All the research, random thoughts and ideas, stuff that doesn't mean anything to anyone but me. Why would anyone want it?"

"That's a damned good question," he replied, hands smoothing down her arms.

"The detectives are on their way," the officer said, "but let's do a quick walkthrough before they get here, and you can see whether anything else is gone."

By the time Jane had ascertained that the thieves had taken nothing but her computer, the detectives had arrived. Her nose was cold, her throat clogged with inexplicable tears, and exhaustion dogged her. Her answers to their questions were undeniably snippy, and at one point Eric slipped from the room and took her favorite thick gray and pink crocheted shawl from the back of the couch. He tucked it around her as he had his jacket earlier. This time, however, as he sat down he took her hand and chafed it lightly between his before lacing their fingers together.

"Are you about done?" he asked the detective. "Dr. Evans has had a long day. I need to get her out of here."

"To where, exactly?"

"I can't tell you because I don't know. If you need to speak with her, call the office and Nash will pass along a message."

The cop frowned. "That's not how we do things, Mr. Sorenson."

"For now it has to be. Honestly, it's best for everyone that way."

Eventually, the detectives took off and she and Eric were alone.

"Pack a bag," he said. "You won't be back until this is over."

Jane pulled her suitcas e from the closet beneath the stairs and carried it up to dump it on the bed. "Where are we going?"

"Didn't you hear me say I didn't know?"

"Yes, and I didn't believe you. Even in college, you were all about strategy."

He shrugged. "It's not precisely a lie. We're going to stay with a friend who occasionally contracts with HSE. He and his fiancée have a place about a half an hour north of here, but I don't know exactly where."

She slipped the throw off her shoulders and folded it carefully before putting it into the bag. No one cared what she wore to work, so the only important outfit was the one for the press conference where they would announce the sale of the drug, if that even happened: gray suit, cream silk blouse, appropriate shoes, even pantyhose. Everything else she tossed in willy-nilly, barely counting to be certain she had enough underwear.

"I have to change."

Eric looked up from his cell phone, where he'd been tap-ping away on the screen. "Go for it. Jake's already here."

In the bathroom, she shucked her pajamas and pulled on a pair of jeans and a T-shirt with a cartoon of a giant microbe on it, along with a zippered hoodie. She gathered her toilet-ries into a travel bag and was out the door in under a minute. With a last look around her room to be sure she wasn't miss-ing anything vital, she snapped the suitcase shut. Eric lifted it from the bed, then led the way back downstairs, where Jane picked up her crochet project bag. No doubt about it, she was going to need the calming influence of a hook in hand.

CHAPTER 3

Outside, the big black SUV idled at the curb. Her neighbors were probably sure she was some kind of criminal. First the explosions and the alarm, then the police, now this. So much for her quiet, anonymous life. Eric handed her into the car, threw her case into the trunk, and crossed the street to stoop next to the hedge they'd hidden behind. A moment later he stood and returned to the car. When he slid into the passenger seat, she realized he was holding a gun.

"I thought you told the police your weapon was in your duffel."

"One of them was. I didn't feel like wasting time explaining why I was carrying, or waiting for them to take the gun and run ballistics on it while trying to see whether it matched anything those guys might have fired with the flashbangs in the house."

"You play fast and loose with the truth." *Way to whine at the guy who saved your life, Jane.* But weren't they all on the same side?

"I tell them as much as they need to know, and I don't lie unless I have to. But you're my first priority." He introduced her to his friend Jake, then turned in his seat so he could fix her with that icy blue gaze. "What's going on, Jane? This is more than a simple delaying tactic. They really want you. And they took your computer, which means they want your thoughts, your ideas as well."

"You're thinking corporate espionage?" Jake asked.

"Aren't you? It's the only thing that makes sense."

"Dammit." Jake pulled the car over and made Jane get out. Eric got out, too, and stood beside her. In the dark, on the side of the road, she wished he'd take her hand again, but instead of reaching for him she pulled the sleeves of her hoodie down over her fingers. When Jake joined them, he was holding a gadget that reminded her of the wands airport personnel used. He waved it over her head to toe, then made her turn around so he could do her back.

"Do you have a purse or anything?"

She nodded.

"Get it."

When she had collected her purse and project bag, he used the wand on them and it immediately began beeping.

"GPS," he said. "Those boys want you badly. They must have seen the purse in your house and figured there was a good chance you'd take it. Same with your phone. We ditch the bug and pull the phone's battery right here. You have a backup of your contacts?"

"Yes. On my computer—well, on the cloud backup of my computer, now."

"Good. We can get you a new laptop and a burner phone at my place."

She handed over her purse, and he dug through it until he found a device no larger than a ticket stub inside the inner pocket. She'd likely never have noticed its presence. He dumped it on the side of the road, ground his heel on it, and then pulled the battery out of the back of her phone. Only then did he pronounce her "clean" and allow her to climb back into the vehicle. To her surprise, Eric slid in next to her rather than returning to the passenger seat.

"How you holding up?" he asked as Jake pulled back onto

the road. "And don't tell me you're fine, because I can see you're not. Tell me what you need."

"I don't know. I'm . . . in shock, I think. It still doesn't seem possible that this could be happening to me. But it is." She picked a piece of fluff off her jeans with shaking fingers. "I'm not handling it well."

"You're handling it better than most would in your position. You should focus on the normal stuff for a while. Tell me and Jake exactly what you're working on so we can get a handle on this. Neither of us knows squat about patents or chemistry, though, so keep it simple like before."

She composed her thoughts. This she could do. "How much do you know about schizophrenia?"

"Almost nothing," said Jake. Eric nodded.

"Okay. Well, first of all, despite the media portrayals, schizophrenics are hardly ever dangerous to anyone but themselves. They have to be medicated to keep them in the mainstream of society, to allow them to hold down a job, pay bills, stuff like that, but if they stop taking their meds most of them aren't apt to go out and murder someone. And we have a number of effective treatments. The problem is that the most effective class of drugs for treating schizophrenics—neuroleptics—have a number of unpleasant side effects, both physical and mental. Between that and the fact that they are feeling 'normal,' schizophrenics often stop taking their meds.

"We don't know what causes schizophrenia. That is, we know there's a genetic component, but we can't fix it or prevent it. As with most mental illnesses, what we do with medication is symptom alleviation, not a cure. So the ideal drug would be one that would allow patients to live symptom free without debilitating side effects. Under Clive's direction, AHI has taken a two-pronged approach to the problem. First, a new base drug, a different chemical compound that would still act as a neuroleptic. Second, an additional compound to alleviate the tics, rigidity, and fogginess that occur for so many schizophrenics on current treatment regimens."

"Sounds logical."

"It is. And we were well on our way to a new drug, one that could change a lot of people's lives, which was why Clive went out and found a buyer. But we ran into a snag that's making it difficult to meet the deadline."

"And that snag is?"

"You said you're not chemists, so this is going to be tough. But basically, the secondary compound isn't reacting properly to the primary compound. We know what we want it to do, and it's *almost* doing that, but when we raise the dosages to the necessary therapeutic levels, something in the neuroleptic makes the secondary drug react badly."

"The theory behind this, could it be used with a different primary? Maybe someone else is working on the same thing and wants your research, wants you to help them finish it before Clive finishes his?"

"The theory is pretty basic. Doctors have been giving patients drug cocktails for years. A little of this, a little of that to get the desired result. This is just more sophisticated. Any decent chemist should be able to help them develop one they already have if they're close enough, but I suppose taking me off Clive's project and stealing our research notes might help them."

She finished her mini-dissertation just before Jake turned off the highway, and they drove in silence down a winding road to a gate set into a tall stone wall. Jake punched numbers into a keypad set into the wall, the gate opened, and they drove through. A dirt road wove through fields of grass toward an old-fashioned farmhouse lit from both within and without. They were still a good hundred yards out when what sounded like an entire pack of wild dogs began barking, yipping, and baying.

"Stay in the car for a minute," Jake said when they pulled up to the house. He slid out of the SUV and jogged over to a fenced area with a low shelter inside it. "Hush," he commanded, leaning over the fence and letting the dogs smell him. Immediately, they quieted.

"Impressive," Jane said.

"It is. I've never been out here, but Jake's a good guy. He and his fiancée take in kids who need temporary placement. There are a bunch of them living here at any given time. You can't see it from the front, but they added a big wing to the back for them. According to Nash, it caused something of a ruckus when they tried to get it past the planning board—this is a pretty ritzy area, I guess, and the idea of a bunch of fosters running around didn't hold a lot of appeal."

"I can imagine."

She was going to ask what had changed their minds, but Jake returned and opened the door to let Jane out. Eric went around and grabbed her suitcase from the trunk, and they all trooped inside.

The scent of baking cookies hit Jane hard. It was so utterly unexpected that she stopped with one foot inside the door and the other out, causing Eric to bump into her.

Jake laughed. "That'll be Tara. Over the past year, she's become convinced that everything's better with chocolate chip cookies. So when we have a late-night run or a complicated case, she bakes." Although he smiled, a note of strain underlay his tone.

"So what you're saying is that after a couple of years, you'll have to quit any fieldwork because you'll be too fat to pass a physical?" Eric slapped Jake on the back.

Jane didn't see the humor. "I apologize for bringing trouble to your door."

A woman with a pile of blond hair stuck up in a knot on the top of her head came out of the kitchen, followed by a striking black cat whose green eyes never left her. "Don't be ridiculous," she said. "When trouble doesn't find us, we go looking for it. It's sort of a way of life when you're a former police officer engaged to a former FBI agent." She strode toward them and held out a hand. "I'm Tara Jean Dobbs. Just call me Tara or TJ." She gestured to the cat. "This is Gomez. He runs the house. And you must be Dr. Evans."

"Jane, please."

"Great. So, Jane, do you want to go straight to bed, or would you prefer to stay up and unwind for a while?"

"I don't think I could sleep just yet, if you don't mind."

"Not at all!" Tara plopped down in one of the chairs, and Jane realized she wasn't wearing any shoes. "Sweetheart, will you take Jane's stuff up to the green room while I get to know her? I made up the blue room for Eric."

"Your wish is my command," Jake said, dropping a kiss on the top of Tara's head before he grabbed Jane's suitcase and led Eric upstairs.

"I need you to tell me if this isn't really okay," Jane said once the men were gone. "I saw Eric in action today in my boss's office, and I know he can kind of bulldoze over objections. I don't want to cause a problem or be a burden."

A buzzer went off in the kitchen, and Tara invited Jane to come along while she switched out the cookies for a new sheet.

"Look," she said once the new cookies were in the oven, "I meant what I said about inviting trouble. It's part of what we do. Both of us are tired of law enforcement, but we still want to make a difference. We have kids staying here. We run a shelter for abused women—and that's not for public consumption, by the way—as well as taking in problem children for short periods of time while their parents are in rehab or the like. It works because Jake and I make sure we are on the same page. When Eric called Jake to ask him if he could drive you guys into the city tomorrow morning, we discussed the possibility of you staying here. I won't have the women or the kids endangered, so if it looks as though your kidnappers are going to come after you guns blazing, we'll find someplace else for you. But for tonight, for the next couple of days, you'll be fine here."

"I'm not sure what to say. Thank you."

"Here, have a cookie. They're better before they get cold."

The guys came into the kitchen discussing timing and strategy for the next morning. Jake put a phone on the table in front of her, then went to stand behind Tara, his hands massaging her shoulders.

"I put a laptop on the bed in your room," he told Jane. "It's less than a year old and completely clean. Already hooked up to the house wireless, so all you should have to do is log in to whatever backup service you use and start restoring from your backup."

"Wow, thanks. You just have a spare computer lying around?"

Tara grinned and tilted her head back to look up at Jake. "I know he doesn't look like it, but my fiancé is a certified geek."

Jake shrugged with an embarrassed half smile, and a peculiar emotion clutched at Jane. They were so obviously happy, so obviously in love. The closed circle was beautiful to look at, but it only emphasized for her how little human contact she had in her own life. Dani was the closest thing to a true friend she had, the only one with whom she shared even a fraction of the hopes and fears in her head. Her only connection to what she considered "reality," the life outside the lab, the kinds of things normal people did every day.

And now Dani was missing. How much *did* HSE charge? Could she hire them to look for Dani? Clive paid well and Jane had fairly inexpensive tastes, so she had a bit put away.

The buzzer went off again, and Tara took the last tray of cookies out of the oven and transferred them to a cooling rack. She yawned.

"Okay, you guys, I am going to bed. I'll be up early in the morning, so I'll see you then. If you want anything to eat or drink, take it. If you finish anything, leave me a note. The kids eat us out of house and home, so we go to the grocery pretty much every day."

Jake followed her up, leaving Eric and Jane alone in the kitchen. Immediately, Jane got up to do the dishes. Eric followed.

"I'll dry," he said, pulling a cloth off a stack by the farm sink.

It took only a few minutes to wash the cookie sheets and spatula. Jane rooted around and found a big rubber container to put the cookies in, and then they washed the cooling racks, too.

"Time to grab some shut-eye," said Eric. "I already told your boss you wouldn't be in until ten at the earliest. Not only do you need the rest, but we have to vary your schedule."

"You could have asked first." But it was a pro forma objection. Under normal circumstances, she hated people telling her what to do, but the situation had spiraled so far out of her control so fast that she appreciated him jumping in and taking over. His obvious experience and comfort with extreme conditions calmed her.

"Sorry. I'll probably irritate the hell out of you with that. Feel free to call me on it. It won't make me change my mind, but if I have time I'll explain to you why we're doing things the way we are. Fact is, we usually ask clients to turn their lives over to us without question. But then, we don't often work with people we know."

"Is it strange for you? Working with me?"

"Yeah, it is. That's why I was downstairs tonight instead of right outside your door, or even in your room. It's also why I haven't read the file Nash compiled on you. If you were an average client, I'd know every man you'd ever dated and how those relationships ended—in case the assaults turned out to be personal rather than professional—whether your family had money that siblings or cousins might be after, all sorts of things. But I asked Nash to evaluate any possible threats and apprise me of them instead of me reading the whole file."

"And he didn't find any?" Of course he wouldn't. She didn't inspire that depth of emotion, and she was sure the kind of research his company did would reveal that. Which made her very glad Eric hadn't read the file himself.

"Nope. So for the rest of it, you'll have to tell me anything you want me to know. Just like normal people do. Later, though. For now, you should really get some sleep." He led her upstairs to a room painted a soft, sandy brown with forest green drapes and bedding. Her suitcase sat next to the four-poster bed, and her purse and crochet bag lay atop the dresser.

"The bathroom's through here," Eric said, opening a door. "And my room's on the other side of it, right through there."

"And you think we're safe here?"

"Absolutely. With the exception of HSE headquarters, there's no place better. I can even sleep here—that's how safe you are."

"Okay, then. Eric?"

"Hmm?"

"How much do you guys—Harp Security—how much do you charge?"

"Nash makes those decisions, but I don't believe there's a standard rate. It has to do with how many operators he has to assign, what kind of resources they'll need, how dangerous the gig is. And, quite honestly, what Nash thinks you can afford." He laid a big, rough hand along her cheek, and she resisted the urge to rub her face against his palm like a cat. "You're worried about Dani?"

Jane nodded.

"I asked Nash to put the geek squad on her trail when I called in this afternoon."

"You did?"

"I saw your face when Clive was talking about her. She's a good friend, isn't she?"

Was she? Certainly, she was the closest thing Jane had, which made Jane herself a terrible friend for not trying to find out about the supposed family emergency in Argentina. "She's one of the few people I can relate to. The scientific community is still very male focused, and Dani had it harder than most because she's gorgeous. Really. She put herself through grad school modeling, which pissed off a lot of her female colleagues, and her grades pissed off the men. I guess you could say when she came to work at AHI, we sort of decided we were kindred spirits. I don't have the looks, but starting out so much younger than the rest of the team and female . . . I understood where she was coming from. I can't believe I've been so focused on work I didn't even try to find out what was going on with her family. I mean, I don't have her parents' phone number in Argentina, but I should have asked Clive to call sooner. Dani has a younger brother who's been in and out of trouble a couple of times. I assumed he was acting out again, but that's no excuse for not trying to find out for sure."

"With a little luck, her kidnappers want her for her expertise, same as they do you. That will protect her."

"She must be so scared."

He tilted her face up. "You can't think that way. Nash's tech guys are the best. If there's any evidence on her computer, her phones, anywhere, they'll find it. And then we'll go in and get her back and you can move on with your lives."

"You make it sound so simple."

"It's what we do. Okay?"

"Yeah. Okay." And oddly, it was. Once he'd left, she rewashed her face, letting her fingers rest for a moment against the spot where Eric had cupped her cheek; re-brushed her teeth; set the alarm on the cell phone Jake had left for her for eight o'clock; and, pajamas on once again, crawled into bed. She was asleep in seconds.

⌒

MORNING CAME TOO soon. What time had she gone to bed, anyway? Jane staggered into the bathroom and took a long shower, letting the hot water sluice the glue from her eyelids and the aches from her muscles. After dressing in jeans and a long-sleeved tee, she followed the tantalizing scent of coffee down to the kitchen.

"Hey," said Tara, looking up from a notebook she was writing in at the table. "Ready for breakfast?"

"I'm not much for eating in the morning, I'm afraid," Jane replied. "Though I'd kill for a cup of coffee."

"Breakfast is the most important meal of the day," said a boy of about twelve or thirteen who stood at the sink, rinsing dishes before putting them into an industrial-sized dishwasher.

Tara laughed. "This is Ricky. Ricky, this is Dr. Evans. She'll be staying with us for a little while."

"Hello," said the boy. "It's nice to meet you."

"Ricky and his twin, Micky, have been here about three weeks," Tara explained, "and they've heard my lectures on the importance of morning nutrition more than once."

"Plus, Miss Tara makes really good oatmeal," Ricky assured her. "It's not like . . . well, not like some places where the food's kind of nasty."

"I certainly can't turn down oatmeal." Jane grinned at him, teasing just a little at his serious demeanor. "Especially not with such a ringing endorsement."

"We're a self-service joint around here," Tara told her. "There's milk in the fridge and maple syrup in the cabinet to the left of the stove."

Jane got a bowl of oatmeal and added syrup. Her coffee she took black. Then she sat down at the table with Tara.

"Where are the guys?"

"Jake roped Eric into helping out with an early-morning self-defense class." Tara glanced at Ricky. "Adult education, though we do self-defense with the kids in the afternoons."

Eric would be good at that. Physically imposing, he probably terrified the women at first. But soon enough they would see that not all men were to be feared. There was a stillness at his core, a deep strain of capable strength that went beyond the physical and radiated reassurance.

"He said they'd be back at nine," Tara said. "Which is pretty much any minute."

"Miss Tara, I'm done. Can I go hang with the horse class?"

"Of course. Thank you, Ricky."

The kid bobbed his head and scuttled from the room.

"He's a good kid," Tara said on a sigh. "They both are. But their mom's an addict, and their dad took off a few years back. The mother's doing thirty days on a Driving While Ability Impaired charge at the moment. Court-ordered rehab while she's inside, then more when she gets out. Ninety-day eval; then they decide whether she gets the boys back."

"Tough row to hoe. Do they get to visit her?"

"Not yet. She doesn't even want them to see her there. Which I understand, though I think she's wrong about it. Once she gets out, she'll have supervised visitation, which will take place here. Jake will go get her, drive her back to the halfway house. Most of our kids have similar situations, so we do a lot of rehab-type training here. How to deal with the addicts in your life and their effect on you." A shadow passed behind Tara's eyes, and her hands formed fists, thumbs rubbing over her fingernails.

"And you have horses."

Tara laughed, as Jane had intended. "We do. Beth and Kevin are in charge of the horses, and we take in older ones, gentle ones, ones that don't serve anyone else and use them as therapy animals both for our own kids and for ones that are brought in. Much like the dogs. And the sheep. And the goats. And the chickens. They also help with community outreach. Allowing class trips to come visit the animals makes our mission more palatable."

"Oh, my."

"Uh-huh. I'd like to believe that our kids miss us when they go home, but I know it's only their four-footed pals who have a *real* place in their hearts."

"How many children do you have here?"

"Right now? Seven. But we've had as many as ten."

"Wow." Jane rinsed out her bowl and, following Ricky's example, placed it in the dishwasher. She'd just sat down again to finish her coffee when Eric and Jake came in.

Jake dropped a kiss on Tara's lips and looked at the notepad. "So how much do I have to make this week to feed the ravening hordes?"

"Oh, stop it, you," she said, laughing.

"You about ready to head down to the city?" Eric asked.

"Sure." Jane smothered a yawn. "Let me brush my teeth and grab my purse."

Eric frowned, touching her face. "You look exhausted. Listen, grab a change of clothes while you're up there. We can stay in the city tonight. It will be easier than making the trip, and it will confuse anyone trying to track you, too."

"Here," said Tara, rising, "I'll get you an overnight bag to put your things in."

She walked out and Jane followed her.

"Do you . . . Does everyone . . ." *Oh God, how to say this without sounding unbelievably rude to a woman who'd been nothing but kind to her?*

Tara stopped halfway up the stairs. "Do we just do whatever the guys tell us to?"

Jane held her hands out in a "you caught me" gesture.

"It seems that way, doesn't it? But no. Right now, you're in danger, and danger is what Eric, Jake, and to some extent even Kevin specialize in. Follow their lead and you'll stay safe.

But if Jake said to me, 'We're going to California next week because I need a vacation,' there would be hell to pay.

"And, frankly, woman to woman, you look like crap. The kids go to bed pretty early, it's true, but you'll be better in one of HSE's apartments. They're very comfortable, have super-high-speed Internet so you'll be able to work, and they're utterly safe."

"Eric told me it was the only place he considered safer than this house."

"See? It's perfect. Then you can come back here tomorrow or the next day when you've caught up on your sleep, and I'll put you to work teaching the kids science. We homeschool because they don't stick around more than a few months, and I *suck* at science!"

Jane felt the tension leave her body. "You're on."

THE DRIVE DOWN to the city took an hour, and Eric didn't miss the fact that Jane hardly spoke at all during the trip. Was she pissed about staying in the city? He would have thought she'd welcome the shorter commute. He could see the outline of the new laptop in her overnight bag, so maybe she was just thinking about work.

At AHI he escorted her to the lab and watched her with her colleagues for a few minutes, then went into the break room and set up his own laptop to scour the files Nash had compiled on all the AHI employees. He skimmed through the support staff first. There were few enough of them and none with any level of clearance other than Ruth, the receptionist. She was a grandmother—though a fertile womb hardly precluded criminal activity—with three children, one in Vermont and two in Maine. She lived well within her means, didn't own a car, and her husband had died years earlier. She had worked for Clive Handler for almost twenty years, having taken a job as his secretary when he was running the company that would become Applied Human Intelligence for the most part out of his garage on Long Island. Clive knew science. She knew people. She'd helped him get his first contracts, and nothing indicated she'd ever turn on him.

Most of the scientists had nothing more serious than a parking ticket on their records. One who was not on Jane's team had a couple of arrests for public intoxication, and another had been accused of embezzlement by a former employer. But Clive had assured Eric that the teams did not have access to each other's research, that only Jane's people could see their own progress. On her team, both Rashid and Sam had weaknesses Eric found troubling.

Two years earlier, Sam had been through what appeared from the court documents to have been an exceedingly ugly divorce. His wife accused him of stealing her jewelry, hiding money, giving her herpes, and infidelity. For his part, he accused her of infidelity, giving *him* herpes, aborting their child, and stealing his money. Whatever money they'd had when the proceedings had begun, they had considerably less when the lawyers were done billing. Since the papers were finalized, Sam had been living well. His credit cards showed a steady stream of late nights at bars and clubs on the weekends, often with tabs high enough it was unlikely he'd racked them up alone. What might he give away during pillow talk?

Rashid had no record in the court system, but in his credit report and card history Eric found the typical signs of a gambling addiction. Long weekends in Atlantic City, many including ATM cash advances. Overdue bills. Large deposits followed by even larger withdrawals. It wouldn't be hard to convince a man like that to give up information, provided he had any.

Eric had saved Dani for last. He could not dismiss the possibility that Dani had chosen to aid AHI's competitors of her own accord, especially since Jane had said Dani's brother was trouble. If he'd found himself in a tight spot, they could be using him as leverage to get her assistance. He double-clicked on the file to reveal a woman whose long, wavy hair, thickly-lashed brown eyes, and smooth skin gave her the look of a fashion model. Before he could begin reading, however, Jane's voice caught his attention.

"I know we're shorthanded and you're all worried about Dani. I am, too. But people are looking for her." Here she looked up and directly at him between the people who stood facing her and the open door of the break room. "Really smart people. That's what they do. This is what we do. And we *can* do it. We *will* do it.

"I realize I can come off like an automaton, though Dani was the only one brave enough to tell me so to my face. And you probably think I am a little crazy, too. There's a better than average chance I am. But I believe in this project. I believe in *you*." She took a deep breath, and Eric stood and walked to the door. Whatever she was about to say was going to cost her, and he needed to be closer. "Clive has been pushing hard because we have a deadline dictated by the sale of a completed drug. I'm not going to tell you that doesn't matter. My salary, all our salaries, depend on keeping AHI solvent. But I push myself, push you, for other reasons, too."

Another breath, and now she was looking down at her feet. "I haven't forgotten Dani. I don't want you to forget her, either. But we have to remember the people we are working to help, too." She paused, then went on. "When I was seventeen, my mother killed herself." Exclamations of surprise and sorrow, but she waved them off. "I'm not telling you this to make you feel sorry for me. I haven't been open about this before because—well, for a lot of reasons. But I want you to understand why this drug we're working on is so important. To feel its value the same way I do. You see, my mother was diagnosed with schizophrenia at twenty-five, two years after I was born. She held it together as long as she could. Long enough to see me off to college. But then she couldn't fight any longer."

Christ. Ten years ago, when he'd met her, she'd been eighteen and already a junior. College must have been hell. Not just too young and too smart to fit in properly, not just resented for busting every bell curve, but suffering the weight of tragedy as well.

"I never knew my mother when she wasn't either twitchy and miserable from her meds or paranoid and delusional from neurotransmitters running riot in her brain. But I loved her. And I miss her. Every. Single. Day. So never believe that what we're doing here is about money. It's about people like my mom and those who will miss them if they go, like me and my father."

A tightness he refused to name clogged the back of Eric's throat as he watched the group around Jane slowly break up and return to their stations. Shaking it off, he sat back down, woke his laptop from sleep, and returned to Dani's file.

Jane hadn't been kidding about the girl's brother. Both Peralta siblings had dual citizenship, as their mother was American and the children had been born in California while their parents worked in the tech industry. They'd moved back to Argentina when the bubble burst—money went a hell of a lot further in La Plata than in Silicon Valley. But both children had returned to the States for college. Dani was already in grad school at Columbia when Alvaro graduated high school, so he had come to live with her in the city. The following year, he'd started at CUNY, but only lasted a few months before being busted for selling pot to his classmates. After that, he seemed okay for a couple of years, but then he was arrested for possession of oxycodone. Dani had bailed him out, but she'd shipped him back to Argentina to get straightened out.

Yeah, the kid was a definite weakness.

What Eric couldn't figure out, what made no sense to him, was why, with all these vulnerabilities, AHI's enemy had gone after Jane instead of blackmailing or bribing or seducing one of the others. Any one of them could have sabotaged the data to prevent Handler from completing his project on schedule. No, the only thing that made sense was that they needed her expertise. Which would explain why they'd taken Dani first—the two women had similar training, but Dani was an easier target. When Dani could not immediately solve their problem, they turned their attention to Jane.

He watched her through the big glass window of the break room as she leaned over a microscope with Stella, making notes. She called Sam and Rashid over, and they all clustered together in heated conversation. *Meeting on the mound.* Strategy sessions always looked the same. Sports, war, apparently even science. Everyone had to know where they stood and what steps to take next.

The day passed quickly, and once again he had to drag Jane from her work when it was time to leave. This time, they were picked up at the service entrance to the building by HSE's receptionist and Nash's assistant, Lexie Morton. Clients saw Lexie as a pleasant woman who brought them coffee and put them at ease. Eric knew she was a former DEA agent and an active HSE operative in her own right.

Jane took a deep, appreciative sniff as she slid into the backseat. "Indian?"

"Yup," said Lexie. "I picked up my own dinner on the way over, so I got extra for the two of you. Hope you don't mind garlic."

"Not in the least," said Jane.

"Have I asked you to marry me lately?" Eric teased.

Lexie punched him in the arm. "You can't afford me, big boy."

HSE was headquartered in a twelve-story building in Tribeca. Eric had become used to the place, but Jane's eyes widened as they passed through the second security gate into the underground garage.

"You weren't kidding about safety," she said.

"More than you can even see," Lexie replied, an unmistakable note of pride in her voice. "This building survived a bomb blast not too long ago." She turned a key in the lock for the private elevator and, when it arrived, used the same key to open access to both the tenth and twelfth floors.

"If you come in through the garage, you need a key," Eric explained. "If you come in through the front door, you go to reception and Lexie or one of the others escorts you wherever you need to be. Among other things, the upper floors have apartments, which is where I live when I'm between jobs."

They got off on ten, and Eric let Jane into his apartment. He didn't spend much time in it himself, and he'd never thought much about personalization. Sure, he had photographs of his mom and sister on the bookshelves and a few books scattered here and there, but otherwise the place was as he'd taken possession: a couple of black chairs, a black leather couch, and a mammoth flat-screen television. It could use a couple of those wooly throws Jane was so fond of to soften the modern lines. Maybe he could convince her to make one for him.

"Yeah," he said when he saw her expression, "it's not exactly to my taste, either. Nash puts these places together, then takes the rent out of our checks if we live in them. Mostly, they're just crash pads."

"Where do you live when you're not here?"

He shrugged. "All HSE operatives have specialties. Mine is kidnap and ransom, which means I travel a lot. Nash has a place in Texas I stay at pretty often because my partner Travis and I end up in Mexico with some regularity. When I'm not on duty, I go back to North Carolina to see my mother or spend time here. But if I didn't work so much, I'd have a place that was a bit more personal."

A grin flitted over her lips. "I have to admit, that's kind of a relief."

"And I have to admit, I was going to ask you to knit—or is it crochet?—one of those afghan thingies to liven the place up."

"I could do that," she said. "But I am far from speedy, so it will be a while."

"That's okay, I don't mind waiting when I really want something." And, boy, that had come out wrong. He busied himself with the food. "You hungry yet? I can refrigerate this if you're not, and we can reheat it later."

"I can eat if you want to, though it's a bit early."

"No problem." He stuffed the food into the fridge and carried her bag into the bedroom, where he dropped it on the bed. Lexie had been there. She'd even changed the sheets, which was way above and beyond the call of duty. Every apartment had stacked washer/dryer units, and there was no such thing as "maid service." But Lexie obviously pegged him for the kind of idiot who wouldn't know he had to clean the place up for Jane to be comfortable.

Having Jane in his space felt strange. He'd never brought a woman here. None of the operatives who stayed at HQ did. Nash never said he *couldn't*, but he didn't have to. Explaining the whole elevator system and the keys . . . It tended to destroy spontaneity and cool ardor.

Jane had followed him and now stood taking in the oversized bed with its bland tan covers and two meagre pillows.

"Shall we set up the new computer and put all your data on it?" Time to get away from the personal and back to business. But for once, she wasn't thinking about work.

"This is the only bedroom, isn't it? I didn't see another door."

"It is. Don't worry, though, I'll sleep on the couch. I've done it plenty of times, and it's actually very comfortable." A slight exaggeration, but he'd certainly bedded down in worse spots.

"What if I don't want you to?"

"Wh—" No way had she really said that. He ran it back through his mind once. Then a second time. "What?"

She came close. Closer. He could feel the heat from her body reaching out to wrap around him. "What if I don't want you to sleep on the sofa?" Her hazel eyes burned up at him.

His heart pounded, and every drop of blood in his body drained into his dick, leaving him light-headed and temporarily speechless.

Her pretty, pink lips twisted. "Never mind." She spun to go, and he grabbed her wrist, catching her despite his erection-induced clumsiness.

"Jane."

"Look," she said, jerking her wrist a couple of times, "I understand. I'm sure it's a rule or something, right? No sleeping with the clients?"

He tugged her around to face him, but still she kept her chin tucked into her chest. What was going through her mind? He could already tell she was going to take the rejection the way she did everything, burying it inside and immersing herself in work. He could see the pattern a mile off. But what he couldn't grasp was why she'd propositioned him in the first place. Not that he had trouble finding dates, but the women who picked him up weren't like Jane. They were abundantly clear about what they wanted, and he made certain they got it. He had no idea what Jane wanted. She'd given him an out, but if he took it, he'd hurt her. And he wasn't willing to do that. No way, no how.

He slid his free hand along her face to cup her jaw and tilt her head up. Her eyelids flinched, but she met his gaze at last.

"You're right. I don't sleep with clients. It's a bad idea in every way and for everyone."

"I get it. I told you."

"Will you please let me finish?"

She squeezed those delicious lips closed.

"Not only do I not sleep with clients, but I'm too old for one-night stands." He could feel her gearing up to argue and pull away again, so he pressed his thumb over her mouth. "But Jane, you won't be a client forever." He watched as his meaning sank in and pink rose on her pale cheekbones. *Much better.* By then, this mad impulse of hers would have passed. It was . . . transference or something. Like Stockholm syndrome. After all, he wasn't menacing her, but he had essentially kidnapped her. Taken her entirely out of her regular life.

"Your deadline for the sale is in eight days. That's not so long, is it?" The question was as much for himself as for her. He just had to keep their relationship professional for another week, and then she could have her life back. He could do that. Hell, he could do anything for a week.

She leaned in and slipped her arms around his neck, bringing her body into full contact with is. "Eric?"

"Yeah?" A frog the size of Montana had settled in his throat, and the word came out a croak.

"Do you ever *kiss* your clients?"

Ah, Christ. He was going to regret this, but he couldn't stop himself. He buried his hands in her hair and pulled it from its knot, then held her in place while he brought his mouth down on hers. She met him kiss for kiss, ragged breath for ragged breath, and he drew away first. "Jesus, woman," he said, tucking her head into the hollow of his shoulder, "you're going to be the death of me."

She snuggled closer for a moment, and he allowed himself to imagine meaning more to her than a life-affirming fuck. Which, okay, he'd been a couple of times on assignment despite his avowal that he never slept with clients. But those women were strangers. When Jane worked her magic and solved Clive's problem, AHI sold the drug for a ridiculous sum of money, and Jane's life went back to normal, she'd wonder what she ever saw in a long-haired, tattooed, glorified security guard. She might be grateful, but he didn't want that, either. No, he'd fade away and let her move on.

"Hey, Eric? I'm only a client until we sell the drug, right, even if we do that tomorrow?"

"Of course."

She pulled away. "Then let's get that computer set up."

CHAPTER 4

THE FOLLOWING AFTERNOON, Jake once again picked them up to drive back to the farm. Jane would rather have stayed in the city—even with Eric refusing to share a bed, the cocoon of privacy had brought with it a comforting illusion of intimacy. Revealing her mother's condition had sucked the life from her. She'd hidden it for so long. All through college, all through grad school. Schizophrenia ran in families, and she was still within the range of onset. If she'd told her classmates about her mother, they'd never have quit watching for signs. The first person she'd revealed her mother's disorder to was Dani, and even then she hadn't dared use the word "suicide." She'd merely said that her mother, now dead, had suffered from the illness, which was what motivated her own studies. The revelation about her mother had served its purpose— she'd put a face to the disorder, personalized a fight that had been purely abstract to that point. But it had left her feeling naked, stripped of all her usual defenses. Now they could all see her. Judge her.

But it also left her freer than she ever remembered feeling. She wasn't naïve. Her degree in clinical psych had come with years of therapy. She'd pushed Eric sexually the night before as a result of that freedom. She'd wanted him, so she'd reached for him. No considering repercussions, just riding the wave of emotion released by the dropping of her guard.

The research, and Eric, had saved her from any awkwardness. Pretending the whole incident had never happened, he'd helped her set up the new computer and, at dinner, had asked questions about what her colleagues had been doing in the lab.

She had followed his lead, but the desire still tugged at her, and sitting in the car she was excruciatingly aware of him next to her.

The sun had not yet set when they pulled up to the house, and she could see both the dogs who ran to the fence to greet Jake and the kids who followed them. There had to be a dozen mutts of all shapes and sizes, and Jane counted all seven of the children Tara had told her about. They ranged in age from Ricky and Micky at the top down to a young girl of about five or six with a dirty face and dirtier hands. When she pushed the dogs out of the way and tried to climb the fence, Jake leaned over and picked her up.

"Selena, what *have* you been doing?" he asked as Jane and Eric joined him.

"Blackie found bunnies, and I helped rescue them."

A round blonde walked over. "Hard life lesson today about bunnies and puppies," she said. "Luckily, some of the bunnies survived." She held out a hand only slightly cleaner than Selena's. "I'm Lizzie. I help out around here. Like with getting the kids ready for dinner." She turned a look that might as well have been a shout on Micky and Ricky, and they set about rounding up all the other children and ushering them toward the house. Jane followed behind, peeling off when they reached the house and the kids walked around to a back wing instead of using the front door.

"Thank goodness you're here," Tara said the minute Jane stepped into the kitchen. "I am so behind. The kids will be in any minute, and dinner's not close to ready." She looked up from the vegetables she was chopping and tossing into a giant salad bowl, and her eyes rounded. "Oops. Thought you were Jake."

"Nope. Just me, but I am happy to help. What can I do?"

"The water should be boiling. If you could toss in two of the boxes of spaghetti out of the cupboard above you, that would be great. I let the day get away from me today."

"I'm just amazed with all you do that doesn't happen every day!"

"No. I swear. I am usually better than this." Tara's left hand clenched into a fist, and Jane saw her rubbing her thumb over her fingernails. How odd that after only a couple of days, she knew that meant the woman was upset or nervous. Jane took a minute to break the massive piles of spaghetti from the industrial-sized boxes in half and drop them into the huge pot, then stepped over to Tara and laid a hand on her arm.

"Better for who? Better against what standard? I think you're amazing, and so does Eric. And obviously your fiancé can't imagine you being 'better.' And neither can those kids. You can say they only miss the animals, but you know it's not true."

Tara smiled, a little shakily. "I have some self-esteem issues."

"Don't we all? But I'm dead serious. I can't imagine doing what you do and making it all seem so . . . normal."

At that, Tara actually laughed. "You have a mighty strange idea of normal."

"I probably do," Jane admitted, "but this is how I always imagined it."

"Imagined?" Tara started to say more, but a clatter sounded outside the kitchen door. "Here comes the stampede."

The kitchen door burst open, and Micky and Ricky flung themselves through it, arguing.

"It's my turn!"

"Nuh-uh. You tossed yesterday."

"Did not."

"Did, too."

"Boys," Tara said. "Enough." She turned to Jane. "Micky and Ricky are going to be chefs when they get older. The only reason I did the cooking tonight without them is that the only thing more appealing than food is baby bunnies. But tossing a salad this size without making a mess is beyond my powers, so they take turns doing that for me.

"Now. Which one of you *really* did it yesterday?"

Two pairs of brown eyes slid sideways as the boys regarded each other. Then Micky sighed. "I did."

"Fine. Ricky, you're up." Tara handed him a pair of tongs, then shifted over to check the texture of the spaghetti. "Almost done. Micky, grab a colander for me and put it in the sink."

A minute later, as Tara poured the pasta into the colander, the kitchen exploded with a riot of children, all talking a mile a minute. They all took places at the big trestle table, nudging and poking each other in a good-natured wrestle that brought a lump to Jane's throat. Jake followed them in, gave Tara a quick squeeze, then raised his hands. Immediately, all movement ceased and the kitchen went quiet.

"Everyone washed up?" he asked. Seven heads bobbed in unison.

"Okay, moment of silence."

Some of the children, Jane noticed, dropped their heads as if in prayer. Others just sat. A minute later, Tara plunked the salad down at one end of the table and a big bowl of spaghetti and sauce down at the other, and the table noise and motion erupted once again as food was dished up and passed around. The older kids, Jane noticed, took responsibility for making sure the younger ones got their fair share.

"Nice setup," Jane said to Tara when the children were all stuffing their faces.

"It works for us."

"And the moment of silence?"

"A few of them are used to saying grace before meals, most are not. We didn't want to enforce any particular religion or way of life. Same thing with bedtime prayers. They all have to spend a few minutes reflecting, but they don't have to say anything."

"Your parents must have been great. You have such a talent for this."

Tara shook her head. "Oh, honey, no. Anything but. They were the *worst*. Whenever I am trying to make a decision, I think to myself, 'What would Daddy have done?' and then I do the opposite."

"Oh, dear. Well, I suppose that's one form of role model."

"It is. And I grew up stronger because of it." Her thumb made a pass over her fingers, and she assessed Jane. "I could be wrong, but my guess is you know exactly what I mean."

"I've never thought of myself as particularly strong."

"Take it from me. You are."

Jane wanted to ask why she thought so, but one of the children knocked over a glass of water and Tara dashed away to help clean up.

⌣

THEY FOUND THE solution to the chemical-reaction issue on Friday afternoon. As she stared through the microscope at the fourth sample proving that they could, indeed, prevent the two reactions from interfering with one another, then annotated the finding and the time — 3:26 p.m. — a rush of tears clogged Jane's throat. Where was the excitement, the triumph?

Stella stood at her elbow, practically bouncing on the tips of her toes, waiting for the final confirmation that they'd created the foundation for a life-changing drug, and Jane had to swallow several times before giving it to her.

"Holy crow, I didn't think we'd actually get it in time," Rashid said when Jane pronounced the final sample clear. "I thought . . . wow."

Clive filed the patent, prepared weeks ahead of time, then joined them in the lab with a bottle of Dom Pérignon. For both Rashid and Stella, this was a first, but Jane and Sam had been through successes with Clive in the past. He never stinted when it came to celebrations. Still, the mood in the lab was somber: there had been no word on Dani's whereabouts.

"I'll call John over at Sundeman Pharmaceuticals and see if we can't move up the press conference to Monday," Clive said as they sipped premium champagne from laboratory beakers. "That way you'll be safe."

"No, don't." She glanced at Eric as she spoke and saw a muscle jump in his jaw. "I mean, call Sundeman, of course. But Eric can take care of me. And if we leave the press conference until Wednesday, that gives HSE a couple extra days to find Dani. After the press conference, whoever took her won't have any reason . . . They . . ."

"Of course," Clive said. "I should have considered that. I'll ask John to be sure our findings stay private until the conference, too. If they're dealing with another lab, they can put off cutting them loose for a few more days."

Stella studied them over her beaker. "This is such a small community, though. The minute we filed the patent application, what we'd learned, the mechanism of treatment and everything became public knowledge."

Silence descended, broken awkwardly by Sam, who asked, "Where are we being reassigned?"

Clive cleared his throat. "You and Stella will transition to Adrian's team. They need the extra hands because the police have asked for help processing a massive amount of evidence from a high-profile homicide. Rashid will go to Alan to work on Project Phobos. Monday, Jane will clean up the reports and work with Ruth on the press release. Tuesday she'll start catching up with the phobia work so she and Alan can lead that team together." He poured another slug of champagne into his beaker, tossed it back in a single gulp, and placed the beaker in a large plastic tub in the corner. "Great work, guys. Take off whenever you like, and I will see you Monday." With a wave, he was gone.

Jane took a sip of her champagne. *This one's for you, Mom. Thanks for fighting the good fight as long as you did.* Then she poured the rest of her drink down the sink, put the beaker into the tub for sterilization, and began to straighten up the lab.

"Hey, Jane, can I talk to you, um, privately?" Stella asked as they catalogued slides.

Behind her, Jane felt Eric perk up. But this was Stella for crying out loud. What could he possibly be worried about? "Sure," she said. "Staff room okay?"

"Yeah, that works."

Jane shut the door behind them, but she heeded the warning in Eric's ice blue gaze and stayed where he could keep an eye on her through the glass insert. "What's up?"

"Umm, so, that guy. Your bodyguard. Sam and Rashid and I were talking. You told us you couldn't give us your new number because he said not to, to just give his office number. But are you sure you trust him?"

"Eric? Of course I do."

"Just because Clive hired him? I mean, what if Clive didn't do his research?"

"No. Seriously, Stel, I had no idea you guys were concerned or I would have told you—I've known Eric for years." Which was a slight exaggeration. She'd known him years *ago*, but not in the intervening time. "We went to college together. I absolutely trust him."

"Oh. Okay, then." Stella glanced out to where Eric stood, very obviously watching them. "So, uh, then, if you trust him and you know him . . . is he single?"

And that shocked a laugh out of her. "Talk about a quick turnaround! You don't trust him; then you want to date him?"

"It's not that we didn't trust him. We're your friends. We wanted to be certain. And as to dating . . . no, he's not my type for a date. But for a night? Absolutely."

God. Out of sync once again. Why was it that although she was younger than most people around her, she always felt so much older? And why were her fists clenched at her sides? It wasn't as if she had rights to Eric's body. He'd turned her down after all, however nicely. She relaxed her hands, but couldn't meet Stella's eyes as she answered. "I don't really talk to Eric about stuff like that. You'll have to ask him yourself." Although she *had* talked to him. And she wasn't out of sync with *him*. After all, he'd proclaimed himself too old for one-night stands.

Stella looked her over as if Jane were under her microscope. "Ah. I didn't realize it was like that. Good luck. He looks . . . intense."

What on earth had the other woman seen? Were Jane's emotions that transparent? She let out a little laugh, ignoring the speculation in the first part of Stella's reply. "I'll give you that. He always has been."

Stella sighed. "Ah, well, it was worth a shot." She shrugged and went back into the lab.

Jane followed her out immediately. If she stayed in the break room, Eric would come in and ask what they'd been discussing, and no way could she handle answering that.

⌒

ERIC WAITED PATIENTLY to ask about Stella. Her posture during the conversation in the break room, and Jane's, had intrigued him. At first, the two had seemed almost adversarial. And then the tension had broken and the mood had changed completely. But when she came out, Jane had ignored him in a way she hadn't since the first day. Whatever had happened, she had no desire to talk about it.

Not that he was going to let a little thing like that stop him. But he did hold his questions until the others had left and he and Jane were alone, waiting for Jake to pick them up. She bit her lip, and pink rose in her cheeks, but she didn't answer.

"Not something having to do with the case, then?"

After a deep breath, she said, "She wanted to know whether you were available."

Well, hell. That was the last thing he'd expected. "Available?"

"For sex," she clarified.

"Yeah, I got that." He shook his head sharply to clear it. "I hope you told her I wasn't?"

"I told her she'd have to ask you herself. But she didn't seem to be willing to go that far." She blushed again. What had Stella said, exactly?

Before he had a chance to respond, his phone dinged with a text from Jake, who had arrived and was waiting to pick them up. *Thank fucking God.* He hustled Jane outside and into the SUV with a little less than his usual caution.

In the back of the car, he watched enviously as Jane pulled the rubber band off the tight braid that had bound her hair all day and unwound the whole mass. His fingers itched with the memory of sliding through the silky strands and the desire to do so again. He glanced up and caught Jake's eyes in the rearview. The man had the balls to grin, as if he could read Eric's thoughts.

"Do your people work on weekends?" Jane asked after about twenty minutes.

From the front seat, Jake laughed. "Doc, HSE operatives work 24/7/365, except for leap years, in which case they work 366. Which is why I am just an occasional contractor."

But Eric knew what she was after. "Don't worry. No one will stop looking for Dani—we don't keep bankers' hours. We've already found a few interesting hints, and no one can track a loose thread like Nash's guys."

Jane sucked in a deep breath and let it out slowly, and Eric braced himself for whatever might be coming. "Can we stay at your place, at HSE? I want to see the data your people are working with myself, see if anything jumps out at me. You could ask if they'd let me work in the research lab to help them."

Of course she'd want that. He'd want it, too, in her place. And he couldn't deny her, despite how uncomfortable the night he'd spent on his own couch thinking about her in his bed had been.

"Not a problem. We can pack up your things and head back tonight if you like. I'll call Lexie and set it up so we can get access to tech." And beg her to toss out all the dead stuff in the fridge and restock while he was at it. For which she'd make him pay in a thousand little ways. His boss's assistant had a cruel streak a mile wide, but she also took care of "her boys."

"Tara will be pissed," Jake said. "She was looking forward to not having to answer science-homework questions. And the experiments you showed the kids after dinner the other night were supercool."

"I was thinking about that. If she's interested, I could probably set her up with people who'd get a kick out of talking about their fields of study with a bunch of kids and designing experiments that would appeal to them. Despite our rigid reputations, a lot of scientists are quite creative and enjoy teaching, especially the kind of teaching that doesn't require grading papers. You'd have to coordinate it, and most of the grad students wouldn't have cars, so you'd either have to pick them up or pay for transportation, but if you're interested I could round up candidates."

"That's quite an offer," Jake said. "Don't make it unless you mean it, because Tara will be all over it. We don't send them to school, as I am sure she told you, because they're not with us long and being the new kid is hard enough without being a foster on top of it, but we like to think they get a more complete education at our place anyway. The courts try to ensure they're going back to better situations than they left, and we try to ensure they're better prepared, both mentally and emotionally, to deal with those situations. Falling behind in school wouldn't serve them well."

"It's really admirable what you guys do."

Eric agreed, but the fact that—despite all the turmoil in her own life and her fears for her friend—Jane had still found a way to pitch in, and to create a plan to do so in the future, impressed him even more.

They turned off the highway, and Jake cursed under his breath.

"Problem?" Eric asked.

"Two cars back. If that's a real county cop car, I'll eat my hat."

"But it's broad daylight," Jane objected.

"Yup. That's why they're going for the ruse this time. All passersby will see is a woman getting arrested." He took a sharp right, then a left, and Jane was thrown into Eric. He held her against his side with one arm, drawing his gun with the other. Behind them, a siren's distinctive, ululating wail warned they'd not lost their pursuers.

"This doesn't make any fucking sense. They're trying too hard and not hard enough at the same damned time."

Jake grunted agreement even as he cut through a parking lot and down a side street.

"Get down, sweetheart," Eric said. He pushed Jane into the footwell, out of danger, out of sight.

"This is the wrong neighborhood for a chase. Too many parks, too many kids, too many chances I could hurt someone. I'm going to double-back and see if I can't get back on the highway." Eric could hear the frustration in his tone and understood: if Jane hadn't been with them, they could have confronted their hunters. Now they couldn't even safely outrun them.

Jane spoke from her crouched position. "If you do, go back to the city. I don't want to lead them anywhere near Tara or the children."

"Don't worry, they won't get on the highway with sirens blaring. That would draw attention from the *actual* county police. We'll lose them."

"No. Please, Jake. I wouldn't forgive myself if anything happened to them." She started to push herself up, but Eric put his hand on her shoulder and held her in place as the car swerved down a narrow road and out, then cut sharply left.

"We won't go to the farm. I promise."

"Hang on," Jake warned. A second later, they took a full U on two wheels. Another minute and they were back on the highway, merging with only a few angry horns to mark their entrance.

They went almost twenty miles north before turning around and heading back south, and it wasn't until then that Eric began to relax. He called Nash and filled him in.

"I'll be here when you get here," Nash said. "Ask Jake to stay, too, if he can, rather than just dropping you off. This job has gone sideways, and I don't like it."

"No shit. We should be there in about an hour."

"We'll be waiting."

⤺

As they rolled into the underground garage, Jane straightened from her position slumped against Eric. After he'd helped her up from her cramped position at the end of the crazy chase, she'd never made it back over to her side of the backseat. Eventually, Eric had holstered his gun, taken out his cell phone, and begun making phone calls. But the arm he'd dropped across her shoulders after determining they'd shaken their pursuers hadn't strayed. If anything, he held her even closer as he talked to Nash, then Lexie.

And now she would be meeting Harper himself. She'd searched out information about him on the Internet the first night Eric had stayed with her, but what she found had done little to sate her curiosity.

In fact, the few pieces of verifiable information and rafts of speculation only piqued her interest. The man would have had to have lived five lifetimes to have done everything people attributed to him.

They took the elevator up to the main office, where Lexie sat behind a large, curve-fronted desk of mahogany and black lacquer with a granite top. Her fingers with their scarlet tips were tapping a mile a minute across the keyboard. She gave them the barest glance when they stepped out, holding up one finger briefly as an order to stay before returning to her work with a frown. A minute or two later, she finished and took the time to examine them more closely.

"Well. Aren't you the motley crew. Nash is up on seven and will be down shortly. He'll meet us in Conference Two." She led the way down a short hallway past one big room that looked to Jane as if it could easily accommodate twenty people around its heavy oval table to a considerably smaller one. She piled some papers at the head of the rectangular table, then took a seat to the right of what Jane figured would be Nash's place.

"Coffee, anyone?" Eric asked, moving to the machine on the wet bar at the far end of the room where a pod brewer sat.

"Count me in. Make it strong," Jake said.

"Decaf for me," said Lexie.

"I'll just have water," Jane said as she pulled a smoothly rolling, ergonomically correct chair from the table and sat down. She'd always considered Clive's office well appointed, but maybe Nash Harper did have the kind of money the websites said he did, because this was one hell of a setup.

Eric brought everyone their drinks, then settled next to Jane while Jake took the seat next to Lexie.

A moment later, the door opened to admit a lean and wiry

man with short salt-and-pepper hair and sharp gray eyes. A silver guitar pick dangled from his ear. If she hadn't read about it on the Net, the jewelry would have surprised her, for otherwise there was nothing decorative about him: he wore a T-shirt, jeans, and work boots.

"Nash Harper," he said, holding out a hand. "Good to meet you, Dr. Evans."

"Jane, please." She shook his hand. "I want to thank you for everything you've done, everything your people have done."

He just grinned at her, revealing strikingly white teeth, and shook his head. "No thanks needed. This is what we do. And your case is an interesting one, which makes a big difference."

"How so?"

Nash moved to the seat Lexie had left for him and sat, shuffling through the papers on the table. Lexie herself passed legal pads and pens to Jane, Eric, and Jake.

"Let's go over the timeline quickly," Nash said. "Your boss called me Sunday afternoon around three to request I send someone for a Monday morning meeting. I got the basics from him at that point—who you were, why he thought you might need protection. From there, I did my own research, both on him and on you, and asked Eric to take the job.

"The next morning, Eric was already on the job when you were attacked. Your attackers did not, in fact, try to kill you. They tried to kidnap you. It was a small, contained operation, designed to be quick and dirty. If Eric had not been there, they could have grabbed you and been gone without a trace relatively easily. They'd scoped the area out in advance, knew there was a loading zone on that block, stole commercial plates for the van so it could sit there. They deemed that a better option than taking you from your home, which would have been my choice. That's one puzzle.

"Monday night's abduction attempt employed a very different tactic. They came in hard and loud. There are reasons to do that. For example, if people hear a small crack of breaking glass in their neighborhood, they might look out the window to see whether there's something going on. On the other hand, if they hear gunshots or explosions, they are apt to *hide* out, not *help* out. But they only sent a couple of guys despite their earlier failure. Any halfway decent crew would assume that you had protection. They might not have known from the morning—Eric could have been a good Samaritan, not a paid protector—but they should have realized that *after* you were attacked once, you'd be more careful and might have hired protection. So, assuming they're well funded, which today's fake cop car indicates they are, why not send a half dozen men? Why take chances?"

Jane looked around the table, but no one spoke up.

"Before tonight," Harper said, "we were working on the assumption that whoever was doing this didn't have the resources necessary for a large-scale op. Those are the leads we followed. Hiring a two-man team—even one with flashbangs and firepower—isn't difficult. With tonight's attack, we've had to change our profile, concentrate on people who can put together a fake police car, uniforms, the whole shebang in short order. And who aren't afraid to go after you when you have serious protection."

"What kind of people can do that?"

Harper answered with a question of his own. "Eric tells me the missing woman, Daniela Peralta, was your friend."

"She is."

"Do you know her brother, too?"

"No." Dani had never wanted to talk about Alvaro, saying only that he'd had to go back to Argentina because she couldn't keep him out of trouble. "I met Dani when she interviewed at AHI, but by the time we became friends, he'd left New York."

"So you'd be surprised that he returned to the city with her after Christmas?"

"What?" But it made sense. For the past couple of months, Dani had become more reticent, inviting Jane out far less frequently. "Was he living with her again? Does he have any ideas about her disappearance?"

"I'm sure he does." Those shrewd eyes never left her face. "Three days before Dani—or whoever had access to her e-mail account—sent that e-mail about going home for a family emergency, Alvaro stopped showing up for work."

"Oh, my God." Jane's stomach cramped. "They took him to make her cooperate."

"That would be my guess. If you want a scientist to work in your lab, you can't physically harm her. Breaking her fingers defeats the purpose. And torture clouds the mind. No, you need a different kind of leverage. Threats against loved ones have a proven track record."

Her stomach lurched. *Oh God, Dani.*

"Jane." Eric put a hand on her knee, calming her, drawing her attention. "This doesn't change anything. In fact, since they have him and she's likely to be giving them anything they ask for, they have no reason to hurt her."

"But she's not getting it done. Or they wouldn't need me."

"No," said Lexie, "but you're more apt to do their bidding if they threaten her, so that's another safety net for her."

"We've had people working this from all directions," Nash assured her. "And when Eric called saying you wanted to help, I told tech to start putting together a data package for you. Working under the assumption that the reason both you and Dani were targeted is that someone is developing a drug similar to AHI's, we pulled articles and patent applications related to schizophrenia, hallucinations, delusions . . . anything we thought might be relevant. But as good as my researchers are, this isn't their area of expertise and there's a lot of data. Sorting the important from the irrelevant takes time."

Finally, a way she could contribute. "I can sort that easily if you can research the few I flag."

Lexie smiled. "They're still putting together the data. I'll give you keys to the seventh floor, which is research and tech, and the tenth, which is the apartment, so you can come and go as you need to. I'll pick you up tomorrow morning at eight thirty, if that works for you, and introduce you to the research department."

She didn't dare express her frustration at not being able to spend the night working. It was enough that they trusted her to help at all.

"We're done here for the moment, then," said Nash. "But Jake, will you stay for a minute?"

"Of course. And Jane, I'll drop your bag off tomorrow. I have to be in the city anyway."

Wow. She hadn't even considered what she was supposed to wear for the next several days. She shook her head to clear the fog. "Thanks so much."

She followed Eric and Lexie out, wondering what Nash had to discuss with Jake. A tiny, paranoid voice in her mind said it was her, that Nash didn't trust Eric's opinions and was asking Jake for his, but she shushed it. Paranoia was a form of obsession she'd succumbed to in the past, and she refused to let it suck her away again.

In the anteroom, Lexie handed over the keys and sent them on their way. Again, concern niggled at the back of her mind. Lexie clearly planned to go back to the conference room once she and Eric were out of the room. But there was nothing Jane could do except wave good night and step into the elevator behind Eric.

As Eric opened the door to his apartment, Jane fingered her new keys. She wanted to lighten the atmosphere with a joke about how she guessed they were living together now that she had her own key, but everything she tried in her mind sounded either awkward or desperate, so she kept her mouth shut.

"Are you hungry?" Eric asked. "I have no idea what's in the fridge, but I need to eat."

She was more tired than hungry, but experience told her if she didn't eat now, she'd wake at three in the morning starving. "I'll eat whatever. I don't need much."

"Okeydoke." He glanced at her, then did a visible double take. "Hey. Come on, sit on the couch." He took her hand and led her, which was when she realized she'd been standing as if planted in the middle of the room. She might even have been swaying. What the hell was the matter with her?

"It's been a long day," he said gently. "Kick off your shoes, put your feet up, and relax. I'll make dinner and we can watch television. What do you like? Biography? Discovery?"

"Bad science-fiction movies." The complete shock on his face surprised a giggle out of her.

"You mean like *Sharktopus*?"

"Exactly. I *adore* those movies. The science is atrocious, the special effects worse. It's a perfect storm of the ridiculous."

"That's so awesome. I was worried you'd want to watch serious programming, and I have to admit I'm not a serious guy when it comes to television." He handed her the remote. "Find the worst thing you can, I'll cook, and we can watch together."

Jane found a movie about supersized, super intelligent sharks and settled in. But before the sharks had eaten even their first person, she was asleep.

Eric looked up from the stove to see Jane fast asleep on the sofa. It was a punch to the gut, just like hearing the story of her mother's suicide had been, just like seeing her name and picture inside the file had been. . . He was beginning to realize Jane Evans wasn't the kind of woman he'd ever get used to. He hoped like hell they'd get a grasp on the case soon. And not just because he worried about Dani, which he did, far more than he was willing to admit to Jane, but because he wouldn't have any peace until Jane was safely back in her life. And out of his.

He flipped the switch to shut off the bacon and went to cut lettuce and tomato for sandwiches. Lexie, bless her heart, had stocked him with steak and potatoes as well as eggs, bacon, cheese, and all kinds of other staples, but even before Jane passed out she hadn't appeared ready for a heavy meal.

He made two BLTs for himself and one for Jane, plopped them on a pair of plates, and carried them over to the coffee table. Jane had slid down so that she was lying, legs curled up, head on her hands. He crouched beside her and smoothed the hair back from her face. Immediately, her eyes popped open. She stared at him for a long moment. Then, just as he was considering asking what was on her mind, she leaned forward and pressed her lips to his. Without thinking, he wrapped an arm around her waist to pull her closer, and they both tumbled to the floor.

Jane's mouth was hot and hungry, and despite her small, light frame, he could feel every inch of her body on top of his. And, Christ, she felt good. Her arms had gone around his neck during the brief fall, and now one hand tangled in his hair, flexing and stretching like a cat's paw kneading his head, while the other slid over his shoulder, outlining the contours of his muscles. Her touch raised all the hairs on his arms, along with his blood pressure, and, inevitably, his cock. If he didn't want to take her to bed, he needed to end things. Now. But her shirt had risen and his left hand rested on warm, bare skin.

Just another minute. He let his left hand stroke her back, cupping her butt with his right and pressing her against the hard-on threatening the zipper of his jeans.

Back off. Get some class, asshole. But Jane didn't seem to mind his rough treatment. In fact, when he loosened his hold, she wiggled closer and her small, hot hands found their way beneath his shirt. She plucked gently at his chest hair, and heat speared through him.

"Janie, Jesus. Give me a minute." He tugged at her hands.

She slid off him and sat cross-legged on the floor. "Why won't you sleep with me? Really."

He closed his eyes. She was so damned direct. It was like a bucket of ice water. He sat up. "Jane—"

She held up a hand, and just the sight of it heated his blood all over again. "Don't lie to me. I've met Harper now, and he doesn't seem like the kind of guy who gives two hoots and a holler about what you do so long as it doesn't interfere with the work. I doubt sex with a client even crosses his mind. So if it's not that, and it's not lack of desire—"

"No, it's definitely not that."

"Then what?"

How was he supposed to explain without insulting her, without sounding patronizing? He rubbed the back of his neck and felt his hair slide over his hand. He never paid it much attention. The hair, the beard—they both helped with undercover work, with blending in most of the places he worked for HSE. But he'd seen the looks in the lab, and that was after he'd cleaned himself up pretty well. Of course, Stella had found him intriguing, but he'd met plenty of women like her in his life.

"Your friend Stella didn't say she wanted to *date* me, did she?"

Jane dropped her eyes and picked at a nail until he leaned over and covered her hands with his own.

"It's okay, baby. You don't have to answer. For the record, I'm not hurt by her lack of interest in me as a long-term partner."

"You're not?"

"Nope. But like I told you, I've had all the one-nighters I want."

"I thought . . ."

Apparently, she couldn't be quite so direct when it came to her own emotions. "You thought I was just saying that to put you off. And partially, I was. Because I do want you. But you're *not* Stella." Now came the hard part. "Have you ever, before the other night, wanted a man for nothing more than sex?"

"I don't . . . It wasn't just about sex. Not the way you mean it. It was about feeling good. Physically, mentally, emotionally. It was about connecting to something solid."

"But none of that is real. Those desires are a product of the circumstances we're in. You'd regret it once you had a chance to think it through."

Instead of drawing inward, as he expected, she shoved him away and catapulted herself to her feet.

"Don't *ever* do that!"

"Do what?" He got up and walked toward her, but she backed away, daggers glaring from her hazel eyes. The pallor he'd noticed when they'd first entered the apartment was gone, as was any sign of exhaustion. She was furious and radiant.

"Don't *ever* tell me what I think. I may not be good at understanding other people's motives or desires, but I have been monitoring my own mental state since I was ten years old and learned what the words 'hereditary' and 'schizophrenia' meant. *Every* idea I come up with gets scrutinized. I watch the faces around me whenever I speak to be sure no one considers what I am saying insane. When I hear a voice, I check to be sure there's a person nearby. I know *exactly* what I wanted and why, and yes, some of it had to be adrenaline and fear and comfort. But there's nothing wrong with any of that. And that wasn't all of it anyway."

Oh, fuck. "I'm so sorry, Janie."

"Don't be sorry. Just don't assume I don't know my own mind, or, worse, that you know it better than I do."

"I won't. I promise. But I am . . . concerned, I guess. It's been years since we were in college." And even then, they hadn't been friends, hadn't even run in the same circles. He'd seen her twice a week for tutoring. But he wasn't going to remind her of that now. "Today is Friday. We've been together since Monday. I asked you before whether you'd ever picked up a man just for sex, so let me rephrase. Have you ever slept with a guy after knowing him a week?"

"No. But most guys I meet, after a week, I've spent maybe two or three hours with them. After a week, it's possible that we've gone on one date. Or maybe not even that; maybe we were assigned to a lab project. After a week, I've never talked to any of the men I've slept with about anything more deep or meaningful than where we went to school or whether we had worked in any of the same places."

Finally, the stiffness left her body and she approached him. "After a week—after a day—I knew everything I needed about you. And what I didn't know, I wanted to find out."

"What do you mean? We didn't talk about anything of importance."

"Knowing someone isn't about learning what their family is like, or whether they love mashed potatoes with an unhealthy passion, or even what sports team they favor. After five days, I've seen you with my colleagues and yours. I've run through the night with you. I know you're careful and methodical—that hasn't changed since we were kids—and that you have a generous heart." He would have protested that, but she reached up and cupped his face with one of those fascinating little hands and stole his power of speech. "I know you see the world through a dark lens and don't realize that you're part of bringing the light. I know you make me feel safe even when people are chasing us. I know that when you smile, really smile, your eyes turn down at the corners in little half-moons, but that doesn't happen often. I know your beard and mustache look rough but feel like silk when you kiss me. And I know I want to find out what the rest of you feels like."

CHAPTER 5

WELL, SHE'D SURPRISED him, that much was clear. She'd surprised herself. Usually, she kept a safe emotional distance from the men she slept with. She couldn't think of a single one she'd ever mentioned her mother's suicide to. It would no doubt shock the crap out of Eric to hear it, but she'd never considered love a prerequisite for sex. She'd wanted to try sex, so she had. The experience had been enjoyable, but she had her doubts that it was worth the risk most of the time. Yes, she was always careful to get to know men before she slept with them, but that wasn't because she was a romantic, for crying out loud; it was simply practical. She didn't need a stalker, an abuser, or a thief in her life. There were so many different ways a man could hurt a woman that she'd basically given up doing much other than window-shopping.

And then Eric showed up. And her life went to hell. Yes, he had a point about her perceptions being skewed because of the free flow of chemicals in her body and brain. Adrenaline came in second only to alcohol as an instigator of bad decisions. But Eric wasn't a bad decision. He wouldn't hurt her. And sex with him, well, she was pretty sure it would be worth any risk.

But she wasn't going to beg. A girl had to have a *little* dignity.

"Jesus, Janie," he said after a long silence. "How the hell am I supposed to respond to that?" He pulled her close, tucked her cheek into the hollow of his shoulder, and nuzzled the top of her head with his chin. His beard felt like the gentlest of brushes tangling with her hair.

"This works," she said, sliding her arms around his waist. It wasn't precisely what she wanted, but she'd take it. Small progress was better than none, and now everything was out in the open. She rested against him for a moment, then pulled away.

"So, let's have dinner. I smell bacon."

"Yeah. Lexie stocked the place for me when I called."

"Wow, I see why you asked her to marry you." She sat on the couch and took a big bite of the sandwich.

He grinned the real grin that lightened her heart and took the spot next to her. "Yeah. I ask her every time I stay. I get the sense most of the other guys do, too. And only about half of them are joking."

"Oh, my God, this is so good." She took another bite, chewed, swallowed. "And what about her?"

"I have no idea. A couple of times I've wondered whether she might be dating Nash, but that seems too far-fetched. Maybe she has no interest in dating anyone, because she's here whenever I am, whenever I call in."

"Wow. Dedicated."

He cocked his head, looked at her. "No more so than you. Don't forget, I've seen what kind of hours you prefer to keep."

"Yeah, well, some might call me obsessive. In fact, there's no 'might' about it. But my career path was set early. How did you end up working for Harp Security? What did you do after college?"

"Army."

"Not baseball?"

"No. I might have made the minors, but I didn't have the power or speed for the majors. The Army didn't pay much, but they provided everything I needed, so it didn't matter. I could send everything home to take care of my mother and sister."

"No father in the picture?" Too late, she realized how stark she sounded, how unfeeling. She'd retreated again, as her psychiatrists had all pointed out, behind a safe wall of facts where emotion couldn't penetrate. But her rudeness didn't seem to faze him.

"He doesn't contribute. I mean, he can't. He and my mother divorced when I was a teenager, but he'd been on disability for years, so he couldn't provide much in the way of financial support even before he left."

"I'm sorry."

He shrugged. "It's the way of the world. We got along fine without him, but by the time I got out of college Missy was sixteen and thinking about her future. Her grades were good, but not stellar enough for an academic scholarship, and she didn't have my athletic skills. Mom was never going to be able to pay for college without help."

"So you joined the Army." Of course he did. He was that kind of guy. "Did you like it?"

He considered that before answering. "Yeah, I did."

"So why did you leave?"

"Because they had a future planned out for me and it wasn't the one I wanted. I had the physical stamina and the strategic thinking for Special Forces, but what was the point of sending money home to my family if I never got to see them?"

"Do you spend a lot of time with them?"

"Enough. Missy's engaged, God help the guy." He laughed, and she could hear the fondness in it. What would it have been like to grow up with a sibling? She remembered begging her parents for a sister when she was about eight, though at the time she'd imagined a sister as something akin to a baby doll.

"And you?" he asked. "I know about your mother—and let me say, in case I didn't before, how sorry I am to hear what you went through—but what else do you have in the way of family?" His blue eyes were warm and softer than she'd ever seen them, more cerulean sea than their usual crystal.

"My father is a professor in Virginia."

"But you're not close."

She laughed, not without a hint of bitterness. "It shows?"

"Just a guess." He reached out and stroked the back of her hand with a single finger. A tiny, delicate thread connecting her to reality, to the messiness of emotion and humanity outside the walls. And, oh, she wanted to reach for it, to grab hold and boost herself over the top, or squeeze through an opening, but then what? No, it was safer to take refuge in fact.

"My mother required a lot of care. And he loved her desperately, so he did what was necessary. But her death . . . It burned him out. He took a sabbatical that turned into retirement. That lasted two years. By the time he was ready to return to the land of the living, I had my own career to consider. We don't see much of each other."

"That's a shame." The single, light touch became a tug, and he pulled her over so she was sitting across his knees, her back resting against the arm of the sofa. He held her against him like a promise of closeness to come. "But that's enough of the serious stuff for the moment. Let's watch the sharks."

THE VIBRATION OF his silenced cell phone alarm against the bedside table woke Eric at seven o'clock. Jane slept half atop him, her right hand beneath his shirt, her right leg tucked between his. He hadn't intended to share the bed, but when she turned those lion gold eyes of hers on him, he couldn't refuse. He'd given her one of his shirts and left her in the bathroom while he tossed her clothes into the washer . . . and poured himself a double shot of bourbon.

But despite the fact she'd been half-asleep during the movie, when he finally allowed himself to slip into bed, she immediately curled up against his side. And he didn't move away. Instead, he wrapped an arm around her and tucked her even closer. What else could he do? She felt so damned good there.

And now he'd be content to lie in bed all day watching her sleep, but Lexie was always on time and Jane would be anxious to get to work. No point in waking her sooner than necessary, however. As carefully as possible, he disentangled himself and went to take a shower.

When he came out, Jane was sitting up in bed, arms stretched out to the side, the neck of his T-shirt slipping over one shoulder. Christ almighty. Could she be any sexier? On the baseball field, on the battlefield, Eric never lost focus, not ever. Runners on, screaming fans, explosions, gunfire — he tuned it all out with ease. But Jane stole his concentration without even trying.

"So today I get to see where you work," she said, cracking her neck and then straightening his shirt so it hid her delicate collarbone. And damn, but he wanted to go muss her up again.

"Not me. They don't let me near tech." He held up his hands and wiggled his blunt fingers. "I'd need a special keyboard."

She laughed and tossed a pillow at him. "Oh, stop." She unfolded herself from the bed and stretched again, and his entire body came to attention. Sometimes he really hated his job.

Because he desperately wanted to touch her and because he knew what a bad idea that would be, he tossed the pillow right back.

"Time to shower, Sleeping Beauty."

"Sure thing, Prince Charming." She dropped the pillow onto the bed and sauntered into the bathroom, her every swaying step raising his blood pressure by a couple of points. When the door closed behind her, he shook himself and headed into the kitchen to make breakfast. With a little luck, that would satisfy the gnawing ache in his gut.

He finished scrambling a big mess of eggs and cheese just as Jane came out of the bedroom dressed in ass-hugging jeans and a white men's dress shirt, which shouldn't have been sexy at all but managed to accentuate the small swells of her breasts and the more generous curve of her hip. His fingers itched to hold her there, to pull her body into his, so he busied them dishing up the food.

"Here you go." He passed her a plate.

"My God, Eric," she said with a little laugh, "this is enough for two people!"

He shrugged. "You need fuel."

"Yes, sir." She gave him a mock salute and took the plate and fork over to the couch.

"Coffee? Juice?"

"Coffee. Lots of coffee."

He knew that. Had seen how much of the stuff she downed over the past several days. If he drank more than a couple of cups, he found it hard to sit still, but she was never jittery or out of control. He poured her a large mug and carried it over to her, then returned to the kitchen to eat his own breakfast standing at the counter.

"You are such a guy," Jane said, watching him. A tiny smile hovered around her lips, and he wanted to touch them, to let the warmth of that little grin wrap itself around him.

"Why?"

"You eat standing up. Women don't do that. I bet your sister doesn't do that."

"No. In fact, one time when she was about fifteen she told me if I ate standing up I'd end up with fat feet."

Jane raised her eyebrows. "Fat feet? What did you tell her?"

"I told her if that was the case, then eating sitting down would give *her* a fat ass."

She laughed, the sound bright in the sterile space. "You must have been a terrible brother."

"The worst." He joined her on the sofa. "Now aren't you glad you never had siblings?"

"Nope." Her smile went wistful. "I so wished I hadn't been an only child."

"Was it hard? With your mother?"

"It wasn't so bad. I mean . . . not most of the time. Other people's parents had fights, got divorced, got drunk. It's not as if I was the only one whose home life had flaws. As long as she stayed on the meds, she was pretty much average. She shook and twitched, but she could talk about normal things and take care of me and keep the house together. But then she'd go off them and . . . I remember one day, I came home after school and she had destroyed all our mirrors and broken the glass in all the picture frames. 'They' were watching us, she said. There was glass everywhere, and she was all cut up, but she didn't even notice."

"Jesus, Janie." He put his plate down, scooted close, and wrapped an arm around her, pulling her into his body. She rested her head against his shoulder. "What did you do?"

"I called my dad. While I waited for him to come home and take her to the hospital, I cleaned her up as much as possible—we didn't have mirrors or photographs in the kitchen and she hadn't touched the windows, so it wasn't *all* glass 'they' could see through. That was our usual game plan. She lost it the first time my dad called an ambulance, so that was out of the question."

So matter-of-fact. Even after her revelation in the lab about her mother's suicide, he'd been considering her smart but sheltered. He hadn't taken the time to imagine what her day-to-day life must have been like. She would have had to be stronger than most of the neighborhood toughs he knew growing up.

"It must have been hard to invite friends over."

Her snort held no humor. "That didn't happen."

"I'm so sorry, Janie."

She reached up and laid a hand on his cheek. "Don't be. It wasn't a bad childhood, I promise. But having a brother or sister would have made it easier."

"Be sure you tell my sister that when you meet her." He tweaked her chin and got up before he gave in to the temptation to turn his head into her hand and kiss her palm. His appetite gone, he dumped the rest of his eggs down the disposal. If Jane noticed, she didn't say so.

At eight thirty on the dot, the doorbell rang. One thing about Lexie, she was fanatically organized and precise. He wondered whether she'd been standing outside for five minutes, watching the time count down on the second hand of a watch just so she'd be on time.

"I'm going to take Jane to tech and introduce her around," she said when he opened the door. "They set up a station for her. Nash wants to see you in his office."

"Is there news?"

"He didn't tell me." Her eyes flicked to Jane. "If you're ready, we can go."

"Of course."

"I'll be up in a few minutes," he promised as Jane and Lexie stepped off the elevator. Then the doors closed, actively cutting him off from her for the first time in days. She was perfectly safe on the seventh floor. Not only because she was in the building, but because the guys who ran tech for Nash were required to train as operatives as well. Every one of them was armed and ready to fight. Still, until he could be sure she was safe, he didn't like not being able to get to her.

That tension might have shown a bit when he strode into Nash's office and found the man tilted back in his chair, loafer-clad feet on his desk, reading a report. Despite having every kind of gadget on earth, Nash still preferred paper, a preference Eric shared except when it hid his boss's face from him.

"Did you find something on Jane's case?"

Nash read for another second, then put down the paper and slowly lowered his feet to the floor.

"Have a seat, Eric."

He sat, bracing himself for the worst.

"You want to tell me what's going on between you and Dr. Evans?"

What the fuck? "She's a client. We're friends."

"So you're not sleeping with her?"

"Would it matter if I was? You've never given a damn about my social life before."

"And if I thought you were just fucking her, I wouldn't

now. But emotional involvement makes people careless, gets people killed. I lost an agent last year, damned near lost this building, all because of *emotions.*"

Yeah, he'd heard about that. They'd chased Mac Brody's girlfriend to some Caribbean island, and it had all gone to shit. That was the case where Hal had died and a bomb had detonated in the HSE garage.

"She's my friend. That's the extent of our involvement."

"Fuck." Nash rubbed a hand across his face. "I'm tempted to take you off this, see if Jake or Mac can give me a few days."

Fury rose, fast and hard, and he beat it back. Anger would only alienate Nash. "You chose me for a reason."

"Yeah. Because she knew you. She would trust you, confide in you."

"So how has that changed?"

"Anything she was going to reveal, she would have by now. Whatever this is, she doesn't have a clue. I can assign Jake to her for whenever she's not at work, and you can go back to doing K and R with Travis."

"You have a case?" Kidnap and ransom was Eric's usual beat. He and Travis, often with a third operative, would make sure the transaction went smoothly. And when it didn't, they'd take back the hostage by any means necessary.

"Would you go if I did?"

So it was cards-on-the-table time. "No." He tried to be reasonable. "Look, Jane is the kind of person who needs everything to make sense, to be explained. I've gotten her to the point where when I say jump, she jumps. Jake would have to start that all over again. He'd say jump and she'd want to know who was coming, which direction they were coming from. . . By the time she jumped, it would be too late. I can't let that happen."

"And what if I ordered you to take a different case?"

"Then I'd quit. And whoever you assigned to her would have to work around me."

"All because you're *friends*."

That didn't deserve an answer, so Eric didn't give it one. He sat, matching stares with Nash, until the other man shook his head.

"Jake said you'd be this way."

"That's what you were talking to him about last night?"

"Partially. He's also going to run some data through one of his algorithms for me. But he was a profiler in a previous life, and even though he says he's a lousy judge of people, I've found he's better than he thinks."

"And what did he say?"

For the first time, a hint of a smile lightened Nash's expression. "I think I'll save that until I decide whether he's right."

⌒

THE NEXT SEVERAL days brought disappointment after disappointment. Jane weeded through the information Nash's guys collected with amazing speed, but Eric could do nothing to help. As he'd told Jane, computers and research were not his areas of expertise. On Monday they returned to the lab so Jane could finish up the paperwork for the patent sale, but once she was done with that she told Clive she wouldn't be back until Thursday. It was a mark of the man's respect for her that he didn't insist she return Tuesday to work with her new team as he'd first ordered.

The only time Eric felt useful was in the evening, when Jane wore herself out with work and worry and allowed him to take care of her. He cooked, teased her out of her funks as much as possible, talked to her about inconsequential things like how she'd learned to crochet from her grandmother, and found the crappiest movies possible for them to watch together. And at night, when they crawled into bed together and she snuggled close and fell asleep in his arms, she made him feel like the only man in the world who could help her. And though he knew it was wrong to take advantage of her vulnerability— to lead her on and let her believe that their relationship would deepen when she was no longer a client when, in truth, he had nothing beyond the moment to offer her—he couldn't bring himself to stop. When her fear dissipated, she would realize she didn't really want him. As long as he didn't give her any- thing to regret, she could move on heart-whole.

Tuesday afternoon, Nash called them both into his office.

"We've run out of leads," he said once Jane had settled into a chair and Eric had taken up a standing position behind her.

Jane squeaked, a tiny sound from the back of her throat, but otherwise did not respond. Eric dropped his hands to her shoulders and felt the tremors running through her body.

When she finally spoke, even her voice wobbled. "I under- stand. Tomorrow morning it will be too late anyway." The defeated tone made him want to break something or, pref- erably, some*one*.

"I'm very sorry, Dr. Evans." Eric had never heard sympa- thy or kindness from Nash. It kind of creeped him out. But he would use it.

"Can we have the office for a few minutes?"

If Nash objected to being kicked out of his own space, he didn't allow it to show. With a brief nod, he left the room.

Eric knelt in front of Jane. "Look at me, Janie." He took her hands in his and waited. "Janie." She met his gaze. "I swear to you, regardless of what happens, I will not give up. I won't allow HSE to give up. I have friends here who will continue to work on finding out what's happened to Dani whenever Nash doesn't have another job for them. No matter how long it takes, no matter where they've hidden her, we *will* find her." *Or her body*. But he figured Jane already understood that part.

Once some color returned to her face, Jane let go of his hands and stood. He followed her up.

"We should give Nash back his office."

"Just say when."

"When." She gave him a wan smile.

In the elevator back up to his apartment, she asked the question he'd dreaded since opening his mouth to make his promise. "If Nash says they're out of leads, where will you look?"

"We'll start with Dani's life away from the lab. She never told you her brother was back in New York, but obviously someone found out if they took him. So maybe she had close friends, people she told about the research you guys were doing who had another idea for it. Did you two ever talk about your private lives?"

"She didn't think I had one." Jane's cheeks turned pink, and he couldn't help the lightening of his heart. Yeah, she talked a big game about having casual sex, but she'd also said her teammates considered her an automaton.

"The last person I know she was really close to was Bryan Axlerod. He worked at AHI with us for a year, and they dated for a while. But he got hired away to work at a lab in California several months ago, and I have no idea whether they still talk. She hasn't mentioned him in ages, so I assumed they'd lost touch.

"She also tried to get me to go out for margaritas with

some friends of hers from a couple of other labs. They got together Thursday nights, mostly at Rosa Mexicano, to drink and dish the dirt. But I don't know whether she was really close to them, either. They sounded more like . . . like . . . well, when I was in college, I hung out with some of the premeds. We'd study and party together. We'd even go to the occasional baseball game together. But I wouldn't call them my friends. I never told them anything meaningful about myself."

"If you didn't tell them, who did you tell?" He'd had more friends in college than he knew what to do with. Getting time alone to study had been the problem.

"Are you kidding? I was younger than all my classmates. I didn't talk to anyone beyond the most trivial and mundane crap until I was in med school. At least by then I'd learned the trick of never mentioning my age, and I'd grown up enough not to look so different from everyone else."

⌒

WAY TO REMIND the guy what a pathetic loser she'd been. Not what she intended.

"After that, I got better," she assured him as he let them into the apartment. "I took a cooking class. Did a couple of yarnathons with other crocheters and knitters to raise money for cancer research, basically became a human being instead of an academic machine."

"Oh, really? And the men in your life. You met them in cooking class, or in the yarnathons?"

"Wow, Eric, sexist much?"

He grinned. "Just giving you a hard time. Who does the cooking around here, Miss 'I took a cooking class'?"

"That's *Doctor* 'I took a cooking class' to you, and don't you forget it!" She snorted, remembering the disaster that class had turned into. "My God, you should have seen it. Seriously. I was so sure before I took that class that there was nothing I couldn't learn. But cooking . . . The science parts of it appealed to me, but it's an art as well, and you can't teach that part. Everything I made tasted awful. I'd think I was following the recipe exactly, but terms like 'cream' the butter and eggs are so imprecise and nothing looked the way the descriptions sounded. And then there was the turkey."

"Dare I even ask?"

"I didn't realize that there were two packages of stuff inside. I saw the instructor reach into the turkey cavity and pull out the bits and pieces, so I did the same. Or thought I did. But there was still one bag left in there. It melted."

"Oh, dear." He was laughing outright, his eyes sparkling with light, and her heart turned over. She wanted him beyond all reason. All his intense focus, those muscles, the laughter that warmed her and cleared the shadows from her heart.

She put her arms around his neck. He hadn't kissed her, except to brush his lips over her forehead when they went to bed, since Friday night when she'd confronted him. But she had only sixteen more hours as a client, most of which would be spent right here at HSE. The only real danger she'd be in would be on the way to the press conference. And it was doubtful anything would happen then—if Clive's competition knew they were making their announcement, they'd also know time had run out and kidnapping her would have no purpose. And as soon as he was off the clock, Eric would disappear. She could practically feel it. Oh, sure, he'd check in occasionally to tell her about Dani—he was a man of his word—but for all intents and purposes it would be as if these days had never happened.

"I watched you in college, you know."

His arms, which had gone around her waist automatically when she hugged him, stiffened.

"What do you mean?"

"Remember when you told me about how baseball was a game of statistics and strategy? And that it was your job as catcher to know all the opposing players' stats and use those stats against them?"

"Not really, but it sounds like me. I was pretty full of myself."

"I went to baseball games when you played. I didn't have much interest in the sport, but I watched you do all that stuff with the hand signals and the different batters. That part fascinated me."

"Why didn't you ever tell me? I thought you wanted to know baseball because it helped you help me. So much of what you explained to me about how to understand my academics was based in the way things worked on the field."

"Absolutely. I learned baseball because I needed a language to teach you science. But if you'd known I did more than learn how it all worked, if you'd known I actually watched you play, what difference would it have made? You were you. I was me. You were . . . Another premed once came to a game with me, and he called you a 'splendid physical specimen.' I was the weird smart kid who was younger than everyone else."

"I never thought of you that way."

"Eric, I'm not stupid. You never thought of me at all. Don't even try to say you did. But it didn't hurt. It *doesn't* hurt. I didn't want a boyfriend—that would only get in the way of my studies—and I was frankly too immature to understand the appeal of a 'splendid physical specimen.' But I'm not now."

"Jesus, Janie." He dropped his head so that his forehead rested against hers, and every word he spoke filled the air between them with the peppermint scent of the gum he chewed. "We're back to this again?"

"Tomorrow after the press conference you'll drop me back at home, and then you'll disappear." She kept all the emotion out of her voice. If he believed for even a minute that she'd become attached to him, he'd rabbit. "You'll get assigned to a job out of the country. Or not. But I won't see you again."

"You don't understand."

"Because you haven't explained." And she hoped he didn't ask her to defend her desire as she wanted him to defend his refusal. It was greedy, selfish, this hunger. She couldn't explain it, had nothing to compare it to. There was nothing reasonable, intellectual, or sensible about it. For once, she wanted something for herself, for no other reason than that it felt good.

He reached up and pried her hands from his neck, then led her to the couch. "I told you, I'm past the age of one-night stands."

"So it won't be one night." *Oh, please, let it not be one night.* She wasn't sure how he'd snuck past all her usual guards, but he had, and if he left—when he left—her life behind those walls would be infinitely lesser for it.

"It can't be anything but. As you said, after this, I'll be assigned elsewhere. But it's not just that." He rubbed a hand across the back of his neck, and Jane tensed. Now they were getting to the truth.

"I don't have anything to offer. The kind of life I lead ... I told you, my specialty is kidnap and ransom. That means I'm out of the country more than I am in it. No, it's not as bad as the Army, and any time I need a break—like if my mother needs me or when my sister gets married—I just tell Nash I'm unavailable for a while. But it's not relationship friendly, either. And then there's the fact that any mission I go on could be my last. I saw what my dad put my mom through. When I was ten, he got drunk and wrapped his car around a lamppost. He lost the use of one arm, but what put him on disability was the brain injury. He had seizures, and the meds that he took to control them, combined with the injury itself, caused memory and cognitive-function problems.

"Any time I leave on a job, I could be injured just as badly. No way would I put a woman through that."

"Your mother divorced him because of his injury?"

"Not according to either of them. They both agree it was mutual. All the usual excuses: they married too young, they grew apart, all the reasons parents tell their children."

She almost asked him why he didn't believe them, but that would lead to a discussion she didn't want to have. No, she wanted to stay solidly where they were. Talking about sex.

"So, we won't have a relationship. Not the kind where I rely on you. You of all people should know what my life looks like. It's complete. I don't need you; I just want you. So why can't we have the kind of relationship where when you're available and I'm available, we sleep together?" She studied him, then went with the most logical argument she could muster. "I don't see how you have much choice."

"No?"

"Well, if you don't want one-nighters, but you can't have a relationship, you either have to have an arrangement like I'm describing, or you have to be celibate. And that would be a crying shame." God, she loved when he got that dazed, surprised look on his face.

But this time he recovered quickly, his blue eyes narrowing on her face. "Are you sure, Jane? Because you need to be absolutely certain."

She leaned in. "Oh, I am very, very sure," she whispered against his lips.

⌒

AND THAT WAS it. No way could he deny her—or himself—any longer. He'd done the right thing. He'd held off and explained and let her make every single move. Now he was going to take her at her word.

At first, he let her keep control. Her mouth against his was light but persistent, her tongue flicking at his lips until he opened them for her. Her fingers explored him, running over his shoulders, down his chest to his waist, then sliding up beneath his shirt. But when she tried to push him back against the arm of the sofa, he stopped her.

"Bed," he said against her lips. "At least the first time, this is going to be in a bed."

She hopped off the couch with gratifying speed, grabbing his hand on the way up to tug him along. *Christ, what a woman.* Somewhere in the back of his mind, he'd expected her to balk at the less-than-romantic shift of scene. But no. Instead, she hurried to the bedroom and threw herself down on her back on the bed, arms and legs outstretched. The invitation was as irresistible as it was unmistakable, and he followed her down, settling his legs between hers, his elbows on either side of her small breasts.

"Hi," she said, grinning up at him.

"Hi, yourself," he replied.

She curled her arms around him and slipped her hands beneath his shirt. "Can you take this off? I'm tired of it."

"Oh-ho? Is that how it's going to be? Well, I'm tired of your outfits, too. Couldn't you wear something just once that doesn't cup that fine butt of yours when you walk? If we're getting rid of clothes, those jeans are number one on my list."

She grinned up at him. "Can we trade? I'll take off whatever you take off."

"Yeah?" He sat up and pulled his T-shirt over his head. She did the same, leaving her in a lacy white bra that made his already hard cock throb with an almost painful pleasure.

"I don't have one of these to take off," he teased, running a finger around the dark areola visible through the lace.

Her breathing sped up. "Oh, well, we can consider it part of the shirt. . . ."

He shook his head, never taking his eyes from hers. "Nope. A deal's a deal. That stays on. Or at least, you don't take it off."

A whimper slipped from her throat. Good God, she was so fucking hot. How had no one snatched her up and tied her down? He bent his head and took one of her fabric-covered breasts into his mouth, and she grabbed the back of his head and arched off the bed with a little cry. He moved to her other breast, and her whole body quivered.

"Jeans," she said. Then, stronger, "*Jeans.*"

"I dunno. I may have decided to keep them on for a while."

"A deal's a deal," she said, pushing him off and climbing off the bed. He watched as she unbuttoned and unzipped the pants. Then she turned her back on him and hooked her thumbs in the sides. Slowly, wiggling that incredible ass the whole time, she began to pull them down. Three inches, four, and he realized she'd caught her panties at the same time. Bare skin was revealed with agonizing slowness as she shimmied out of the jeans, bending over when they reached her knees to hold them down while she stepped out of them entirely.

He couldn't breathe.

She turned her head and grinned at him over her shoulder. "Your turn."

He'd never stripped so fast in his life. He couldn't give her the same kind of show she'd given him—he simply wouldn't last if he tried. Maybe next time. Naked, he faced her across about two feet of space. She turned around, stripping off her bra as she did so, all the fun gone from her expression, and the first thought through his head eased a little of his tension. So he spoke it aloud, hoping to help ease hers.

"I see you haven't changed quite as much as you'd have people believe." He waggled his eyebrows.

It took a second for her to follow his gaze, and then she laughed. "Nope. Very expensive color treatments. It was hard enough to get taken seriously at my age without having traffic-cone orange hair as well. The highlights and lowlights free me from the whole Raggedy Ann look."

He crawled onto the bed and she joined him, pressing herself against him as if she wanted to absorb him right into her body. Her desperation drove him over the edge, and he flipped her to her back, sliding a finger inside her at the same time he invaded her mouth with his tongue. She squirmed against his hand, hot and wet and frantic. He lifted his head and reached across her with his other arm, tried to grab the knob on the bedside table drawer. And almost fell off the bed.

"Fuck."

She giggled. "Smooth, Romeo." But her face was rosy and her breathing harsh and fast.

He grabbed a condom out of the drawer. "Watch out, Juliet.

I'm coming for you." He got on all fours, the condom in one fist, and moved toward her.

Her lips twisted as she tried to restrain a smile. "Oh, I hope so."

He pounced, knocking her flat while keeping his weight mostly on his own hands and knees so as not to hurt her. "You first."

And then he was inside her and all the humor was gone and it was just heat and passion and the clawing, questing climb to the top. Her legs were wrapped around his waist, her arms around his shoulders, one hand tangled in his hair. Every thrust forced a sob from her throat, and the pitch wound higher as her body tightened around him.

"You first, baby," he said, fingers finding one tight nipple and rolling it.

And she went, sobbing his name, the most incredible thing he'd ever seen, the sweetest sound he'd ever heard, and he couldn't even appreciate it because her contractions sent him flying over the edge into a blinding orgasm.

By the time Jane caught her breath, Eric was already striding to the bathroom to dispose of the condom. Dusk's light gleamed on his damp skin, setting the smooth muscles rippling beneath his skin into stark relief. Holy hell, the man was hot.

And the sex . . . She'd never had sex like that before, or she might have changed her mind about the risk/reward ratio. It wasn't just his body, though there was no denying the appeal of all that muscle. No, her first lover, a doctor who swam, ran, and lifted weights to relieve stress, had had plenty of muscle but had never generated the same kind of havoc in her system. He'd been considerate, too, always making sure she was satisfied, so it wasn't that she'd never had an orgasm in the past.

Maybe it was the humor. She'd never actually laughed in bed with a man in her life. She tried to imagine laughing with the doctor and failed. But then, she couldn't imagine watching *Lake Placid 3* with him, either.

No, Eric was special, though he'd disappear the minute she said so.

When he slid back into the bed, however, reaching for her and pulling her up against his solid strength, she could not resist asking the question dominating her mind.

"Is it always like that for you?"

"Is it for you?"

Against his chest, she shook her head. Fearing what he might find in her eyes, she pressed a kiss to his clavicle and watched her own fingers toying with the sprinkle of rough hair spread across his chest.

But of course it didn't fool him. "Janie, look at me." She did. "It's never like that. Never. Think about it like baseball. Or chemistry. If you taught me anything, it was that seeing a chemical in one state in no way predicts how that chemical will change when exposed to others."

"So we are chemicals?"

"Or baseball players. A guy can play for Florida for five years and bat a solid .385, then be traded to Colorado and drop to .270. What just happened wasn't you or me; it was us."

"Scientists don't believe the results of a single experiment, you know," she said, lowering her lids so she could peek up at him through her lashes.

His lips twitched. "No?"

"No. You have to repeat it several times."

"Well," he said, a devilish grin in his sparkling eyes, "I wouldn't want to be accused of being unscientific."

CHAPTER 6

JANE WOKE BEFORE the alarm, which came as a surprise, given how thoroughly Eric had exhausted her the night before. At one point, he'd insisted they break for dinner. He broiled steak and baked potatoes because he swore Jane would need her energy for what he had planned, and he'd been right. She had no idea what time she'd dozed off, only that he'd lost the battle first, allowing her to study him for at least a few minutes before curling up next to the heat and strength of his body and falling asleep.

While she slept, her legs had twined with his and his arms had wrapped around her so that she couldn't imagine how she would get loose without disturbing him.

"You worried about the press conference?" His voice rumbled in his chest beneath her ear.

"I should have known you were already up."

"I wasn't. But you're thinking so loud, you disturbed my perfect slumber."

She scooted away. "Yeah, right. And no, wasn't thinking about the press conference. I was thinking that I needed to pee. And shower. And get ready. And go over my notes." He raised his eyebrows. "Yeah, okay, I was sort of thinking about the press conference. *And* other stuff."

She ran for the bathroom and locked the door behind her just in case he got any ideas. He'd mentioned showering together the night before, but they hadn't gotten around to it. And this was definitely not the right time. She allowed herself the luxury of a long shower. After all, there would be at least one photographer, so she had to shave her legs. She had to stand up for her colleagues—no allowing any comments about how a scientist couldn't be both intelligent and fashionable.

"Your turn," she said, unlocking the door and walking out into the bedroom wrapped in one of Eric's giant bath sheets. He still lay in bed, but his arms were folded beneath his head, emphasizing the bulge of his biceps and the sheet lay crumpled at his waist, showing off his six-pack. "You're just trying to get me to come back to bed," she grumbled.

"Is it working?" He wiggled his eyebrows and she laughed. "Afraid not."

He huffed. "Fine."

She watched him saunter into the bathroom, all those muscles gliding gracefully beneath the skin. Only after he closed the door did she turn to her bag and dig out her underwear and a T-shirt. She'd wait until her hair was dry before putting on her clothes for the day, but despite the previous night's intimacies, she didn't feel right walking around the apartment undressed.

"What happens at these things, anyway?" Eric asked as he came out of the bathroom a few minutes later. He rummaged through his drawers and pulled on one of his typical outfits of olive cargo pants and a black T-shirt.

"Well, Sundeman called this one. They're big enough to attract attention, so at least a few reporters will show up to hear their news. Their representative will announce that they've bought the drug from AHI, which will only be of interest because they had a spectacular failure about five years ago with a similar drug that had to be taken off the market. Clive will talk a little bit about the development while a publicity person hands out data sheets and press releases, and then we'll open it up for questions. Since I was lead on the research team, I'll answer whatever research-related questions arise."

"Wouldn't most of the questions be about research?"

"Not really. Under normal circumstances, companies don't even bother with an actual press conference. This kind of deal shows up in the financial papers because of how it's apt to affect investment in Sundeman's stock. But because of Alophil—that was the drug that had to be taken off the market because it caused aneurisms after long-term use— they're doing a big promotional push for this one. They're going to invite scrutiny at every step so that no one accuses them of malfeasance or not doing their due diligence if any-thing goes wrong."

"You don't expect a big crowd?"

"Not really. Sundeman will have told them enough to bring the right reporters, the psych folks rather than the sports-medicine folks, for example, and schizophrenia isn't a huge draw. It's not as if they were announcing an Alzheimer's breakthrough."

"Gotcha."

THEY LEFT FOR the press conference at eight fifteen, having agreed to meet early at Sundeman in case any last-minute issues cropped up. Eric parked in a garage a couple of blocks away, and as they walked to the office, he took her hand in his. Was that how he treated all the women he slept with? Did none of them ever get attached to him? How did they avoid it? He let go only when they were close enough to attract attention.

Two news vans were setting up on the corner in front of the Sundeman building, and a few reporters had gathered already when they arrived. Clive and his contact, John, were waiting for them in the lobby.

"Welcome to Sundeman Pharmaceuticals, Dr. Evans," John said. "We're very impressed with your work."

"Thank you. This is my friend, Eric Sorenson."

Eric and John shook hands.

"I was telling him we could never have completed the project without you," Clive said.

"Can I get you a drink or anything before we face the piranhas outside?"

"Maybe a bottle of water, if you have one." Jane wished Clive would have left her in the lab and done the conference by himself. She hated being the center of attention. Teaching in grad school had been pure hell. She shifted and fidgeted, and Eric brushed his fingers briefly over hers.

At nine o'clock on the dot, Jane, Clive, and John walked out and stood before the small crowd that had gathered. Eric hung back, watching from off to the side, but she could feel his eyes on her.

The conference went on considerably longer than usual, though luckily most of the questions weren't for her. She and John explained the mechanism of the drug and how it differed from Alophil, but most of the reporters wanted to know about the lawsuits from Alophil and how soon the new drug would go into testing and how long it might be before they'd see it on the market.

When it was over and the reporters had dispersed, Jane, Eric, and Clive went back to AHI.

"Honestly, Jane, I didn't think we were going to make it," Clive said after they had settled in his office and gone over the questions asked at the press conference. "I wouldn't say so to the team, of course, but I was pretty sure we'd lose the Sundeman contract."

"Never count them out, Clive. Especially Rashid. He's a brilliant scientist, and he and Stella worked a ton of overtime."

"I know they did. But we couldn't have done it without you. Thank goodness Sorenson was able to keep you safe." He looked at Eric. "If there's ever anything I can do for you and your boss, please let me know. I know HSE's lab is second to none, but I'd be happy to help if you need extra resources."

"I'll keep that in mind," said Eric. "But for now I'd like to get Jane home so she can relax in peace. It's been a stressful ten days."

"Of course! Jane, can I at least call a car service for you?"

"No, I'm fine. Eric will take me."

"Oh?" Clive eyed her, waiting for her to elaborate, but she didn't. What could she say?

"All part of the service," Eric said easily.

"Great." Clive stood and held out a hand. "Again, my thanks, Eric. Jane, I'll see you tomorrow."

Eric didn't say much as he drove her home, but his hand rested possessively on her thigh. Its warmth comforted her, and she drifted off a bit until they pulled up in front of her house. The door was her same, bright blue paneled wood, but the frame had been replaced with a new, unpainted oak one, and as they walked up the steps, Jane was filled with memories of how they had left.

"When they broke in, the door held up great," Eric explained. "The frame not so much."

He held her back, placing her bag inside the door and

drawing his gun to check the entire house before allowing her inside.

"But I'm safe now," she protested.

"Let me be sure, okay? I don't want to take any chances with you."

Oh. That was very sweet. She waited patiently while he searched, then plopped down on the couch when he allowed her inside.

"The crew cleaned up upstairs," he told her. "The glass is gone, but the windows are just boarded over. I figured you'd want to work through it all with your insurance company, but they couldn't be left the way they were."

"No, I really appreciate that. The house is old. I probably should put in better windows anyway. My heating bills are astronomical. I can't imagine what it's like for those people who live in the giant Victorians in this neighborhood. Of course, I can't imagine cleaning those places, either, so clearly I'm not cut out to live in one."

"People who live in those places don't worry about cleaning them. They have maid services for that."

She shuddered. "Is it weird that I wouldn't want that, even if I could afford it? Having a stranger in my space all the time?"

"Nah. Privacy's important to me, too. But my mom cleaned houses like that. And one of the families she cleaned for eventually hired her full-time. They didn't consider her a stranger. She was special to them. When she had a heart attack a couple of years ago, it was the daughter who called me and my sister."

"I suppose I could manage that. Around here you mostly see services. Like 'Happy Clean Maids' or whatever." The conversation wasn't about maids, or even about his mother. It was about not letting him leave.

Apparently, he came to the same conclusion. "Have dinner with me tonight?"

Thank God for direct men. "Sure. Down by you, or up here?"

"Here. I hardly ever bother with eating out when I'm in New York, so I'm not up on the good places."

"Okay."

"I'll pick you up at seven?"

"That works."

"Great." He pulled her into a hard, fast hug and pressed a hot kiss to her lips, then left.

Holy hell. She was in deep. She took a breath and waited for her heart to slow down. Checking her watch, she saw it was only one o'clock. She should have lunch, then clean the house. With a little luck, that would keep her busy until Eric came to pick her up, because if she had too much time to ponder what might happen on an actual, honest-to-goodness *date*, she'd go mad.

She ordered Chinese because she could stock the extra needed to make the delivery minimum in her fridge, which needed a clean-out after a week away. While she waited for it to arrive, she changed out of her fancy clothes into jeans and a tee and stripped her bed. She was transferring the first load of laundry into the dryer when the doorbell rang. Her stomach growled in anticipation.

It took a minute for her to process the fact that the man wearing a ball cap with "Harry's Hunan" on it and holding a bag smelling of soy sauce and sesame oil in his left hand held a syringe in his right. Before she could slam the door, he'd stepped inside and jammed the needle into the side of her neck. She screamed, or tried to, but no sound emerged, and then she was falling. . . .

Eric sat in the driver's seat of the HSE SUV he'd borrowed for the evening. What kind of man didn't even own his own car? Everyone told him that owning a vehicle in New York City was more trouble than it was worth, and under normal circumstances he agreed. Public transportation was fast and comprehensive, and parking prohibitively expensive. When he went home to North Carolina, he flew and then rented a car at the airport. And next time he and Jane went out he'd rent a car, too, because asking Lexie to borrow the SUV was like stroking a viper's belly. Of course, there might not be a next time. Now that the pressure was off, Jane would get bored with him soon enough.

But he'd worry about that when the time came. For now, he'd enjoy what they had. He jogged up the steps and rang Jane's doorbell. He waited a few minutes, then pressed his ear to the door. With another woman, he'd assume she was in the bathroom getting ready and hadn't heard the bell, or even that she was simply making him wait so he'd appreciate her more when she answered. But neither of those explanations suited Jane's character. The hairs on the back of his neck rose.

He rang again but didn't wait before making his way around the side of the house to peer through the window into the living room. No movement, but nothing particularly out of order, either. Still, he couldn't ignore the increasing knot in the pit of his stomach. He went around the back and tried the door. It opened easily.

Fuck.

"Jane?" He headed for the front of the house and the stairs and saw, lying just inside the front door, out of view of the windows, her purse lying next to a spilled bag of Chinese food. His mind played out the ambush scene all too easily. He'd done the same thing himself more than once, rushing in on the heels of a delivery guy or taking him out as he approached a house using his uniform as an entry pass.

He was back in the SUV in seconds punching a button to connect him directly to Lexie.

"They took her," he said the minute she picked up.

"But the press conference. She should have been safe now."

"This isn't about the schizophrenia drug. It never was." *Damn, damn, damn.* If he hadn't been racing to HSE at top speed, he'd have bashed his head into the steering wheel at his own stupidity. "I'm such a fucking idiot. The timing was a *cover*. If she disappeared before the conference, people would assume there was no reason to look for her afterward. They'd believe she was dead, the same assumption we've been making about Dani."

"Oh, hell. I am so sorry."

"Is Nash there?"

"He is. Do you want to talk to him?"

"Not now. I'm headed back. I should be there in half an hour. Can you get me some time with him then?"

"Of course, Eric."

"And get the tech guys working on it. I want to know who would want Jane. She's been the object all along. If they need a client number, you give them my name. I'll settle with Nash on how I'll pay the debt."

"Don't worry about that, for God's sake. I'll be sure Nash is waiting and research will start on Jane's background and contacts. They'll be happy to. They all really liked her."

"Thanks, Lex." He hung up, his heart pounding, and had to blink a couple of times. What the hell was that? He was a fucking warrior. Warriors didn't cry. But the idea of Jane held against her will gutted him. He'd been in too many horrible places, seen too many kidnap victims, witnessed the bits and pieces sent back to family members. He shoved the memories and the images they inspired out of his mind. *Hang on, Janie. I'm coming.*

Amazingly, he made it down to HSE headquarters without getting a ticket. As Lexie had promised, Nash was waiting for him, his face set in grim lines.

"Come on in the office. Lexie, you, too."

Lexie took a seat, but Eric remained on his feet, pacing the carpeted floor.

"Goddammit, Nash, I should have known."

"We're good, Sorensen, but we're not psychics. We have to work with what we're given. And what we were given was a client in need of protection because of her research."

"Do we have any leads at all?"

"Maybe."

He froze. "Maybe? Like what?"

"The name Jane gave you, Bryan Axlerod. Research just told me they don't think he went to work at a lab when he left AHI. Or if he did, they're not paying him in the usual fashion. No employment records exist after September of last year. Proving a negative is impossible, as you know, so we can't be sure someone didn't hire him under the table, but no one's paying taxes on him."

"Are you saying he was abducted, too?"

"No," said Nash. "After all, he told Jane and the others he was moving, right? But what happened after that will take some more personal investigation, which means calling people, which we cannot do at eight o'clock at night. At least not for people like his former landlord, whose offices are now closed.

But I can call Clive Handler, and I will. I was just waiting for you." He pressed the speakerphone button and dialed.

When Clive picked up, Nash explained the situation as succinctly as possible, but Eric noticed he didn't mention Bryan Axlerod by name.

"So the timing is coincidence? But Jane's association with AHI was all about Project Calm. I mean, yes, she came on board with us before it got off the ground, but we discussed it at our first meeting. If another company wanted to poach her, all they had to do was wait. She was dedicated to this project because of her mother. She doesn't have the same connection to anything else we're working on."

"I'm going to want to talk to her lab group. Can you give me their phone numbers?"

Clive read them off, and Lexie scribbled them down. Not that they didn't already have the information—Nash's files on each of the lab's employees had addresses, phone numbers, even birthdays and social security numbers—but comparing what Clive gave them to what they already had might provide insights.

"Now that we know the attacks weren't specifically aimed at the schizophrenia solution you were working on, I need to ask a couple of other questions before I let you go."

"Whatever I can do," Clive said.

"Has she worked on any other projects over the last, say, year?"

Eric understood why Nash was being so roundabout. He no longer trusted Clive and didn't want to alert the man to the fact that they were looking at Bryan. Still, impatience gnawed at him.

"No."

"And her team members. Have they always been the same?"

"No. People move around depending on what's the most urgent at any given moment. As I mentioned during our earlier conversation, I'd only recently moved Dani to Project Calm."

"Right. So that's one change. Any others? New hires? Fires? Transfers in or out?"

"We did have one guy who left. Got a better offer from a place in California. Bryan Axlerod."

"Did he have reason to resent Jane? Or to want to hurt your company?"

"I can't imagine why. He was successful at AHI, and we parted on good terms, I thought."

"Anyone else?"

"No. Rashid has been off and on the team depending on what we need, but he was part of it in the beginning and he's never left the company, just worked on other things for periods of time. I suppose Alan Michaels, who's running the project Jane is transferring to, might resent the fact that they'll be heading it up together, but he knew that when I assigned him and I've always thought they had a good relationship or I wouldn't have asked them to work so closely together."

"I'll need his information as well."

"Of course." Clive read it off.

"And that's it?"

"Yes. Honestly, I can't think of anything else."

"All right, then. Oh, one last thing: Do you by any chance remember the name of the lab Bryan Axlerod went to work for?"

"I'm afraid not. It shouldn't be hard to find out, though. Research and development is a small world. I can look into it, if you like."

"That would be great."

But, of course, Clive wouldn't find anything. Because Nash had already checked and Bryan Axlerod had simply disappeared.

⌒

JANE'S HEAD HURT. And not with the "all I need is a cup of coffee and a hot shower" pain she often felt after a long night in front of the computer. What had happened? Her eyes were crusted shut, and when she opened them she didn't recognize her surroundings. The bed she was lying on was not her own. The last bit of moisture in her mouth dried up. When she sat up, the scream of her neck muscles brought memory rushing back.

How long had she been unconscious? And where had they brought her? Clearly, they had no fear of her escaping, as she was not restrained in any way.

She jumped off the bed and rushed to the door but found it locked. Not a big surprise. The second door she tried opened, revealing a bathroom that she made use of before continuing her exploration. The bedroom appeared utterly normal. Under other circumstances, she might even have called it beautiful with its whitewashed walls, high ceilings, and oversized windows. A large wood and wrought-iron ceiling fan circulated humid, green-scented air. *You're not in Kansas anymore, Jane.*

A scraping by the door sent her scrambling for any object that might serve as a weapon, but before she could grab anything, the door opened, Dani was shoved in, and the door closed again, the latch clicking with finality behind her.

"Jane?" Dani's eyes filled with tears. "Oh my God, this is

my fault. It never occurred to me that if I didn't work fast enough they'd go after you!"

"This isn't your fault. Come and sit." She led Dani over to the bed. "I'm just . . . Thank God you're alive. Are you okay?" Jane had often envied Dani's shiny, bouncy hair, but now it lay flat and stringy, all sheen gone. Heavy purple circles smudged the skin beneath her eyes.

"Tell me what you know. Where are we? What's going on? How are you being treated? Have you seen your brother?"

"I saw him once." Dani shook her head, and the tears fell. "Only once in person. But they bring me a picture every morning. Him and the newspaper to prove they still have him and that he's still alive." Dani rubbed her hands over her arms, shivering despite the heat. "We're in a house — a mansion, really — in Mexico somewhere. I don't know where. But there's a full lab built into an addition, so you don't have to leave the house to get to it. The grounds are heavily patrolled. There's no point in trying to run."

"So you stay inside and work . . . on what?"

"It's Bryan's project. And he's lost his mind."

"Bryan Axlerod?"

Dani nodded. "He didn't go to work in California. He came here. I don't know who's running the place. He makes like he is, but he doesn't have this kind of money. This . . . Well, after Alvaro got involved in drugs, I learned more than I wanted to about the creation and sale of illegal drugs. Everything about this setup screams 'cartel.' People think cartels just deal in cocaine and heroin, but they make other things, too. They have full-on manufacturing plants for off-label pharmaceutical pills and liquids."

"But Bryan wouldn't need you for that. Don't they just take the patents and create their own drugs? I mean, they're criminals; it's not as if they're worried about intellectual property."

"No. I mean, yes, that's what happens. But no, that's not what Bryan is doing. When I say he's lost it, I mean he's completely insane. No conscience whatsoever."

"What's he working on?"

"It's some combination of the schizophrenia and phobia research we were doing at AHI. He's trying to eliminate realistic fear, replace it with something else, a kind of amorphous paranoia. No fear of real-life death or pain because they are subsumed beneath the fear of this vague supernatural threat; no memory of love, no guilt, no conscience can survive in the face of that paranoia. The only thing left is total loyalty to the person or thing that can protect you from the threat. In short, sociopathology in pill form. Or maybe IV."

For a long moment, Jane couldn't speak. The idea was so heinous, so antithetical to her training and beliefs, that she couldn't even wrap her mind around it. "For God's sake, why?"

Dani grimaced. "Money. He says a drug like that could create an army."

It was a type of bioweapon she'd never considered. She'd refused two job offers because the labs offering her positions made their money primarily in government contracts. On the surface, all three were developing defensive drugs, but Jane had enough of her mother's paranoia and her father's academic mistrust of authority to see that the only way one could develop a countermeasure was first to come up with the weapon.

The latch clicked, and the door swung open to reveal two bored-looking men with guns. They were both short and dark haired and could have been brothers. One had had his nose broken at least once, because it had a distinct misalignment, while the other had a mustache.

"You are to come down to the laboratory," said Mustache.

"Frick and Frack," muttered Dani. "They follow me everywhere."

Mustache led the way through the house while Nose took up the rear. Dani hadn't been kidding about the mansion. The place had been let go for far too long, but the soaring ceilings, intricately carved columns and archways, and massive chandeliers all spoke of its former glory. Recent owners had brought in hypermodern, obviously expensive furnishings that clashed hideously with the old-world grandeur of the home itself.

Mustache took them through a thoroughly modernized kitchen and out a side door into a short, low-ceilinged corridor. The walls were stucco, as was the ceiling, but there were no windows or decorations and the floor was cement with two two-foot-square tiled panels and a large drain in the center. Jane could imagine it as either bunker or kill room all too easily, and neither made her comfortable. She hurried to the other end.

They emerged into a large, well-equipped lab. A half dozen men worked at various clean, well-organized, and amply lit stations. No one spoke except to examine readings, and the few words she could catch were in Spanish. She found Bryan hunched over a microscope and marched over to him.

"What the hell is this, Bryan?"

"Ah, Dr. Evans." Her name was a verbal sneer in his mouth. "This is your new lab, where you'll be working for the foreseeable future."

"And if I refuse?"

"I've been asked to keep you undamaged, at least for the moment. But Daniela here has no such protection. She will suffer for your disobedience, as her brother suffered for hers." He smiled then, a grotesque rictus, and spoke to Dani.

"Go ahead, my darling, tell them what happened when you said no."

Dani trembled and wrapped her arms tightly around her own body. Jane's first impulse was to comfort her, but a warning deep in the primitive, lizard brain part of her mind she seldom heard prevented her. This man would see compassion as weakness, and to show weakness here was to lose any slim advantage she might have.

"There are cells," Dani said at last. "They took me to one. It's the only time I've seen Varo in person since I got here. They wouldn't let me near him, but they made me watch and listen while they broke his index finger. They never told him why, just said it was my fault he was being punished." She turned pleading eyes on Jane. "Do you think he blames me?"

"No, I do not. You've been his big sister his whole life, and he knows you would never do anything to hurt him."

She focused on Bryan. "Why me and Dani? Surely there are people you could pay to do this work. That has to be easier than having hostages."

"But you're the best, Dr. Evans. And this research is right up your alley. No one else will be able to make sense of it as quickly, to develop a functional protocol with such efficiency. And, frankly, anyone else we'd want to do this would ask for too much money. No, you're not going anywhere. You'll be allowed to sleep in a comfortable space, and we have brought in clothes for you. You have no need to fear that we'll drug your food or otherwise dull your brain. We need you functioning at the top of your game. But don't mistake these courtesies for a lack of vigilance. If you sabotage anything in the lab, Dani will suffer. If you try to escape, Dani will suffer. If you do manage to escape, *you* will suffer. The jungle around this compound is inhospitable to say the least. It is also controlled by a very vicious cartel, Los Hijos de la Madre Muerte. We have protection, but outside these walls you'd have none. They'd take you, break you, and sell you to the highest bidder."

Not good. No wonder HSE hadn't been able to find Dani. Not only were they working off the wrong premise, but she'd been taken far from the bounds of civilization as well. Jane had seen a television special on the Hijos that showed how the cartel had survived the deaths of various leaders. The narrator had sounded hopeful that the death of the current leader—a woman, no less—in the United States would signal the end of the Hijos for good. But apparently it hadn't happened. Dealers in drugs, weapons, even people, cartels like the Hijos guarded their privacy fiercely.

But Bryan was here. And Jane had given Eric Bryan's name, thank God. Eric wouldn't give up. He'd promised that much even when only Dani was missing, when there was no reason to believe she was still alive. He might not want a relationship with Jane, but he would never let her disappear.

So she had to stall. And spy. Because sooner or later HSE's resources would dig up a trail, and she needed to be ready. But she couldn't afford to let down her guard or act out of character. They had to believe she did not think anyone would come for her.

Luckily, taking the easy way out was distinctly out of character, so she didn't have to do it.

"If I'm going to help you, I have a few demands of my own."

"You don't get to make demands," said Mustache. But he was the hired help. She ignored him.

Bryan held up a hand. "Let's hear the good doctor out."

Her mind whirled. What to ask for first?

"I want Dani as my assistant."

Bryan shrugged. "Easy enough."

"And she shares my room."

His face went thunderous at that, confirming her worst fears about what Dani might be suffering. It had been the 'my darling' that told the tale. Bryan Axlerod *was* a psychopath, and she would bring him to his knees if it was the last thing she ever did.

But she maintained a bored expression. "Both my assistant and I need to be well rested to do our best work. If she's out of my sight, I will be concerned and won't sleep."

"Fine. Whatever. You two lesbos cuddle up."

"And last, we want to see Alvaro every day. Maybe you could arrange to have him take breakfast with us. No more 'proof of life' photos—they don't suffice to keep my assistant calm and productive."

"Is that all? Or does the queen have other demands?"

"That's all for the moment. Unless you'd like to introduce me to your boss?"

He barked a laugh. "Wouldn't you love to know who's financing this op."

"I'd like to thank him for telling you not to abuse me."

"No thanks necessary. If he thought beating the shit out of you would be more effective, he'd have ordered that. In fact, he might change his mind tomorrow if you don't produce the results he wants in short order."

She swallowed the bile in the back of her throat and kept her voice even. "Then I guess I should look at where you are in terms of development. I'll need all the paperwork and history files to catch up."

Which she'd go through as slowly as possible. *Hurry, Eric. Please.*

Bryan set Jane up at a desk while he assigned Dani to work with one of the others.

"You don't need her yet," he said when Jane complained, "and everyone here earns their keep. Dani already knows what we're doing. She can join you when you're caught up." He pulled a laptop off another desk, opened it up, and set it down on the desk he'd assigned Jane. She watched for a network icon, but none appeared. That would be too much to hope for.

"We've entered the fourth research phase," Bryan said, opening a window that filled the screen. The picture flickered like an old movie, but then the pixels resolved and Jane realized she was looking into a darkened room, where half a dozen young men lay on cots. An IV pole stood sentinel over each bed with three bags attached, slowly dripping liquid into the veins of the sleeping men.

"These men are Group Two. We tried many, many individuals before Group One, and some of those individuals have gone on to do great things. Group One should have been a success. And at first, they were. Strong, focused, dedicated. But then they self-destructed." Disgust coated his words. "Every single one. That's when our backers agreed to bring you in."

"What on earth do I have to do with them?"

"Everything. Your research provided the key to shaping perfect soldiers out of our crop of young local men desperate for a few extra bucks. You see, not so long ago, recruitment into a group like the Hijos de la Madre Muerte would be enough to guarantee loyalty to a cause. But loyalty is in short supply these days. Fear of a common enemy is the only effective motivation." He tapped a key on the laptop, and a constant murmuring whisper almost like white noise came from the speakers. Concentrating, Jane could make out a few words in Spanish, but nothing that made sense.

"Oh, right," Bryan said, "language isn't your thing." He brought up another window. "This is the script." While Jane read, he lit a cigarette and breathed in the smoke. Jane tried not to cough when he blew it back out, but cigarette smoke always made her throat itch. She focused on the screen.

The Black is coming. Only the Hijos *can protect you from the Black. The Black will swallow you whole. The Black will destroy your family. The Black will consume you. Velasquez will save you. The Black will try to seduce you…*

It went on, more and more of the same. The end was coming in the form of "the Black," and only fealty to the *Hijos* and their leader, Velasquez, would save them. No wonder she hadn't been able to understand the Spanish. The English barely made sense, though the words felt like spiders crawling up her spine.

"This isn't anything I would touch. Ever."

"Oh, but it is. Those IVs are filled with solutions we developed by reversing the principles used for Project Calm and Project Phobos. Essentially, we've found a way to give our… volunteers…a variant of schizophrenia. Unfortunately, the first group who successfully completed the training couldn't live with the repercussions and they self-destructed."

Jane's stomach lurched. He'd caused six men to commit suicide and had not an ounce of remorse.

"This batch is doing better, but they need constant reinforcement. It's not practical. When Clive patented his new formula, we realized we needed to add a stabilizing chemical to our compound. We tried one before you got here, but it caused a reaction with what they were already taking."

"You do realize that exact issue forced us to change *everything* with Project Calm. I can't just slap the same buffer chemical we used into your formula like a Band-Aid. There's no guarantee I'll ever be able to stabilize those men, not with what you're doing to them."

"If you can't, you—and Dani—will suffer for it. Clive was fond of bonuses. Velasquez, your new employer, prefers consequences to rewards. So if I were you, I'd think really, really hard as you read the research. Your best work is the only thing that will save you."

CHAPTER 7

Jane paged through the research slowly, which proved harder than she anticipated. Science had always been her savior. If the other kids didn't want to hang with her, there were always books to read. She had started with history, seduced into reading by the Arthurian legends, but then she picked up a book on medicine and magic and became fascinated. A couple of books on the history of medicine taught her about genetics, and by age ten she understood that she might end up like her mother, though she still wasn't certain what that meant. Her parents, although they saw her intelligence, refused to discuss her mother's condition. The following year, a therapist recommended she deal with her ever-increasing fear of schizophrenia by learning more about the disorder on her own.

Taking the advice to heart, she'd asked her father to take her to the library directly from the therapist's office. The first books she tried assumed a far greater knowledge of biochemistry than she had, so she traded them in for beginner texts in chemistry and biology. Psychology came later, as she tried to understand her classmates and herself. She'd gotten a grip on the chemical and electrical bases of brain function—and dysfunction—but she'd never managed to make sense of people themselves. Their motives and behavior remained a mystery.

So she continued to study. And in one respect, Bryan had been correct: the research *was* right up her alley. Someone on this team had imagination. Not Bryan. Not only was the scope of the project beyond him, but also the solutions they'd already tried were far from anything he would—or could—come up with. In fact, she was hard pressed to believe anyone trained at an accredited institution would conceive a program like this one. It combined light therapy, drugs, torture, sleep deprivation, hypnosis, and mild electric-shock therapy. Traditional labs would never bother with such a complex system,

because they were seeking real-world solutions, treatments people could access without too much difficulty. Every additional step in a treatment, every hurdle, even a single extra pill in a day made patients less likely to remain compliant with their routines.

The people who volunteered to be altered at the fundamental level at which Bryan's project—Project Warlock—changed them were unlikely to go off plan. They'd also probably be supervised constantly, although the original project description discussed the possibility of long-lasting injections, implants, or even gene modifications.

The first skim through, done as slowly as possible, took four hours and gave her all the information she needed, especially since she had no intention of helping Bryan succeed. Of course, he wouldn't know that. He had always struck her as a worker bee, a follower. But maybe that was just a disguise? If he'd been planted at AHI to grab the phobia and schizophrenia data, playing the dullard would have been a smart move.

She flipped back to the beginning of the large sheaf of papers and called Bryan over.

"Can you mark for me who did each of these trials so I can talk to them? From my admittedly brief skim of the data, the results descriptions are not complete."

"That's because they failed."

So the dullard thing hadn't been an act. How the hell did the lack of that natural curiosity that was the hallmark of a good scientist get by Clive? He must have been on really good postgrad teams where others took up his slack. "You know how it works. If I know the exact reactions in each trial, the results might give me an idea of a new direction. So I'll want to interview the scientists and make my own notes."

"Bullshit," he said. "You're stalling."

Yup. "For crying out loud, Bryan, you've *seen* me work. This is how I do it. You're the one who brought me here. If I can't talk to the others, how am I supposed to advance the project?"

"*I* didn't bring you here. *I* don't think we need you. And I don't believe you *want* to advance the project. Why the hell should you?"

She shrugged. "Because the science is fascinating. What you're doing here is completely new. Sure, people have experimented with bits and pieces before—using light to change memories from bad to good, testing Ecstasy and emapunil for PTSD, propranolol for guilty memories, gene doping for all kinds of performance enhancements—but nothing on this level. Not even close." At least, not since MKUltra. But that would probably not be a wise comment to make.

THEY BROKE FOR the day at six, and Nose led Jane and Dani back to their room. A garbage bag containing Dani's few possessions, all jumbled together, had been tossed on the bed. When Jane opened a dresser drawer to begin helping Dani put away her shirts, she found clothes in her own size already there. Including underwear. More than anything that had happened to that point, even the kidnapping itself, the sight of those clothes brought home her complete lack of privacy.

Bryan had said there was nowhere to run, and after dropping them at the room Nose did not bother to lock the door, making clear his complete lack of concern about the possibility of escape. Still, they might be being watched. Or at least listened to. *Damn.* She'd hoped to be able to tell Dani about Eric and HSE, provide her a glimmer of hope, but if the room was bugged that was out of the question.

"How did you guess about . . ." Dani's eyes went to the bed. "Because you did, didn't you? That's why you asked to have me stay with you."

Jane's stomach rolled and every muscle tensed. She could barely look at Dani for fear the anger would consume her. "Believe me," she said through clenched teeth, "I didn't guess. I'm not good at that kind of interpretation. But Bryan practically held it up in front of my face. Even when the two of you were dating, he never called you by pet names, at least not in the lab. And what I said was one hundred percent true: I'd get no rest at all thinking of you dealing with him."

Dani nodded. "I'm sorry I wasn't a better friend. You know, before."

"Don't be ridiculous. You were great. You invited me out, made me feel as if I was part of your life. That was amazing. It was totally my fault that I never accepted, didn't know how to be a proper friend."

"Sure, we were friend*ly*, but that's not the same thing. I didn't tell you when Alvaro came back, didn't share the important things. And since I've been here, Bryan's told me stuff you and I never talked about, like how your mom died. If I'd been more open with you about my crap, you would have trusted me with that. I assumed your father lived far away, like mine, because you never mentioned him, but I didn't realize you were actually estranged."

A chill set the hairs on Jane's arms on end. "Why would he tell you about my family?"

"He asked me who you cared about. They wanted a relative to threaten, the way they're holding Alvaro over me. Bryan said you were a sucker, that if they could find the right person, they wouldn't even need to bring them here; they could just take a few pictures, maybe kill a pet, and you'd fall in line. But you have no siblings, and by all appearances you're estranged from your father, and you never date—" She huffed a laugh. "That pissed him off, by the way."

"That I don't date?"

"That you wouldn't date *him*. He tried to get your attention long before he settled for me."

"He did?"

"Totally."

"I never even noticed. He was probably only interested because I had access to more data on the project than anyone else."

"I wonder whether he planned all along to steal the research and come out here, or whether he was approached once he was at AHI because he already had access."

Time to change the subject. If Bryan was listening, she didn't want to spend too much time discussing his motives or possible employers.

"Speaking of access . . . I need access to a pad and some pens. I mean, I understand why they wouldn't want to give us a computer, which would be *really* useful, but I often come up with questions—and answers—in the middle of the night. Remind me to ask for that tomorrow."

"You can ask tonight." Dani checked the ornate clock hanging on the wall. "Dinner's in about an hour. Every night at seven thirty, we're expected to meet Bryan and assorted others in the dining room."

"Others?"

"Yeah. They're not always the same people. A lot of times, it's guys you'll recognize from around the house, but occasionally others show up. I never ask who they are or why they're here. Doesn't seem too smart to pry."

"I imagine not."

When the time came, Dani led the way to the dining room. Along the way, they passed armed men meandering through the house. Although the men gave them only the briefest of glances, each one sent a needle of fear up Jane's spine. Even if Eric did come for her, how could he possibly get her away? He wasn't Superman, and while HSE might be willing to let him take off on his own to rescue her, Nash Harper had no reason to expend the kind of resources in both men and equipment it would take to bring this place down. She needed to find an escape path for herself and Dani and Alvaro. . . . If they could get free of the mansion, Eric could get them home. And then she'd spend every penny she'd saved to hire HSE to bring Bryan down.

At dinner, they were joined by four men, all dark haired and dark eyed, ranging in age from mid-twenties to mid-forties. At least two of them, the oldest and the youngest, were undoubtedly related. Both had classically Mexican, even Mayan features, with flat-bridged noses, widow's peaks, and the same slightly elongated jawline. Father and son? Uncle and nephew? Crime was a family business, apparently. But then, Eric had said they were in cartel country, and the cartels were big on family.

The older man examined Jane with a disturbing and acquisitive thoroughness, and she mentally thanked Bryan's superior for instructing she not be harmed. Bryan himself, she felt certain, would turn her over in a second for profit or power.

The meal was served by two silent women Jane hadn't seen either in the lab or on their way to it earlier that day. When she thanked one, the girl damned near jumped out of her skin. Her eyes flicked over to the older man before she ducked her head in acknowledgement of Jane's words. Interesting. Was this Bryan's boss? The home's owner?

She drew breath to ask, to introduce herself as if this were any other dinner, but beneath the table, Dani kicked her. Hard. *Okay, then.* No introductions. But how was she to gather information if she couldn't speak? Patting Dani's thigh in reassurance, she started again.

"Bryan, is it possible to get a pad and some pencils or pens sent to our room? I'm one of those people who wakes up with ideas that flit away if I don't get them down right away."

Say yes, say yes. But she kept her expression carefully bland. Paper would allow her to communicate with Dani even if the room was bugged.

Bryan's eyes narrowed, and all four of their guests scrutinized her.

"I'll think about it," he said at last. Then he returned to his meal, signifying the conversation's end.

Although the food smelled spicy and Jane's stomach demanded she eat, she could taste nothing. Mechanically, conceding the need for nutrition, she shoved bites into her mouth, chewed, and swallowed, all the while watching the dynamic among the men. They spoke in low tones, mostly in Spanish, which she could not understand. Could Dani? She glanced at the other woman, but she appeared totally absorbed in her dinner, cutting the meat into ever-smaller pieces before forking minuscule slivers into her mouth. She chewed each sliver so long Jane was certain it had liquefied by the time Dani swallowed.

Damn. Dani was losing it. No surprise, really. It was amazing she'd held up as well as she had. But they needed to get out, and soon.

⌒

"Do you know who those guys are?" Jane asked the minute she and Dani were back in their room. Bryan would expect her to be curious. If the room was bugged, she needed to keep to a normal script.

Dani shook her head. "Some bigwigs in the cartel. They don't address each other by name, but they've been here a couple of times."

"Could you understand what they were saying?"

"Not really. The accents and dialect . . . It's Spanish, but it's like asking a Texan to eavesdrop on a Brit. Without context, it's tough. From what I understand, there are a couple of investors in Warlock. One's an American, who just puts up money but doesn't come down here; the other is the head of the Hijos cartel. This is his place."

Interesting. Jane wanted to know more about the American investor, but she didn't dare ask. "It's a beautiful house. Have you had a chance to look around the grounds at all?" Was there any chance for escape? Dani seemed to understand the question she didn't ask aloud.

"A bit. Bryan wasn't kidding when he said we were in the middle of the jungle. There's a big road that runs in front of the property, and they truck in supplies every few days. There must be a city or town relatively close, because I've heard the guards talk about going drinking and picking up prostitutes, but you wouldn't know it from what you can see here." She frowned. "You can't be considering running?"

Oh, how Jane wished she could explain, but she didn't dare. She had to wait until she could be certain no one would hear.

"I'm not considering anything. It's always good to know your options, though."

"I wish we had any. But even if I thought we could escape the house and grounds, I couldn't leave my brother."

"You said he was in a cell?"

"In the basement. You can see the little windows from around the back of the house. There's a door in the kitchen, but any time I've gone through there I've seen at least one guard hanging out."

"And what about the . . . subjects?"

"I'm sure Bryan will take you to see them tomorrow." Her lips twisted into a grimace. "They sleep on the main floor in what used to be, I think, a ballroom. Half of the second floor was converted into a sort of medical center. That's where they get physicals, meds other than those in their IVs, and where you'll interview them."

"The file says they get HGH and vitamins as well as the hallucinogenics?"

"Yeah. The steroids are to help with their physical training but also to increase their aggression — which seems ridiculous to me, since they're all plenty aggressive when they join up. They train constantly. Running, lifting, weapons. You'll see it on the grounds during the day. And they're totally focused. It's part of having all their other emotional connections chemically erased. They give me the creeps."

"I can totally see that. How much humanity do they have left?"

"Not a lot. I know failure to stabilize them could get us killed, but I almost hope you can't figure it out. Because I'm not sure who Warlock is worse for—the kids who sign up to be 'enhanced' because it gets them out of poverty, or the world they're unleashed on."

No need to worry on that account. Jane would kill herself before she contributed to such a project. Again she squelched her desire to tell Dani the truth.

"I caught up on what was done with Group One in my reading today, and Bryan said they all died. Were you treating them? Do you know what happened, exactly?"

"Yeah, I was. They'd 'graduated' from the first phase, and Group Two was starting out. They went off the compound for four days. No one would tell me where they were going, but it was the second week they'd been off IVs and out of the dormitory. Bryan had moved them into one of the cabanas instead, and we were dosing them daily with what was supposed to be a maintenance series of medications in pill form.

"Anyway, they went away, and when they came back Bryan spoke to them at length without me. I was watching them train the next day, taking notes on physical changes from the drug regimen, when one of them put his gun under his chin and blew the top of his head off." She swallowed hard. "I've never seen anything like it. It was horrible. And the others . . ."

"What did they do?"

"Nothing. The other two who were doing weapons training with him just kept firing at their targets. The three who were running didn't even pause to see what he'd done. They ran right by."

"Jesus."

"I couldn't breathe. I stood there and thought I was going to throw up. It was like the world suddenly stopped."

"What happened to the others?"

"Within a week, they were all dead. Two of them stopped eating and drinking. We put them on IV nutrients and rehydration, but they'd given up. After a couple of days where they simply wouldn't move, Bryan euthanized them. The other three all used weapons."

"Good God. But surely you talked to them?"

"I did! For that week, it seemed like that was all I did. I monitored their levels, of course, but I also spent hours and hours talking to them about what they were feeling. The thing is, I don't think they knew. The regimen kills their emotions, punishes them for feeling anything except fear and loyalty."

Jane had seen that in the notes. The combination of strobes and electroshock was used to supplement the chemical suppression of normal emotions.

"So they couldn't tell you what they were feeling, or why. What would you guess?"

"Bryan says during their four days away, they invaded a house run by a competing cartel. By their accounts, the job was a success. Two of them were injured, but not seriously, and they killed the eight guys who were there and brought back a ton of cash, drugs, and weapons. Apparently, that had been an Hijos stronghold before it was taken over, and Velasquez wanted it back."

"So it could have been guilt over killing the other men, or shock at the brutality of which they were capable, or self-disgust, or even plain-old depression. Or it might have been something more chemical, having to do with taking them off the IVs."

"Exactly. If Group Two were to follow Group One's

schedule, they'd be off the IVs next week and onto the mainte-nance meds. But I suspect he'll want to do some stress testing with them before they transition to pills to see what happens, how effective the drugs are against emotional overload. Of course, that means sending them out to kill again."

"Hell." What could she do to stop him? She'd have to tell him the IV drugs needed tweaking, buy a couple of days for the new formula to kick in before sending the guys out, and then hope she could continue to stall from there. "Has he spoken to you about his plans?"

"No, but I bet that's part of why those guys were here tonight. They came before Group One went on their mission, too. But they don't discuss particulars at dinner, as far as I can understand. Bryan gets his orders later."

"Okay." Jane touched Dani's hand. "Just hang on. I promise, I won't let him hurt you."

"You'll do your best. I believe that."

"I will."

CHAPTER 8

THE NEXT MORNING, when Jane and Dani descended the stairs and entered the dining room, they found Alvaro seated at the table, a guard standing right behind his chair. Jane had never met the boy before, so she leaned over to introduce herself, holding out her hand. Alvaro glanced over his shoulder at the guard before taking it.

"Are you feeling okay?" she asked, allowing her gaze to drop to the splinted finger on his left hand. The bandage was clean, at least, and other than that injury he seemed unharmed.

Again, he checked with the guard. "I'm fine."

"They're treating you all right?" Dani asked.

"Yeah. Fine." Alvaro began shoveling food into his mouth. Dani watched him for a couple of seconds, then served herself from the platters on the sideboard and sat down to eat.

Jane followed suit. A couple of times, she tried to start conversations with Alvaro, but the boy concentrated on his food and answered in monosyllables. As soon as he was done, the guard ushered him away. Not, much to Jane's surprise, toward the kitchen and the stairs Dani had noticed down to the basement, but out of the house entirely. Did they allow him exercise time? She'd hoped by insisting on the breakfasts that he would be kept alive, at least, but it had never occurred to her that Bryan might be seeing to it that Alvaro was kept healthy. Did they have long-term plans for Dani that required having him on hand?

After breakfast, Jane and Dani made their way back to

the lab. At the kitchen island, an armed guard sat drinking coffee and reading a newspaper. Dani flicked her eyes at a door in the corner that stood cracked slightly open. *The basement.* Dani didn't need to explain, couldn't if she'd wanted to, for the guard's eyes followed their progress until they exited down the corridor to the lab.

Bryan was yelling in rapid-fire Spanish when they came in, gesturing to one of the stations where something had clearly gone amiss. Shards of glass littered the counter along with grains of white and tan dust. At the sight of Jane, he wound up his tirade with something she assumed meant "clean it up and don't let it happen again."

"We lost one of the Group Two subjects this morning," he said. "Dr. Santiago autopsied him and said it was heart failure. Congenital problem, nothing to do with our treatments. So it's not our fault, but it is our problem. Velasquez likes six-man teams. Once the program is in full swing, it will be easy to replace a man when we lose one. But for evaluative purposes, we can't do that. They all have to be at the same stage. So for the next couple of days I'll be interviewing candidates for Group Three.

"We will need new dormitory space, so we'll be gutting a couple of the rooms on your floor and building them out into a dorm with the appropriate electronics and medical supplies. Don't let the construction give you any ideas: every man on the crew is completely loyal to Velasquez. They won't help you."

Maybe not intentionally. But disruption could only benefit her, especially if the noise masked any conversation she wanted to have with Dani.

"I'll have to examine the remaining members of Group Two before I start fiddling with the chemical or psychological routines," she said, as if the news of yet another set of young men signing away their souls was of no consequence. "You'll arrange it?"

He nodded and called over one of the lab rats. "This is Liandro. He'll be your liaison to the subjects while I am gone. Tell him what you need and he'll set it up. I will be back no later than six every night, so you can report your findings. And needless to say, any and all contact with the subjects will be recorded."

"Of course."

"Daniela, show her to the clinic. Liandro and I will send up the first subject."

Dani took her back down the cement-floored hallway, past the hard-eyed kitchen guard and the still-ajar door to the basement, and up the stairs to the second floor. The first door at the top of the stairs opened into a large space remodeled out of a couple of bedrooms. The beautiful hardwood floors had been covered with cheap, easy-to-clean vinyl, and the plaster walls had been drywalled over and painted a pale gray. In two spots, she could see where the paint had been scrubbed but rusty stains remained. *Why would there be blood on the walls?*

Two hospital beds took up the space in one half of the room, while an exam table and workstation dominated the other.

"The interview room is across the hall," Dani said.

"I don't suppose the computer's hooked up to the Net?"

"No. There's an intranet so you can access the men's medical records and the research data, but you can't get to the outside world."

But someone had to. She could accept that Wi-Fi was too insecure, but the data had to be backed up off site—no way would they risk losing it to a fire or a raid. Which meant she might be able to get a message out if she could figure out which computer was wired for access. Of course, it also meant that even if she and Dani managed to escape, the results of all the experiments Bryan had conducted would still be sitting out there for Velasquez and his investor to pick up. They could disappear in the night, set up half a world away, and be up and running again in no time.

Liandro arrived with a young, strong, sweaty man in tow. The first of the Group Two subjects. Liandro was sweating, too, and panting, but just from climbing the stairs—he could use some exercise.

"This is Juan," Liandro said. "When you're done with him, send him down and he'll bring the next guy up for you."

"Okay, thanks."

Juan hiked himself up onto the exam table, biceps bulging beneath his T-shirt. She'd seen the training schedule in the research: three hours every other day in weight training; cardio and weapons training every single day. Strict diets, hypnosis sessions, hand-to-hand combat, and work details filled every waking moment, while subliminal messages and drugs filled their sleep.

Juan's chart noted that he spoke English, so she sent Dani over to the computer to track her findings and interviewed him without a translator.

"How do you feel, Juan?"

"Good. I should be training."

"I know. But this is part of the program, too."

He shrugged.

"Tell me, what do you think of the training you're getting?"

"It's good." He flexed his biceps. "I am getting more strong. Healthy. Not like Manny. He was weak."

After a brief physical exam, Jane had to agree. He was strong. She drew blood, asked him to go into the bathroom and provide a urine sample, but it was stalling. He was a perfect physical specimen — she could see that much from his chart.

When he came back from the bathroom, they adjourned to the room across the hall, where four chairs were arranged in a tight circle next to a small desk with a laptop on it. Jane took one of the chairs while Dani sat behind the desk and booted up the computer.

"So tell me, Juan, do you know what the program here is about? What you're training for?" The study documents showed that all the young men signed up being told very little beyond what they would be paid and that they would have to live in the compound and work hard."

"I am going to be a top man among the Hijos. To guard Velasquez and help him expand."

"And has anyone explained to you what that position entails? What you will do?"

He shrugged.

"Have you ever killed a man, Juan?"

"Yes."

Interesting. Only one man's application showed violent crime in his past, and it wasn't Juan. Had he killed as part of the program already? "Can you tell me what that was like?"

He shrugged again. "What's to tell? What's it ever like?"

"I don't know. That's why I'm asking. Was it spontaneous, or did you plan it out? Were you alone, or part of a group? Did you shoot him, or stab him, or strangle him, or beat him to death? Give me some details."

His eyes flicked back and forth several times, and he cracked his neck. Was it possible he didn't even remember the killing? Then his expression cleared. "I shot him. I am good with a pistol."

"And how did you feel afterward?"

"Feel? I did my job."

Oh, yeah, the psychiatric aspect of this was going to be a cakewalk.

"So you wouldn't mind doing it again if you had to? The blood, the gore, doesn't bother you?"

Another shrug. "It is the world we live in."

"Do you dream, Juan?"

"Dream?"

"*¿Sueñas?*" asked Dani.

"No. Or if I do, I do not remember."

"Okay. Just a couple more things. If you were free to go anywhere, do anything, what would it be?"

Flat, affectless brown eyes stared at her. "I am where I am supposed to be."

"I know, but that's not what I asked. What if things could be different?"

He stared at her for a long moment. "They're not."

Yeah, okay. And there was a reason she hadn't gone into clinical psych.

"Thanks, Juan. Go on down and ask Liandro to send up the next person in about ten minutes, okay?"

"Okay."

As soon as he was out of earshot, Jane turned to Dani. "What is this about a shooting? There was nothing like that in the records."

"That's because it didn't happen." Dani rubbed her forehead with two fingers. "After Group One suicided, Bryan thought the subjects should be proactively desensitized to killing. He'd assumed they could all handle it—part of the interview process was weeding out anyone with a noticeable moral center and finding the more calculating customers. The aggression from the constant combat training and steroids should have taken care of the rest. And it did, up to a point. That is, they all managed the actual takedown operation just fine. It wasn't until later that it seems to have come back to haunt them.

"So he started adding false memories to hypnotherapy. Suggestions that they had killed before, that it didn't bother them, that it was a run-of-the-mill activity. He's got a couple of guys working on scent desensitization, too, so that no one breaks down smelling blood after their first kill."

"It's not in the notes."

"You can find it, but you have to tunnel into each individual subject's chart—it's not in the overall project write-up you read yesterday. He set it up like that so they could alter individual bits and pieces."

"Okay. I'll read all the charts tonight, then."

⌒

INTERVIEWING AND EXAMINING the men of Group Two took the rest of the day. In between subjects, Jane tried to sneak out and explore, but the number of guards inside the house had risen in Bryan's absence and she didn't dare do much beyond run down to the kitchen to fix herself a snack and peek into a couple of rooms along the way.

At a quarter to five, Bryan returned while Jane and Dani were talking through the last of the subjects, the project targets, and the various ways the individual men had been altered as they became more integrated into the group. Each revelation in the men's charts sickened Jane further.

"How did it go today?" Bryan asked.

"It went fine. I didn't realize you'd individualized treatments for the men, so I have more reading to do."

"The drugs are the same. And most of the treatment is the same. We just compensate for individual weaknesses to keep them all on track."

He made it sound so clinical, so abstract and uncomplicated, as if they weren't dealing with people, with emotions and psyches and altering the very stuff that made up the human soul.

"Don't spend too long catching up, Jane. Velasquez is losing patience. I saw him this afternoon, and he expects results, especially since he's going to be shelling out for two sets of recruits at once."

"What happened to the American investor? I thought it was his money? Why should Velasquez care how much he spends?"

If Bryan was surprised that she knew about the American, it didn't show. So more than likely he *was* listening to her and Dani at night. "That's none of your business. Did you discover anything useful today, or did you just waste the entire day?"

"For God's sake, Bryan, it's *science*; it doesn't keep to a deadline."

"You managed Project Calm under a deadline."

"Not really. We thought we had it under control, which was why Clive went into negotiations. The problem cropped up later, and we almost didn't make it. This is a much bigger project. I hope you didn't make promises about a timetable, or you'll get us all in trouble."

"We're close enough. We almost had it with Group One."

"But you *didn't*. That's precisely what I mean. We won't know what is going on with Group Two until we get them at least past their first trials, and I wouldn't recommend that for another several days at the very soonest."

"Really? Why is that? I had plans for them for tomorrow."

Oh, fuck. What to say?

"Well, you can do whatever you like, of course. But I didn't realize what you'd been fiddling with in those men's heads, so I'd layer in a few more days of hypnotherapy first. My questions about the histories you've given them to replace their real pasts could have shaken something loose, left them vulnerable to emotional injury."

"They're not supposed to have emotions at all by this point." He frowned. "But I take your meaning. I'll wait a couple of days before sending them out. In the meantime, I want you to take what you found out today and use it to reinforce their training. This batch will not fail, or there will be hell to pay. Is that understood?"

"Yes."

"Good."

Since they had more than two hours before dinner when Bryan left the interview room, Jane decided to take the opportunity to snoop.

"I need to get some air," she said for the benefit of the recorders keeping track of all subject interaction. "I don't think well cooped up all day like this. You want to come?"

"Sure, I guess," Dani replied.

They went down the stairs, past a guard stationed at the bottom, a machine gun of some sort slung casually across his shoulder. He watched them, but his hands didn't move, even when they approached the door. Jane's shoulders twitched, and the back of her neck developed a sudden itch as she reached for the door handle. Would he stop them, or was escape so impossible that no one cared if they left the house?

The warmth of the wrought-iron door handle shocked her bloodless fingers. No one yelled; the guard didn't point his weapon; even the heavy hinges on the elaborately carved door remained silent as she swung it open and walked out into a large courtyard. A high wall encircled the grounds. The gate lay about a hundred yards directly in front of the door, no longer than a New York City block. She could run the distance in seconds if not for the armed men hanging about.

A heavy iron gate blocked access to the wide road Dani had described to her. The bars were set about four inches apart, from what she could see — definitely not wide enough to squeeze through, even if she could sneak out in the middle of the night when the men weren't running and shooting and wrestling on the grounds. Two vehicles were parked next to the house on a patio in front of a three-car garage. One was a standard-issue Jeep, a bare-bones, beat-up model, while the other one looked like some kind of oversized pickup, the kind the landscape companies at home used to carry their equipment, only with a set of tall posts running up the side that rounded over at the top. Perhaps to hold a canopy? To protect equipment from rain? Neither of the vehicles looked particularly fast, and both were bulky. If she made it off the property and into the woods, she might have a chance.

Of course, if she made it off the property and into the woods, she'd be . . . in the woods. With snakes. And spiders. And all kinds of poisonous critters. And that was without considering the various Hijos men sent in after her. So maybe it didn't matter whether she could get away.

Still, she had to try. She refused to simply give up. She led Dani along the curving gravel path that branched away from the driveway and around the side of the house. A few small buildings originally intended as guesthouses dotted the property. On the third floor, where she slept with Dani, she had seen no other bedrooms in use, which was borne out by the plan to use the space for a dormitory. And while she knew that Bryan slept on the floor below hers, farther down the hall from the clinic and interview area, she had no idea where the guards had their quarters. Probably at least some of them were housed in the bungalows.

And how many of them were there, anyway? She was going to have to start counting. If—when—Eric came for her, she wanted to be useful, and he'd probably want a head count.

On what appeared to have been a tennis court in a former life, a group of men practiced some sort of martial arts. Kicking, punching, throwing each other to the ground, they paid no attention as Jane and Dani passed. Christ, there were a lot of them. Way more than she'd seen around the house. Around the back of the house, they passed a drained pool fronted by a structure larger than the bungalows. Just as they walked by, two men came out dressed in fatigues with guns in shoulder holsters. So the former pool house was in active use. That meant the north, west, and south faces of the house had serious guard action. The path stopped at the pool, and the east side of the yard seemed to be grass and over-grown garden, not currently in use. That would be where Eric would be forced to sneak through the defenses if he wanted to get onto the property. Her bedroom, of course, was on the front corner, the northwest, in easy view of the guards. That had to be deliberate. Not that she could exactly rappel down the building from her window anyway, not without hoard-ing sheets for months to rip up and make a rope.

"It must have been a beautiful property once," she said to Dani, more to hear her own voice than for any other reason.

"Absolutely. Look at that garden." Dani walked over to the edge of the pool surround. "If this were a place for actual therapy, the men would be working in there. And playing tennis on those courts."

It was true. Jane could almost imagine the property as a high-end rehab center. If it weren't in the middle of land owned by a drug cartel.

"It's too bad the pool's dry," Dani said. "If we're stuck here, I'd like to swim."

Jane stared at her.

"Okay, look. I know I sound crazy. I'm just trying to make this a little bit normal, okay? I . . . It's been . . . hard."

Of course it had. Much harder on Dani than on Jane. She put an arm across her friend's shoulders. "Swimming would be good. Tanning would be good, too, but they don't seem to have any lounge chairs for our use. What kind of low-class establishment is this?"

Dani choked out a laugh. "Well, you can't have everything. At least the sheets are clean."

"And the food is good."

"Yeah. And it's cheap."

"It sure is." Jane squeezed Dani's shoulders, and the other woman let out a little sigh.

"I guess we should go back inside."

"Probably." Jane glanced around. They were alone. And outside, where they were not likely to be overheard. "Don't give up hope, Dani. Help may be coming."

"What?" Dani stopped, almost tripping over her own feet. "What kind of help?"

"I have a friend. He was protecting me because Clive thought you'd been kidnapped to prevent Project Calm from being completed. They kidnapped me after he left, but he'll know I am gone. We were supposed to go on a date. He won't believe I stood him up."

"But how would he figure out where you were?"

Should she explain telling him about Bryan and Dani dating? What if Bryan threatened Alvaro? Would Dani spill the beans? She hated mistrusting her friend, but she couldn't afford to make a mistake.

"He might not. I mean, he probably can't figure it out. But if you can't have a swimming pool, you have to hang on to hope."

⟳

WHEN NASH CALLED him in, the last thing Eric expected to find was a conference room full of people. After five ago-nizing days during which he questioned everyone Bryan Axlerod had ever known, followed up on every lead, and spent hours a day in the company gym taking out his frus-trations on the heavy bag, he was pretty sure Nash was going to cut him loose. Or at least tell him he had to work on something else.

But an assignment would mean Nash, Lexie, and who-ever he was partnering with would be at the table, not Jake and Tara, Marco, Jimmy and LeRon from research, and Jake's friend Kevin from up at the farm.

"What is it?" he asked without even sitting down.

Lexie got up, took him by the hand, and led him to an empty seat. Obeying the unspoken command, he sat, but his body remained on full alert. "We have information," she said, resting her hands on his shoulders, "but we don't know where she is yet. So relax. . . . We have a lot of work to do."

When Lexie was back in her own spot, Nash gave LeRon the nod.

"Once we had new search parameters," he said, "we started from the beginning. What did Daniela Peralta and Jane have in common aside from the schizophrenia research? Who did they know in common? Obviously, there were the people at AHI. Jimmy focused on Bryan Axlerod, and he's going to talk about that in a sec. But in addition, in relation, we started to think about what someone might want with a pair if biochemists, one who was particularly versed in psychopharmacology. The obvious answer there is designer drugs."

"Who the fuck kidnaps two chemists to create a disco drug?"

"Things go in cycles," Nash said. "Right now, the most popular and problematic drugs on the street are prescriptions. Both uppers and downers. But heroin is on the rise again. Ecstasy has never entirely gone away. Meth users tend to be lower on the socioeconomic spectrum, so if you want to make big bucks, you do it with party drugs like cocaine."

Eric ran a hand around the back of his neck. Okay. They were the experts. When it came right down to it, he was just muscle. Smarter than your average thug, but nothing like the brainiacs sitting around the table. And clearly this line of research had led to an answer, or they wouldn't be here.

"So what did you find?"

Jimmy answered. "Last month, Bryan Axlerod sent flowers to his mother for her birthday. Doesn't matter what kind of asshole you are, I guess, you still have a soft spot for mom. Anyway, the flowers were sent via FTD and paid for with a debit card in the name of Bryan Dominguez drawn on a bank in Mexico."

"She's in Mexico?"

"It seemed likely," Nash said, "so we focused our resources there. Kevin is former DEA, like Lexie, and they both worked their contacts hard. We have a pretty good idea who has Dr. Evans, but we haven't been able to track down where yet."

"Who?" He could barely force the word out past the combination of rage, fear, and excitement tensing the muscles of his neck and throat.

"Los Hijos," said Jake.

Oh, fucking hell. Not what he wanted to hear at all. But it explained Jake and Tara's presence — they'd taken out the cartel's leader, but not before Tara had almost died.

"You know how it goes," Jake said, as if hearing his thoughts. "With those guys, you cut off one head and two grow back. I've been keeping an eye on them in case anyone was out for revenge, but now that the original bloodline is gone, loyalty doesn't seem to be a high priority. It took several months of feuding and bloodletting, but Enrique Velasquez emerged the victor. He'd been running the organization in everything but name for years anyway, but the challengers thought that without the family backing he might go down. They were wrong. He took out at least a dozen men to get that job and has no compunction in taking out another dozen if it gets him what he wants. We're not currently on his radar because, frankly, he figures we did him a favor killing his bosses so he could move into place, but the minute we get in his way, that will change."

"We need to be ready to move the minute we find out where Dr. Evans is being held," Nash said. "I'm sending Marco with you. Trey's already in Mexico City finishing up a short job, so he'll be available to help any minute. Frankly, I'd prefer you didn't go at all, but I've learned from experience forbidding you guys to do shit like that doesn't work. So since we don't know who's down there and whether they were watching her and saw you, use the time to dye the hair dark and shave the beard. They see you like this in town or whatever, the gig is up."

"I know the drill." *Hang on baby, I'm coming.* "How do we get to Mexico?"

"Commercial flight tomorrow morning into Mexico City. Trey's been working with a contact we have in Mexico, Miguel Perez. He'll pick you up at the airport and get you settled. We'll set pickup when we figure out where you're going to have to leave from."

"You trust this guy?" Corruption hung like smog in the Mexican air.

"He's solid," Jake said.

"He has every reason to hate the cartels," Nash said. "Trusting him beyond that . . . well, I don't trust anyone completely."

"What the fuck? You expect me to put my life—not to mention Jane's and Marco's and Trey's—in the hands a guy you don't trust yourself?"

"Miguel has his own problems," Nash said. "He has to live in Mexico, which means not making too many waves. But he lost his daughter five years ago when warring cartels took their beef to a club. His seventeen-year-old daughter was out dancing and was shot to death when the place was turned into a battlefield. He'll help you."

Jesus. What a way to live. Of course, it could happen just as easily in the States. Just look at all those kids at Jake and Tara's place. Every one of them had some horror in their past or they wouldn't be there.

"I'll be driving you to the airport," Jake said. "I'll pick you up—" His cell dinged, interrupting him. He dug it out of his pocket and frowned at the screen.

Now, that took some balls. Eric couldn't imagine answering a text while in a conference with Nash.

"Give me a sec," Jake said, tapping at the screen.

A few minutes later, he looked up from the phone. "We may know where she is."

CHAPTER 9

Every day, Jane interviewed men and watched them train in the morning, while spending her afternoons with the lab rats. When Bryan would ask about sending the group on a mission, she used any excuse to declare them emotionally or physically unfit for the stress.

She'd learned fairly quickly that documentation was the weakest area for the men in the lab. They preferred to write down the details of each test after they'd performed it rather than before. So one time she'd repeated the wrong numbers back to one guy who'd asked her to look at his results, and, sure enough, those were the numbers he wrote down. When he tried replicating the results, he couldn't make the experiment work. In another instance, she knocked most of a setup off the table with an elbow. Bryan had screamed about that one, but since the chemicals had yet to be mixed at the time, he let it go. Unfortunately, that one had been too easy to reconstruct, and since then Bryan had been watching her more closely.

Every morning, Alvaro appeared at the breakfast table flanked by a silent guard. Although his bandage was clean and he appeared well treated, he was becoming more and more sullen, and Jane didn't know how to help him.

Twice, Dani had asked her about Eric, and each time Jane's prevarications weighed on her. She was a bad friend. She should be trying to bolster Dani's hopes rather than doubting her strength. But under pressure Dani might break and tell Bryan that Eric knew who he was. Or she might trade the information for her brother's freedom, especially if Bryan took it in his head to threaten the boy further. All she dared ask of Dani—conversing via the pad and pens delivered to their room the second afternoon—was to be on the lookout for any information they could use to get themselves out of trouble, any secret passages in the house or ways off the grounds.

And truth be told, if she allowed herself to think too hard, her own hopes of rescue slipped away. What if she never got out of here? What would happen to her once she no longer had any value to these men as a scientist? They were damned close to finding their magic supersoldier regimen. A better scientist, a more imaginative crew of researchers would have put the pieces together already and would have begun a fourth group with gene doping and deep hypnosis.

She figured she had a month at the outside before one of the researchers put together the various pieces of the formula to come up with a pill, hypnotherapy, and electroshock combination that worked. It would require constant monitoring, not what they wanted for a long-term solution, but enough to get a foothold. In a month, they'd have trained a group and be sending them on their first mission. And once they came back from that mission, once the blood and violence didn't break them, her life was over.

Tuesday evening, the older man who'd been at dinner the first night showed up again with his entourage. He and Bryan were laughing at something when she and Dani came in, and nerves fired beneath her skin. Why were they so happy? Had Bryan called him because of a breakthrough?

"Miss Evans," the man said when she and Dani sat down.

"*Doctor.* Dr. Evans."

He smirked and raised a single eyebrow. "Indeed. My mistake. How goes your work?"

She considered not answering but settled for asking a question of her own. "Since you know my name, might I know yours?"

"Ah, of course. Enrique Velasquez. And this"—he indicated the young man with similar features—"this is my nephew Eduardo."

Oh, hell. Head of the Hijos cartel himself. This can't be good.

"Mr. Velasquez is your employer," said Bryan.

Like hell. "No, he's *your* employer. I'm not being paid, so I don't have one."

"Watch your fucking mouth, Jane."

"No, no," Velasquez said. "It is better to let her speak her mind for now." But the eyes he turned on her were flat, as was his voice. There was so little inflection in his words, she almost missed the threat. "Though the time is coming when speaking in such a way will get your tongue cut out."

The serving women, who Jane never saw during the day, stood by the kitchen door, watching the whole exchange with fearful eyes. Every night, Jane thanked them. Every night, they nodded but did not speak. Velasquez's threat put a new, terrifying spin on their actions.

"She doesn't need her tongue to work on Warlock," Bryan pointed out.

"Ah, but she is of less value without it later. Women always are."

Bryan laughed coarsely. "There is that."

Velasquez turned his dark eyes on her. "You do not wish to help me, Dr. Evans. I understand that. But you will help me. My preference is to retain you here, working on my projects. But it is not necessary. I cannot sell you to my best American customer, but I have a customer in Thailand who would pay a great deal to break you. A great deal. And the more you fight back, the better he will enjoy it. And once he has fin-ished, once there is nothing left of you, he will allow you to get pregnant and begin again with the next generation.

"You think your life here is terrible. You believe I am evil. You have never met evil, never tasted pain. But if you do not perform adequately here, you will."

⌒

ERIC AND MARCO landed in Mexico City at 2:40 in the afternoon. Trey met them outside the baggage area and intro-duced them to Miguel when they all piled into the man's Jeep.

"I went by the place late last night, after Nash called me," said Miguel. "It is heavily guarded, and word in town is that Velasquez himself has been spending time there of late."

"That's never encouraging," Trey said.

"No, but he always brings his own guards, which means the regulars get the night off."

And being local, and feeling secure in their environment, they gossiped. It was the kind of intel Eric sought on missions, and the professionalism of the approach allowed a fraction of tension to leach from his body. Whatever personal beef Miguel had with the cartels, he knew how to keep his cool.

"What have you heard?"

"I haven't had much time and did not want to appear anxious, but I gather the men feel Velasquez is becoming impatient."

"For fuck's sake, even if they brought her here by plane, stopping for nothing but refueling, it's been less than a week!"

"For you. Velasquez cleared the house last year. They built a new addition, outfitted a lab."

Last year. They'd been planning this a damned long time. Way too long for a simple club drug, no matter how much they hoped to make off it.

"So you're telling me this isn't all Bryan Axlerod's plan? It was in the works before him?"

"Definitely. There is at least one other American they talk of who came even before the renovation of the house. I could get no details without appearing obvious, but the men are frustrated. That American apparently made promises to them over and above what they get from Velasquez. Now they are wondering whether he will ever return, whether they should ask for better assignments since nothing has happened at the house and they have been given no bonuses."

"You got all that in one night?"

"No. I have been working with Trey on a kidnapping case. He's been in Mexico City, but I have stayed in Tenancingo, so I've been hearing about the house for a couple of weeks now. We thought at first it might be where they were holding the young man they'd kidnapped, but that did not turn out to be the case."

"Are you certain, as Nash says, that this is about developing a drug?"

"We're not certain of anything," Eric replied.

"Why?" It was the first thing Marco had said since leaving New York, and his voice sounded almost rusty. Eric hardly ever worked with the guy, a former Marine sniper, but on their few missions together, he'd been a virtual ghost. He followed orders, showed up whenever you needed him, but rarely spoke.

Miguel shifted in the driver's seat, glanced at Marco in the rearview, then returned his attention to the rutted road they thumped down.

"Some of the renovations rumored at that house have less

in common with a medical laboratory than with a place of torture."

Eric went cold. "Like?"

"One of the rumors includes a room with electrical chairs and tables. There is also talk of human subjects. Volunteers who are put through testing, though what kind of testing no one ever says."

"Jesus." What the hell was happening to Jane? "How soon do we go in?"

"We need better information before we can try anything," Trey said. "The hacienda is enormous, and there are out-buildings, too. We have to suss out where they're keeping the prisoners. Right now, we'd get ourselves and everyone else killed."

Goddammit. He knew it was true, but the thought of wait-ing . . .

"I'll go in alone and scope it out tonight."

"No," Trey said.

"Look, Godwin, I know you're used to being in charge, but this is my mission. Jane was my responsibility from day one. I go in by myself, I have a lot better chance of not getting caught. And if, by chance, I figure out where they are being held, I'm the one she won't freak out over seeing. She's never met the rest of you."

"It's a good plan," Marco grated in that rusty voice. "I'll tag along, scope out an aerie. Miguel, you're recognized in town already anyway, so you'll have better luck getting people to talk to you."

Trey gritted his teeth. Even from the backseat, Eric could see the tendons in his neck tense, but he capitulated. They pulled up to a rundown apartment building, and Trey led them to a second-floor apartment."

Mi casa es su casa," he said.

"Casa my assa," Eric grumbled. "How many roaches you share this place with?"

"You know how it is."

And he did. Kidnap and ransom could go south fast. You wanted a hidey-hole no one would consider worth a rich man's attention. This place definitely qualified.

"How far are we from the lab?"

"Twenty kilometers, more or less."

"And from there to the nearest landing zone?"

"Twenty-two, twenty-three."

"Terrain?"

"Inhospitable. Start with your basic jungle with all the attendant vicious and poisonous critters. Add in the fact that this particular jungle is Hijos territory and smack in the middle of one of the heaviest human-trafficking zones in the world. Makes for a rough landscape to traverse."

"Fuck." The distance was doable—in training, he could run thirteen miles in his sleep, and probably had. But with two women and a young man, one or all possibly injured, through hostile territory . . . it would be tough.

"It's going to be a long night," Trey said, pulling food out of the refrigerator. "Eat, then get some sleep. Everyone knows I was the designated American ransom coordinator for the last drop, so I'm no good in town. I'll leave early, head out to the property, and start tracking guard movements."

Miguel opened a closet, then pried the back wall off, revealing an entrance to the apartment next door. Furnished more nicely, the second apartment had a heavy wooden dining table with wrought-iron detailing. Putting his shoulder beneath the overhang of the top, Miguel lifted it to reveal a large cache of weapons.

"Batcave. Nice," said Eric, picking up a Glock and feeling the weight. It wasn't his favorite weapon, but beggars couldn't be choosers.

"I do my best. I own the building but don't live in it. It suits my cover to be what you would call a slumlord. People I know one way or another stay here when they are between jobs, between apartments, between wives. When Nash needs someone like Trey to stay in one, I make certain these apartments are vacant."

Eric and Marco loaded themselves up; then they went back to the rat's nest next door and Miguel replaced the false wall in the closet and rehung the umbrellas and clothes that hid it. They ate sandwiches and talked over logistics for a few minutes before crashing.

MIDNIGHT. TIME TO go. Miguel had taken Trey out just after seven as the sun began to set, then left for town himself at ten to hang out in a bar and see what intel he could pick up. Eric wouldn't even consider approaching the actual house before two or three, but he wanted plenty of time to scout through the area first. Miguel had supplied them with a Jeep, and he and Marco parked it deep in the woods about two miles from Velasquez's property. No point in announcing their presence.

Eric's backpack held climbing equipment, and the Glock rode at his hip in a quick-draw holster. Night-vision goggles turned the world to shades of eerie, electric green. He hated NVGs. They screwed up his depth perception, but they were a necessary evil.

He and Marco made a full circuit of the property. A nice, thick stone wall with plenty of handholds and a beautiful flat top encircled it. The lack of electricity or barbed wire surprised Eric, but he supposed few would dare attempt an assault on a home owned by the newest, most brutal leader of the Hijos.

On the northwest side of the property, Trey dropped from a tree as they passed.

"My guess is they're keeping the women up there," he said, gesturing to a third-floor window. "I saw them pass by a few times before they turned out the lights. Not sure if they're both in one room or what."

"No sign of Alvaro?"

Trey shook his head. "I can't say for certain that he's not in the same room, but I didn't see him near the window."

"And the guards?"

"Lax. They wander around on no particular schedule, which complicates planning, but they smoke and talk to each other. Bringing a large force in would be a big problem, but a few of us should be able to slip through."

Eric studied the building. He'd have to climb, but the window Trey had pointed out was at least near a corner, which would make the process easier. He could rappel. . . .

"Did you see anyone else on the third floor? If I shoot a line up onto the roof, are they apt to hear the hook landing and come running?"

"The other rooms have been dark. A few of the second-floor rooms have had lights on all night. One still does. I'd guess that's where the more important guests stay. Keeping the women upstairs means they can't get out without passing by the men."

"That'll work, then."

Eric switched out his boots for climbing shoes, leaving the boots with Trey. Marco high-fived him for luck, slipped in the earpiece that would allow them all to talk to each other, then disappeared into the jungle, a deadly shadow with a rifle slung over his back.

It took only seconds to scale the wall.

"You've got two guards coming from the left," said Trey's voice in his ear. Sure enough, a moment later two men appeared, talking and smoking. One looked up at the window Trey had pointed out. Eric could guess what he said by the coarse laugh it elicited from his companion.

Not on your life, asshole.

Once they'd passed, Eric dropped from the top of the wall. The landscape was largely lawn, dotted here and there with bushes and short palms. None of them would provide actual cover, but he could blend with the shadows easily enough if no one were actually looking. He plotted his course and dashed from one to the next until he reached the building.

Like many a fancy Mexican home, Velasquez's property had a tile roof and stucco walls. Stucco was a fucking bitch to climb. This had seen better days, so it was possible no one would notice the prints and scrapes he would have to leave if he free-climbed, but if they were holding captives, they'd be paying more attention than the average homeowner. Rope was a much better idea. He flattened himself against the wall and pulled the rope launcher from his backpack. He'd practiced with it plenty but had only actually used it one other time, so he sent up a brief prayer and fired. The hook stayed on the roof, which was better than the first time he'd tried to use the damned thing and almost lost an eye when it came flying right back down at him. He tugged the rope, heard the metal skitter over the tiles, the sound as loud as a train bearing down on him, and froze. But no one else seemed to have noticed. Cautiously, he tugged again, and the hooks caught.

Thank you, God.

Now he just had to worry about anyone who might look up and see a large, black figure against the white stucco. Hand over hand, he climbed as fast as he could, looping the rope over the hook at his belt as he went so no one would discover it hanging, until he reached the window Trey had pointed out. He pressed himself against it and took a deep breath. Here he wouldn't be seen nearly so easily from the outside.

From his precarious position, NVGs in place, he could see both Jane and Dani, their bodies outlined in alien green glow. Jane was sitting up in the bed. She held a book, a big one, but she wasn't reading. A chair was propped with its back beneath the bedroom door, but she held the book like a weapon. She squinted at the window. Without taking her eyes off him, she reached out and shook Dani awake. When the other woman started to speak, Jane clapped a hand over her mouth and put a finger to her own lips. Then she indicated Dani should hide behind the side of the bed opposite the window. Dani obeyed, but her head kept popping up to watch Jane.

Jane flattened herself against the bedroom wall and approached cautiously. She might not be a trained operative, but she learned fast—her position would make it difficult for him to fire upon her, should that have been his intent. He yanked off his cap and shoved the NVGs up on his head. Not much he could do about his dark hair and lack of beard, but maybe she'd recognize him anyway.

He saw the minute she did. Her fingers flew to the latch, and she unlocked the window and shoved it up. The screen popped out easily, and Eric slipped into the room as quietly as possible, bringing the rope inside with him. Jane threw herself against him. *Fuck.* There were so many things he wanted to say to her, but what if the room was bugged? Her earlier actions, silencing Dani, indicated it might be. So he settled for wrapping his arms around her and holding her tight against his heart. She was safe. For the moment, she was whole and well.

When his breathing stabilized, he loosened his hold on Jane and detached the rope, hitting the button on his belt that retracted it. The hook and rope would still be on the roof, but at least no one would see it from the ground.

Dani popped up from behind the bed. She grabbed a pad from the nightstand, scribbled on it, and held it up.

What's going on?

Jane looked at him, and for the first time he realized tears dripped down her face. *Ah, Christ.* Holding her hand, he sat on the bed, drawing her down beside him, and took the pad from Dani.

I can't get you out tonight, but we're coming for you. I promise. Do you know where Alvaro is being kept?

Dani wrote down what she knew about Alvaro's basement cell, and Eric nodded.

I need as much information as you have about what's going on here. He tapped the pen against his lips. *Jane had a nightmare. It woke you up. Talk about the experiments. The more details we have, the better we can plan.*

Jane nodded. She drew a breath and let it out in a little shriek. Not enough to bring anyone running, but enough to have startled Dani from sleep.

"Jane?" Dani did a credible job sounding freshly woken.

"Oh God, Dani, I just had the freakiest nightmare."

"What was it?"

"We did it. We completed Warlock."

"Were they . . . selling us?"

Every nerve fired in screaming fury. He should have expected it. With Tenancingo home to so much human trafficking and the Hijos involved up to their collective necks, it was the most logical way to get rid of two women who no longer served any purpose, but he still had to clamp down with all his strength to prevent himself from tearing open the door and going after their enemies barehanded.

"No." Jane stroked his thigh, silently begging him to calm down.

"So what was the nightmare?" Dani asked.

"That *was* the nightmare. You know what we're working on, Dani. Let's pretend for a minute we find a way to create a conscienceless, fearless killing machine. The first time one of those 'perfect soldiers' turns on Velasquez, which would totally happen despite all the subliminal sleep messages in the world, you know who's going to be blamed."

"Even with the data they made me steal from AHI before I left," Dani said, "it's not likely we'll actually find a combination of drugs and behavior mods that will work. Not that that's such a happy thought, either. I mean, how long do you think they'll keep us around if we don't? Velasquez seemed pretty impatient at dinner."

"He wants his supersoldiers. They're closer than I'm comfortable with, and it's not like you or I are in any position to stop them. If we don't help, Alvaro will suffer. At least for the moment they seem to be keeping him relatively comfortable despite having broken his finger."

Dani wrapped her arms around herself, and Eric touched her shoulder in sympathy. She was blaming herself for her brother's injury, which was, of course, the way psychological torture worked.

What a clusterfuck. They couldn't leave the lab standing. It and all the associated research had to be destroyed. Which meant they had to find the American investor, too, if he existed. No way could they afford to let a cartel — or anyone else — create an army of sociopaths.

Jane picked up the pad. *Is that enough? We don't know any more.*

It's enough. We will come for you at night. Probably tomorrow, the next night at the latest. Be here. He underlined the last word three times, and she nodded.

ONCE ERIC HAD left, hugging her fiercely before sliding three stories to the ground down a long rope that she then tossed down to him, Jane tore up the paper they'd written on and flushed it down the toilet. Dani had questions, Jane could tell, but she wasn't ready to discuss Eric, what he meant to her, why he might be there, because she didn't have answers. He'd referred to others being with him. How many? Were they on an assignment from Nash Harper, or just doing Eric a favor? How could they possibly rescue her, Dani, and Alvaro with just a few guys against all the armed men she'd seen around the compound?

Although, with his ropes and the big black pistol in his shoulder holster and the knife in his belt, Eric seemed a little better equipped than she would have expected. How had he gotten from New York to Mexico with the weapons when she still had to take her damned shoes off in the security lines?

So maybe, maybe there was hope. She'd felt it when he held her. For the first time since waking up in this place, her heart had settled back out of her throat, her nerves had calmed, and the promise of security seemed within reach.

She lay awake for the rest of the night, counting the bumps in the plaster ceiling and listening to Dani—who finally gave up staring at her and fell asleep—snore softly.

CHAPTER 10

THE FOLLOWING MORNING, much to Jane's dismay, Velasquez and Bryan were both at the breakfast table when she and Dani went downstairs.

"What's going on?" she asked.

"Where's Alvaro?" Dani added.

"Your brother has a little something he'd like to show you," said Bryan. He nodded to Nose, who stood at the kitchen door. "He's been helping us out, and I'm really quite proud of what we've accomplished together."

Nose led Alvaro into the room, and Bryan held up a Taser. "Alvaro, what would you say if I told you I was going to use this on you?"

Jane studied Alvaro's dark eyes but saw no reaction. He shrugged.

"Very well," said Bryan. He pressed the small device into Alvaro's side, and the boy folded, collapsed into a twitching heap. Dani shrieked and ran to him. Bryan yanked her up, a gun to her head. "Get back. He doesn't need your pitiful mewling." He held out a hand and Alvaro took it. When the boy was standing, Bryan smiled at him.

"Did that hurt?"

Alvaro shrugged.

"Do you want me to do it again?"

Another shrug.

"What about if I told you to go over there and do it to your sister?"

Alvaro held out a hand for the Taser. Jane stepped in front of Dani, who was still sobbing and calling her brother's name. Instead of handing the boy the Taser, however, Bryan asked another question.

"What if I told you to shoot your sister?" He put the gun into Alvaro's hand, and the kid pointed it straight at Jane's face.

"Get out of the fucking way," he said. They were the first words she'd heard him speak.

A guard yanked Jane's arm and dragged her across the room, leaving Dani exposed. Jane shouted at her to run, but she stood there, tears running down her cheeks, her lips moving soundlessly.

Alvaro steadied his good hand with his bad one and fired.

Jane's knees went out from under her, and she hit the floor, choking on bile. Dani, however, remained on her feet. Alvaro fired again and again until the magazine was empty.

"Oops," said Bryan cheerfully, "must have been blanks."

Dani crumpled and Jane crawled over to her. She was out cold, her breathing shallow, her pulse fast. Shock.

"You see, Jane," Bryan continued, "I don't think you're working as hard as you could be. You need a little more inspiration. So Daniela here is going to join her brother in our human-subjects trials. She doesn't have the physical strength we are after for most of our work, but she's damned good-looking. A woman who proves as biddable as young Alvaro here could bring a good price. No worries about keeping her locked up, no fear she'll go to the cops, just a hot body ready to please . . . or, of course, kill your enemies on command."

Jane swallowed the acid in her throat. "How's that any different than what you have planned for us if I do manage to work faster?"

He considered. "I'll make you a deal. You finish Warlock

before I break Dani down and retrain her, and you can have her back and you can both stay here as scientists."

"Finish it? It looks to me as if you finished it just fine without me."

Velasquez stood. "Don't play games with me, Dr. Evans. Alvaro represents a fine start, but broken men are nothing more than cannon fodder. We have been creating them for decades. Dr. Axlerod has sped the process up considerably. In fact, I am quite happy with his progress in that area, but we need soldiers, not drones. Men who can think for themselves, who retain the ability for reason and creative thought. Alvaro Peralta has neither.

"However, we will provide you with his history so you can see how he was broken. Perhaps it will . . . assist your research. You must remember that whatever is necessary to activate the reaction you are searching for can and will be done. If a person's own brain does not create enough electricity to provide the reaction, we can give an external, shall we say, boost."

The Taser flashed through Jane's mind. She'd seen a few notes on electrical-shock treatments in the research the first day she'd paged through the research, but she ignored any potential use of that, strobe lights, or the other behavior-modification regimens discussed. Yes, the brain was basically just a big electrical system, and yes, sometimes sending a brief shock through it was beneficial, but she had a feeling that wasn't what Velasquez had in mind.

The literature on what had been done to Alvaro proved her correct. It also set her guts on fire. How could a sane person do these things to someone else? She understood mental illness. Psychosis, obsession, even rage, either outward or turned inward as depression—these were the causes she could understand for torture and rape and murder. But the cold, logical decision to hurt others for your own bene-fit? It was beyond her.

In the lab, experiments continued. Midafternoon, two of the lab rats chattered excitedly in Spanish at one of the stations. She couldn't understand them, but whatever had them so intrigued, it couldn't be good. They didn't call her over, however, asking for Bryan instead. He examined their findings through a microscope, then repeated whatever they had done.

"Can I help?" Jane asked finally. She had to find out what they'd discovered or she couldn't derail it.

"I don't think so," Bryan said. "This… beautiful. One of those elegant answers that only arises when people think in truly big terms. One of these men, you see, has a child. That child learned yesterday that fire was hot as well as bright. It's a lesson he won't forget. Manuel realized that when we use the kind of desensitization techniques we've been using on Alvaro, we burn out their will. That's a bad idea. But if they aren't afraid of pain to begin with, if they learn that pain doesn't hurt, well, that's a different matter."

There it was, the very thing Jane had been terrified they'd figure out. She'd understood it from the first, though only because she'd known a woman in med school whose twin brother had hereditary sensory and autonomic neuropathy, which had prompted her interest in medicine. As rare as the family of HSAN disorders was, however, CIP—congenital insensitivity to pain—was rarer still and yet more devastat-ing. She'd never met an actual case. Congenital analgesia had no known cause, though researchers had identified two sep-arate affected genes.

Still, being able to predict the disorder based on affected genes and the proteins they did or did not create was very different from being able to change those genes or proteins at will. The reminder calmed her. If Manuel had only made his realization the night before, they couldn't be very far along. And Bryan was a chemist, not a medical doctor. What were the chances he'd kept up with any of the research? Even if he had, she hadn't heard of anyone working on synthesizing new analgesics from the genetic research, so he'd have to start from scratch. And before he could do that, Eric would have gotten her out. So today, she had to pretend to help, enough so she could possibly see Dani again.

"But pain is necessary," she said. Bryan would expect that. "Kids who don't feel it do things like bite off their tongues and fingertips. If you create a group of guys that don't feel pain, you'll lose a crap-ton of them to minor injuries that get infected. A guy who doesn't feel a snakebite won't get the antivenin shot. They have to be able to feel it. . . . What you want to do is dull it, so they feel it but not badly enough to stop what they're doing if it's important."

"Interesting. That's the first time you've said anything useful since you got here. But overdosing these men on oxy isn't a viable answer."

"It wouldn't matter. Prophylactic use of analgesics doesn't help with sudden pain. Especially for long-term users. If you want a guy to keep going after he's been stabbed, which is I assume what you're after, you have to dull his reaction to pain, without dulling his reflexes. That's a neurotransmitter issue."

"Do you know *which* neurotransmitters?"

"Not off the top of my head. Pain isn't my field. It shouldn't be too hard to find out, though, assuming they've been iden-tified in the journals. Have your guys do it. Or have me do it. Give me Dani and we'll do it twice as fast."

"You'd like that, wouldn't you?"

"Of course I would."

"Sorry, that wasn't the deal."

"Fine. Give me a computer, and I'll get to work on the research."

At that, he actually laughed out loud. "And have you contact your friends at HSE and tell them all about us?"

Her stomach dropped. How did he know about Eric?

"Clive did well hiring HSE after we took Dani. Velasquez was decidedly pissed off that you proved so difficult to abduct. Waiting isn't his strong suit, but I knew they'd leave you alone after the press conference. So no, you won't be getting anywhere near a computer with Internet access. I'll provide you with a typist. You tell him what to search for and where, and he will look it up. He'll print the results, and you can go through them."

"That will take forever!"

"Best I can do. It's your own fault for not figuring this out until you and Daniela had been separated."

For the rest of the afternoon, Jane sat with a pen and pad, industriously writing down what to research and where, passing sheets to her new assistant whenever he came by to drop a pile of paperwork next to her. She also scanned his findings, throwing most of them out but keeping a few that looked promising. Bryan had to believe she was actually working, actually trying to help.

When they were released to get ready for dinner, Jane took a pile of the paperwork with her. She'd managed to keep the majority of the good stuff to herself, putting it aside for "further attention." Not that Bryan couldn't re-create her searches and find the articles again, but if she could slow him down by taking the work with her when Eric came, she'd give the proper authorities—and she had no clue who that even was at this point—more time to clean out the house and lab before Bryan got too far along in his research.

⌒

BRYAN DIDN'T ALLOW Dani to come to dinner. Since Jane hadn't eaten breakfast, and the crew ate only light lunches in the lab, she should have been hungry. She wasn't. Thoughts of Dani, of Eric, of the day's discoveries filled her mind. She forced herself to chew and swallow—what if Eric came tonight? She would need her strength.

Upstairs, she propped the chair under the doorknob and took a quick shower. Usually she slept in shorts with whatever tee came most easily to hand, but she needed to be ready to run, so she slipped into underwear, jeans, and the darkest tee she could find to blend well into the night. She opened the window and removed the screen from its snaps but left it loose in the frame, allowing her to leave the window itself open in case Eric came for her. *Please, let him come tonight.*

Nerves kept Jane awake for a few hours, but eventually exhaustion had its way and she slept. Her dreams were filled with dark figures, and she woke twice, sure Velasquez was coming for her. The third time, she woke to a gloved hand over her mouth and Eric's bright blue eyes staring into hers. The minute she stopped her instinctive struggles, he let go and reached for the pad by the bed.

Where's Dani?

They took her prisoner this morning. She's with her brother, I think.

He nodded once, decisively, as if the information were of no consequence. He helped Jane up and watched while she donned the Crocs that were her only footwear since she'd been barefoot when abducted. At the window, he showed her a rope leading up to the roof, knotted at intervals. Oh, hell, this was going to be worse than gym class in high school. Sure enough, he jerked his thumb upward. With a deep breath, Jane reached out and grabbed the rope just above the first knot over her head. She hauled herself upward and felt Eric behind her. The minute he was out, he began speaking.

"Yeah. I've got Jane. Are you in?" He listened. "Change of plan. His sister is down there, too. Or Jane thinks so."

Jane climbed up onto the clay-tile roof, thankful for the grip of the rubber shoes.

"Got 'em?" Eric asked. "Great. Marco, give us three minutes, then go." He took Jane's hand and helped her up and over the ridge of the roof, then collected the grappling hook and reset it on the opposite side of the roofline, attaching a much thicker, unknotted rope.

"Why didn't we just go down from my window?"

"Because any minute, Marco's going to create a big boom to draw the guards' attention so they don't see where we go. The magic of misdirection. They will head for two places: toward the bang and toward their most valuable asset—you. We will be on the opposite side of the building when they do. He can't wait for us to go down because we need to draw the guards off before we go down." He leaned over the edge of the roof, checking below them for guards, then tossed the rope down. "You're going to have to climb on my back. You don't have protective gloves or the strength to go down as fast as I can. Arms around my neck, legs around my waist."

They were halfway down the side of the house when the night exploded. Light flared and the house shook. And then they were on the ground and running for the wall, skirting the pool and the dark cabanas, ignoring the shouts of guards. Leaving her at the foot of the wall, he free-climbed up and dropped her a rope.

"Wrap it around your waist and tie it before you start climbing," he ordered. "I'll pull you up at the same time."

Once they'd landed on the other side, Eric took her hand and darted the few yards into the deeper shade of the thick woods. He dug in his pocket and handed her a small object. "Put this in your ear. You'll be able to hear us; we'll be able to hear you."

Jane placed the device deep in her ear and immediately heard a vaguely familiar male voice.

"We got a problem. The kid wasn't so eager to be rescued. I had to knock him out, so we're off schedule by a couple of minutes."

"Marco?" Hearing Eric next to her through her right ear while the earbud gave her his voice through her left was peculiar, and Jane shook her head slightly, trying to bring the two in line.

Another male voice answered. "On it. Trey, head to your right, and I'll put a few little distractions between you and trouble."

A minute later, shots rang out and then a tremendous crash reverberated through the air. More shouting followed, and over it Jane heard Bryan yell at his men to stop what they were doing and find her.

"We're over," came the voice she now realized was Trey Godwin, who'd driven them back to her house the first night Eric had stayed with her. "We'll meet you at the rendezvous in twenty."

"Ten-four," said the other voice.

"We're gone," Eric said. "ETA fifteen." He took her hand

and led her deeper into the jungle. Occasionally, he glanced at his watch and made adjustments to their path, and after a while they came to a rocky, slow-moving stream. Not long after, they were joined by Dani, Trey, Alvaro, and a stranger with long dark hair she assumed must be Marco. Alvaro had his hands bound with climbing rope and duct tape over his mouth.

"I explained to him that if he kept shouting behind the tape I'd have to knock him out again," Trey said. "It's mostly worked, but he's pretty fucking uncooperative."

"He'll do better," said Dani. "He's confused is all. They tortured him. You didn't have to do the same."

"That wasn't torture; that was practicality. If we'd waited for you to convince him to join us, we'd all be dead."

"Let's go," Eric broke in. "Trey, you lead. Dani, you're behind him. Alvaro, follow your sister. I'll take center with Janie behind me, and Marco, you cover our six. We're going two miles upstream. Watch your footing, but keep up your speed. We can't lead them in a straight line, so if we keep to the optimal course for evasion, we have seventeen miles to the extraction point, and we can't afford broken ankles."

Upstream was also uphill, and Jane almost fell three times in as many minutes, grabbing on to Eric's shirt to hold herself upright. Mud, sand, and slime filled her shoes and soaked the legs of her jeans as she picked her way along through the sluggish water. They couldn't be making good time—at this rate it would take days to get to the pickup spot.

Eric winced when Jane grabbed him for the third or fourth time. It would be a whole lot easier if he could simply carry her, but that plan had gone out the window the minute he'd gotten a look at Alvaro Peralta's eyes. That flat, dead look meant the kid couldn't be trusted at all. Yeah, he'd been a prisoner and Eric felt sorry for him, but his wiring was seriously screwed up. The sister stumbled along behind Trey, fury in every line of her body. He guessed he understood; it had to be hard to see your own sibling as a potential danger.

After a couple of hours, they crested a small rise and came to the pool that supplied the stream they'd been wading through. It, in turn, was supplied by two separate sources, one to the east and one to the west. The plan had called for taking the western route, the whole purpose of the upstream trip being to diffuse scent trails. Once they were tracked to the stream, the hunting force would split in two, one going up and one going down. The idea here was to divide them again between the east and west streams.

But, as usual, incomplete intel forced Eric to rethink. Either direction took them uphill. He'd expected that, given that water flowed with gravity, but they hadn't had time to do a full survey, and he hadn't seen aerial views or elevation maps. The western route was going to be tough. The water came down into the pool as a thin fall about thirty feet high.

"Hold up. No one break cover." They all stopped.

"What do you think, Trey?"

"Rangers lead the way."

"Yeah, fuck you, too," said Marco from behind them.

"And look where you are, Marine." Trey laughed.

"Cool it. Who's got rope and hooks?" He'd used all his getting Jane out of the compound. They all carried paracord, but that wouldn't do for climbing the cliff face with amateurs.

"I've got rope," Trey said. "I'll find a tie-off at the top."

"Go."

Trey looped a long length of rope over one shoulder and across his body, handed his backpack to Marco, then dove into the pool and disappeared. Eric moved to the head of their little group and surveyed them. Dani was drooping visibly, Alvaro still looked sullen, and Jane kept flicking her eyes back and forth, as if expecting their pursuers to attack without warning from the darkness around them. He'd agree with her if he were fighting guerrillas, but in his experience cartel soldiers didn't value stealth, only strength.

"Find a rock, take a seat. It's going to take Trey at least half an hour to make that climb, even not going up the face itself, and this may be your last chance to rest for a while." He grabbed a handful of protein bars out of his backpack and passed them around, along with a bladder of water. He untied Alvaro's hands but sent Marco a visual command to keep an eye on the kid. Marco nodded and shifted slightly, putting himself between Alvaro and the rest of the group.

It had only been about twenty minutes when Marco's head came up sharply. "Company."

"Fuck." He'd thought they'd have more time. "Okay, Marco, see what we're up against. Everyone else, in the water. Stay to the edge, in the weeds, but start making your way around toward the waterfall. Move quietly. Jane, you take lead. Dani, you're next." He didn't plan on taking his eyes off Alvaro. He was tempted to gag the kid again, but if they had to swim the taped mouth could be dangerous.

A few minutes passed, and he heard Marco in his ear.

"I can see four. I can take them out no problem, but there won't be any way to hide it."

Eric considered the group making their slow way around

the edge of the water. "Do it. We need the time." He saw Jane stumble slightly—she'd be rethinking getting involved with him now—but this was what he did. Would be prefer not to kill anyone? Absolutely. Every life had value. But the simple fact of the matter was that this was kill or be killed.

"Ahoy below," came Trey's voice. "Operation rope and scope under way. All's quiet now that Marco's cut off the tail, so time for you guys to head up."

"Good. Marco, head east and leave a few obvious tracks, then double-back to us."

"Will do."

"They're not going to let you get away," said Alvaro. "You have no idea how pathetic you look compared to them."

"Shut your mouth and move your feet, or I'll show you pathetic," Eric replied. For a moment, the kid didn't budge, and Eric feared he'd have to knock him out again, but at last he turned around and trudged along behind his sister.

At the cliff face Eric sent Marco up with Dani clinging to his back like a monkey. Trey fast-roped back down, leaving Marco at the top, where his sniper skills would do the most good. Without being told, Jane clambered back onto Eric's back, and he went up. At the top, Marco gave him a hand over, and he sent Jane and Dani into the jungle to hide while he crouched at the edge of the cliff and watched Trey getting Alvaro into position. The climb was a treacherous one even without an extra buck seventy-five of ill-distributed weight from a reluctant passenger.

Trey was halfway up when Marco cursed under his breath. "Double time," he said. "Company's coming." He steadied his AR-15 on a rock, and his whole body went still. As often as Eric had seen snipers work, he never got over the way they seemed to stop breathing, to transform into stone or brick or earth.

"Dani, Jane, get further back behind the tree line and lie down. If they fire, they'll be shooting up." Eric leaned over the edge and saw Trey a good ten feet down but moving fast. Eight feet. Six. Four. A shot rang out, and stone chips flew inches from Trey's shoulder. Marco returned a single shot.

"Got him. But there may be more. And they'll know which direction we've taken."

"No shit." Eric helped Trey over the lip of the cliff. "Time for plan B."

"What's that?" asked Jane.

"Run like hell."

CHAPTER 11

THEY RAN. AND ran. And ran. The sun rose and the jungle around them went from black to a series of deep, rich greens. Although direct light never reached her skin, the air heated and thickened with humidity, clogging Jane's breathing. Her feet squelched in their own sweat inside the rubber shoes. But she refused to quit. They'd abandoned their line and now spread out, as they forced their way through the brush, though Eric still took the lead and Marco held up the rear.

It seemed hours before Eric called a halt. Dani had given up, and Trey was carrying her in a fireman's hold across his shoulders. Both he and Eric appeared unstoppable, barely fazed by the conditions. Trey let Dani down, and Eric passed around more protein bars and the canteen.

"Scouting," Marco said, and disappeared into the woods.

Eric sat next to Jane and tapped at the device on his wrist, which Jane could now see was far more than a simple watch.

"How far off course are we?" Trey asked.

"We're doing okay, but we can't stay on a direct trajectory or they'll figure out exactly where we're headed."

"Where *are* we headed?"

Both Eric and Trey looked at her as if they'd forgotten she was even there.

"An airfield about twenty klicks from here. Small, used primarily—ironically—by cartel flyers. Nash has a friend who can get his hands on a little cargo plane. Once we get close, I'll give him an ETA and he'll pick us up."

"How long do you think it will take us to get there? And what's going to happen to the lab?"

"Nash identified the lab as a terrorist enclave to Homeland Security. We figured that wasn't far off, given what they were trying to develop. So we'll leave that in their hands and they'll work it with the Mexican government, or, if they can't get assistance from the Mexicans, they'll probably send in a black-ops team to shred the place. Marco knocked as much of the communications system as he could identify offline when he was firing on the compound to give us space for our escape, and sent a couple Stingers into the lab itself as well."

Okay, so she could breathe a little easier on that score. It wasn't perfect. She'd have preferred to have burned the place to the ground on their way out and stirred the ashes with the bones of Bryan Axlerod's dismembered skeleton, but at least Nash was working on containing the problem.

"As to how long it will take, that's what Trey and I were talking about. The airfield isn't far as the crow flies, but we can't afford to put a neon arrow on our path so they can hang out there and wait for us. If we head east first for a couple of klicks, then northeast, we should be able to cut straight west and hit the airstrip. We're not moving as fast as I'd like, though."

"Um, Eric . . ."

"I know, Janie. You guys are doing your best, and I appreciate it. But there's no way we make the pickup today at this rate."

Oh, great. Another night in the jungle. Exactly what she needed to complete the current nightmare.

"Five minutes, everyone," Eric said. "We need to get moving again."

Dani groaned. "I should have joined a gym instead of spending my money on mocha lattes and margaritas. That's the top of my to-do list when I get home."

"The top of my to-do list is a hot bath and a massage," Jane said.

"Well, yeah. *After* that."

"Why are they even wasting manpower chasing us?" Jane asked. "Why aren't they dismantling the lab, saving what they can, and getting out while the getting's good?"

Eric shook his head. "Because Velasquez heads up the Hijos cartel, which means the law on both sides of the border would love to bring him down. He operates with relative impunity because he never performs any of the acts himself. On the local level, people are either bribed or bullied so that on the national level—where prosecutors would be willing to take him on—nothing can be proven. But this operation was too big and too personal. He got involved. He showed himself to you. He needs to eliminate the threat you pose if he wants to get back to business as usual.

"Failing to deliver on the supersoldier project isn't fatal, but allowing a woman to destroy his lab might be. He needs to prove he can still lead the cartel, and the best way to do that is to bring you in and make an example of you. The second best is to kill you outright and display your body as proof of what happens to those who cross him."

Oh, wow. So there would be no talking them out of the pursuit. She didn't bother replying, and Eric touched her hand. "We're not going to let them get you."

Jane nodded.

Once again, Eric led them through the dense underbrush. Jane watched his body move gracefully but forcefully forward and tried to step where he did before the grass and brush could spring back up and grab at her legs. Marco had not returned, but through her earbud she could hear him giving Eric updates.

Fear and monotony combined in the thick, humid air, weighing down her eyelids and her feet until every step became a chore, every breath a struggle. She inhaled tiny insects and choked them out. Her legs cramped, and she wished she could ask Eric to pick her up and carry her, but she refused to give in. He needed his hands free to defend them.

"Company," said Marco's voice in her ear. Eric held up a hand and they all stopped.

"Where?"

"Nine o'clock, thirty meters out."

"Incoming?"

"Hold. They've stopped. Arguing about something."

Eric held his hand out parallel to the ground and mimed for them all to get down. Jane crouched next to Dani but didn't take her eyes off Eric. He and Trey had dropped as well, but even beneath the long-sleeved jackets they wore, she could see the tension in their muscles. Both unholstered weapons.

"Heading away. Don't move yet."

Alvaro coughed.

"They heard that."

Alvaro looked as if he might cough again, but Eric, next to him, knocked him in the temple with the butt of his gun and caught him as he fell over.

"Talk to me, Marco," he whispered.

"Can't figure out how they heard that. I only got it through my bud."

Eric glanced at Alvaro's prone body. "Fuck. I know how. Keep an eye on them." He went through Alvaro's pockets, then checked the seams and hem of his shirt. At last, inside what looked like a label sewn onto his jeans, he found a small electronic device. He crushed it between two rocks. "Short-range transmitter," he said. "They were probably hoping that Dani would tell him whatever she knew if they were locked up together. We're just lucky they didn't GPS tag him."

"They're standing still again. Maybe trying to figure out what happened to their signal."

"Fuck," said Trey. "You think he knew?"

"No way to tell," Eric said.

"Of course not!" Dani said.

"These assholes are armed for bear," Marco said. "I can see AKs and M16s. Unless this kid has some value no one's bothered to tell us about, calling attention to himself would be fucking suicide."

Eric dropped the pack from his back and pulled out a folded strip of duct tape. He tore off a two-foot section, peeled off the backing, and re-gagged Alvaro, wrapping the tape all the way around his head. Dani hissed a protest, but his glare silenced her.

"Still not moving?"

"Nope. But they're not arguing, either. Wish I had ears in there."

"No getting closer, Marco. That's an order."

In her earbud, Jane heard Marco grunt agreement.

"Okay, they have a plan. They're circling outward, looking for a trail."

"Which we definitely will have left." Eric hoisted the unconscious Alvaro into a fireman's carry. "Everyone stay close together and be as quiet as possible. Step lightly."

They inched forward, taking pains not to disturb the ground more than absolutely necessary. That a two-hundred-pound man carrying another could leave so little trace of his passage amazed Jane, and she did her best to imitate him.

"They found part of your trail," said Marco, "but then they

lost it. They may pick it back up if you're not careful There are six of them, and they have comms. I can't take all of them out without one sending up a flare."

"Can you get out?"

"Yeah, I'm good. I'll keep you posted."

It seemed hours before Alvaro stirred, trying to kick free of Eric's hold, but it had probably been only ten or fifteen minutes. Eric set him down but held him still. He shoved his face right up to Alvaro's, so close their noses practically touched.

"Maybe you believe the men behind us intend to spare your life. Or maybe you have a death wish. I don't know and I don't care. Make a move to alert them again, and I'll kill you myself." He spun and forged ahead, leaving Alvaro to follow.

Did the kid believe him? Jane did, and it freaked her out more than a little. If Eric killed Alvaro, it would be in her defense. Hers and Dani's. She glanced over her shoulder at her friend, but Dani was trudging along completely absorbed in her own thoughts and Jane couldn't catch her eye.

The shadows were lengthening, and the patches of actual sunlight had completely disappeared by the time Eric allowed them to stop again. Marco had kept them apprised of their pursuers' location through the afternoon, allowing Eric to set an opposing course. As they sat down in a minuscule clearing, he joined them.

"They stopping?" Eric asked.

"Looks like, but they could be waiting for reinforcements. They know they're close. We've gained some distance, but they'll close it soon enough."

"We keep moving, then," Eric said. "Jane, Dani, if we rest for an hour, can you go on?"

Could she? She ached in places she hadn't known she had

muscles and itched in places she couldn't scratch in public. The stupid shoes had rubbed raw spots in her feet, and she wanted to give up. But she wasn't ready to die, either.

"Whatever we have to do," she said, settling next to Dani, who'd plopped herself down on the trunk of a fallen tree. "Dani?"

Dani shrugged. "We don't have any choice, do we?" The grime on her face was streaked with tears, and the flat tone of her voice contradicted her statement.

Jane slipped an arm across her shoulders. "You're doing great, Dani, but if you can't go on you need to say so. The guys will figure something out."

"It's just walking. Anybody can walk." She stared down at her sneaker-clad feet, comparing them to Jane's. "Oh my God, Jane, you're bleeding!"

Eric's eyes followed Dani's gaze, and he cursed. "Trey?"

"On it." Trey opened his pack and pulled out ointment and bandages.

"So you're a doctor as well as a Ranger?" Dani asked.

"Medic. We all have multiple roles. I patch people up and fly them around. Marco's a sniper and tracker. And our fearless leader for this mission is an expert strategist and tactician, as well as the king of SERE."

"Seer?"

"Survival, evasion, resistance, escape," Eric said. "In other words, I'm good at games."

Jane figured it meant a whole lot more than that but kept her mouth shut. Trey slathered salve on her feet and wrapped them in gauze, creating socks to prevent further damage from the ill-fitting shoes.

"You should have spoken up sooner. The jungle's no place for an open wound. Bacteria love it here."

"Trey fucking hates the jungle," Marco said, the jab the first touch of humor Jane had heard from him. "'Scuse my French."

"Who doesn't?" Trey groused. "There's all kinds of crap that can kill you here. Plants, bugs, snakes. Give me a good chase through the city any day." He studied Dani. "I don't think an hour's going to be enough, Eric. They need two."

"Marco?"

Without a word, the other man disappeared back into the thick forest around them. Trey pulled a packet out of his bag and shook it out to reveal a survival blanket. He kicked together a bunch of fallen leaves, then laid the blanket atop them, silver side facing down, olive green side showing. "Lie down. Get as much rest as you can."

Jane didn't have to be told twice. She and Dani both lay on the plasticky sheeting, and in a couple of minutes, Alvaro joined them. Despite the twigs poking her and the musty, damp smell of the forest floor, she drifted off to sleep.

⌒

Eric wished he didn't have to wake them, but Marco had seen too much movement among their pursuers. He leaned over Jane and shook her gently. Her eyes popped open, full of fear. He put a finger to his lips.

"Time to go."

She nodded and touched Dani on the shoulder. Within minutes, they were moving. At least both Jane and Dani had managed forty-five minutes of rest. While they'd slept, the sun had disappeared completely and the jungle had gone black, the shadows broken only by glints of silver where the moonlight hit moisture-covered leaves and branches. Marco could tease Trey about his dislike of such areas, but Trey wasn't alone—Eric had grown up a country boy in many ways, but this kind of environment creeped him out. Snakes both human and reptile infested the landscape.

"Do either of you know how to shoot?" he asked.

Jane shook her head, but Dani said, "I do. My father used to take me target shooting."

"Good." He handed Dani a pistol and magazine from his backpack. "It may be bigger than what you're used to, but it's better than nothing."

Dani checked the gun, then slapped the magazine into place with practiced ease.

"Don't shoot anything unless you have to—we don't need the noise. That said, if you do need to, just go for it and we'll worry about consequences later."

"Gotcha."

"Let's go."

They headed out, winding around the trees and picking their way through the dense undergrowth. In the distance, Eric heard the distinctive howls of a pack of wolves. *You stay on your territory. We're just passing through.*

"They're catching up to you," Marco said in his ear. "Not a lot, but you guys should move faster if you can. And head west."

Well, fuck. They couldn't go west for too much longer, or they'd be putting an insurmountable distance between themselves and the airstrip. He picked up the pace a bit, and the others followed.

He heard a rustle and then a feminine "damn" behind him and turned to see that Dani had tripped over something and fallen to the ground. Alvaro leaned over to help her up, and before Eric could stop him, the kid had her gun. Had it and pointed it right at his sister, jabbing it into her stomach, his finger tightening on the trigger.

The shot that rang out surprised even him. The kid's eyes widened, his brain seeming to take a second to catch up to the fact that it wasn't working any longer, and then he fell over.

Dani started screaming. Her face was white in the night's darkness, all color leached away. Her shrieks went on and on as she stared at her brother lying on the ground, a gaping hole in his forehead.

And then she leaped on Trey, pounding her fists into him and yelling at him.

"How could you? He was just a kid! You monster!"

"That kid was about to kill you."

"He wouldn't have. He was my brother!" She crumpled, all the fight gone out of her, and crawled back over to her brother's body.

"You have to shut her up," came Marco's urgent command. "They're headed straight for you."

"Give them something else to think about," Eric said. "We've got a problem." Immediately, the sound of gunfire came from his left.

Trey had a hypo out. "Jane, she's not going to let me near her, but she needs a sedative. We can't do this here, now. Can you get her to take it?"

Jane, tears running down her face, took the needle and vial from him, along with an alcohol pad to wipe down Dani's arm. Eric had to blink moisture from his own eyes watching them.

"Dani, sweetheart, give me your arm," Jane said.

The other woman stared at her, her face a frozen mask. "What am I supposed to tell my parents?"

"I don't know, sweetie. But we can worry about that once

we get home. Right now, you need to make sure you stay alive so they don't lose both their children."

"They'll never forgive me. Never. This is my fault."

"No, it's not."

"If I hadn't gotten involved with Bryan, he wouldn't have taken Varo."

Jane wiped the grime off the inside of Dani's elbow and injected the sedative from Trey's kit. "You know that's not true. Bryan would have found a way to get what he wanted, whether you dated him or not. He's evil. He played on the fact that you loved your brother. That's not your fault."

Dani started to say something else, but then her eyes fluttered several times and she simply keeled over. Trey stepped forward and caught her, then passed her off to Eric while he picked up Alvaro's lifeless body.

"Janie, we're going to have to do this at a run for a while. If you stop being able to keep up, say so and we'll slow down. But we cannot stop again."

God bless her, she just nodded even though he knew she had to be in shock. Eric settled Dani as comfortably as he could across his shoulders and beat feet.

Daniela Peralta didn't weigh as much as some packs he'd carried over the years, but even with his NVGs the darkness, the unstable footing, and the thick, heavy air made the going rough. He could hear Jane's ragged breathing behind him and wished he could stop for her, but safety was his priority. He'd like to ask Trey to leave the kid behind, for that matter, but he understood his friend's need to bring the body home. It was a gesture that would be lost on Dani now, though she might appreciate it later. But even after Trey had done his best to patch up the wound, there was no doubt they were leaving a blood trail, and the deadweight was slowing them down.

How in the hell had a simple rescue op gone so badly wrong?

The GPS on his wrist vibrated. They were within four hours of the airstrip. Thank God. He called a halt, laid Dani down to let Jane fuss over her, and pulled his sat phone out of his pack.

Miguel answered on the first ring and assured him he'd have the plane there and ready for them when they arrived. They needed to get the fuck out of this country. Jane wouldn't be safe until all the men involved in the experiments were locked up or dead, but at least back home he could provide her with protection. Here they were entirely too exposed.

Trey had his own pack open and was digging through it.

"I'm out of sedative," he said. "I wanted to knock her out until we got at least as far as the plane, but it doesn't look as if that's going to happen. She'll be waking up in a half hour or an hour."

"Okay. We'll deal with that when it happens. With a bit of luck, she won't be screaming."

Unfortunately, they had no idea how many others were coming after them. Marco had taken out all six of the previous hunters, but not before they'd radioed their position, calling for reinforcements. And they had no choice but to head for the airstrip, which meant that the new group would figure out their plans with relative ease.

"I'll try to keep her calm," Jane said. "But . . ."

"But?"

"It might be best if Trey and Marco traded positions. If that's possible. I don't think she's going to want to see you right now."

"Of course," Trey said. "I'm not as good as Marco is, but we've only got a few hours left. We can manage."

Eric spoke to Marco, who appeared, wraithlike, from the jungle a few minutes later. He passed off binocs and a rifle to Trey without a word and hoisted Alvaro's body onto his back. Trey slipped into the woods, and Eric picked up Dani and led the way once more toward to the airstrip.

As Trey had predicted, about an hour later, Dani stirred. Eric let her down while Marco set Alvaro's body down a few feet away and backed off. Dani blinked a few times, and then her eyes opened, but her gaze remained unfocused until it caught on Alvaro's body.

"Oh," she said, but she didn't scream. Instead, her body shook with quiet sobs. She looked at Eric. "You brought him?"

"Trey did. We'll take him home for you."

If she noticed that Trey wasn't with them, she didn't mention it. She stood up somewhat shakily and nodded. "I want to go home. So let's get going."

Two hours later, Eric could almost taste safety. This was always the most dangerous part, the part where people got sloppy. The airfield was damned close, and as much as it represented their way out, it was by no means a secure location.

"Trey, let's find out whether any of our friends are currently using the strip for cargo."

"On it."

They slogged through a muddy stream and paused at the top of a small hill for Marco to pass Alvaro over to Eric so he could pull out his rifle. Jane sucked in a deep breath, and Eric wondered whether she'd ever get over all the killing. Maybe once she got home, she would be able to put all this behind her.

Of course, that would mean forgetting him, too. But he'd have to deal with that. There was no way she could look at him the same way she had in the past.

"No one here," Trey said in his earbud. "There's a sweet little Bear 360 two-seater housed in the hangar. Fully fueled and ready to go, which means someone's actively playing games out here. So keep your eyes open."

"Okay, we're coming in. Marco, cover us from up here." He led the women slowly down toward the airstrip.

"I can hear Miguel's plane," Marco said after a couple of minutes.

He could, too. A dull hum on the horizon. "Let me know when it's in sight. We've got no visual under this canopy."

"Gotcha."

They forged on until they got to the airstrip. Eric set Alvaro's body down, leaning it up against the hangar wall. Rigor had begun to set in. The heat wasn't helping either that or the smell of the boy's blood and body fluids. It was going to be unpleasant as hell in the closed environs of the plane.

He stretched his back, working out the kinks, then pulled binocs from his pack to search the sky for Miguel's plane.

"Fuck!" Marco yelled just as he spotted the plane. "Abort! Get the hell out!"

The plane shuddered, then exploded, fire raining down from the night sky into the jungle. Jane screamed; Dani shouted. Eric blocked it out.

"How far out are they, Marco?"

"They'll be on you in eight. Max ten. And you're between me and them. I can't get them for you. I'm on my way."

"Trey, get in the damned hangar and get that plane started. You're putting both women in the passenger seat and flying out. The rest of us will get out as we can."

Trey ran for the hangar.

"This isn't a fucking '76 Oldsmobile, you know. I can't hot-wire it."

"Yeah, you can. Rangers lead the way, remember."

"What should we do?" Jane asked. "Get in the plane?"

"Not until Trey starts it. If he can't and they have SAMs, that whole hangar is a death trap. Find cover." He gestured to the side of the building, where a rusted Jeep with no doors or tires rotted into a cement pad and four large barrels lined up to create a small wall. "Over there."

Marco came in on the run.

"How many?"

"A dozen. Maybe more. Pretty sure Miguel ejected, but didn't stop to see."

The engine of the plane in the hangar coughed a few times, then roared to life. Trey brought it rolling out onto the short runway.

"Jane! Dani! Get out here!"

The first shots hit when the women were halfway across the tarmac. Two whistled by Eric's head, embedding themselves in the wall of the hangar behind him with dull *thunks*. He fired back a few times, though he couldn't see the shooters, who had yet to emerge from the jungle. Marco dropped to the ground beneath the belly of the plane and laid down a steady stream of suppressing fire, giving Eric the chance to run over and help boost the women up into the plane.

Dani went first, pushing herself up with one foot resting on Eric's shoulder as she clambered into the small second seat. The second the pressure from her foot lifted, he leaned down to help Jane. More shots cracked and pinged around them, one sending bits of pavement flying up to slice into his hands.

Jane ducked and scrambled away from the bullets, which were coming from a new direction.

And then Dani toppled backward out of the plane. He reached out instinctively and caught her before she hit the ground. Blood poured from a bullet crease across her temple.

Holy fucking hell. He fired off five more shots in quick succession.

"Put her back inside!" Jane shouted at him from the nose of the plane, where she'd taken shelter. "Trey can fly her to a hospital!"

"You first!"

But she shook her head. "No time! Give me a gun and put her in the damned plane!"

No arguing with that. Their position was becoming more tenuous by the second. Marco slapped a new magazine into his rifle, and Trey stood up and began firing in a semicircle around the plane in every direction except toward the hangar. Eric slid his weapon across the tarmac in Jane's direction and hoisted Dani in his arms. With Trey covering, he plopped her into the seat as best he could.

"Jane! Get in! *Now!*"

Jane inched her way around toward him, but a volley of bullets sent her running for shelter beneath the plane. One slammed into his vest, knocking him to the ground. He rolled and came up firing just as three men with AKs came out of the woods. They were out of time. Someone in this group had SAMs, and if the plane didn't move, both Trey and Dani were dead meat.

"Go!" he shouted at Trey. "We'll catch you stateside!"

He grabbed Jane's hand and sprinted for the corner of the hangar where the jungle encroached on the airstrip. Marco took down one of the men and followed, firing constantly. The men concentrated on trying to stop the plane, but Trey was a hell of a pilot and it took off in a steep, smooth ascent over their heads even as they fired.

Eric couldn't stop to watch, but after a few minutes of running, he realized he hadn't heard it explode, which meant they'd avoided the surface-to-air missiles. He sent up a brief prayer for both Trey and Dani. Trey would have a hard time dealing with killing Dani's brother, let alone what would happen to him if the girl died on his watch. Jane wouldn't deal well with Dani's death, either. He'd been around survivor's guilt often enough to know how corrosive it could be.

⸺

ERIC'S HAND ON hers was the only thing that kept Jane going. She could see nothing in the darkness of the forest after the bright lights of the airstrip. Any minute now she expected men to pop out of the underbrush and murder her. *Please, God, let Dani and Trey be okay.* She hadn't seen their plane take off, too busy trying to keep from falling down as she stumbled along behind Eric after returning his gun. She'd managed to fire four shots in the time it took him to put Dani in the plane. They had nearly dislocated her shoulder, and she had no clue whether any had hit their targets. All around her, the crash and boom of weapons combined with the rumbling roar of the plane's engine into a chaotic symphony of menace.

Where would they go? Did Eric have a backup plan? They were deep in the middle of the jungle. They couldn't possibly walk out. And even if they did, what would happen to them? The local authorities would likely shoot them on sight if Velasquez was as powerful as Eric seemed to think.

"Hold up," said Eric after a while. "I think we've lost them. At least temporarily."

Marco flipped a switch on the big eyepiece goggle he wore

and scanned the woods. "Nothing human nearby," he confirmed.

"Okay, then. We can head for Extraction Bravo, but if they knew about Alpha, we might be in trouble. Keep an eye out, and let me see if I can get a signal on the sat phone."

He pulled what looked to Jane like an oversized cell phone out of his pack and extended a long antenna. In minutes, he had Lexie and Nash on the line and was explaining their situation. By putting her own head right next to his, Jane could hear both sides of the conversation.

"I heard from Miguel," Nash said. "He made it out before they blew up his plane. He's gone underground for the moment while waiting to figure out whether anyone knew he was the one flying. He did see Trey get away. They sent missiles after him twice, but he avoided both of them. The explosions drew a lot of attention, though. There will probably be a fair amount of military and police presence in that area for a while."

"Yeah. We're on the move."

"No one's injured?"

"We lost Alvaro. I'll tell you when I get back. Dani's injured, but Trey has her. You haven't heard from him yet?"

"No. He'll be in touch when he's secure, I'm sure. They may still be in the air. What's he flying?"

"Fuck if I know. Two-seater. He called it a Bear?"

"Bear 360."

"Yeah."

"Okay. Lexie, see what you can find registered. Or not registered. We'll try to track them down in case he loses comms. Eric, I want you, Jane, and Marco to head to LZ Charlie. With Alpha shot, Bravo is apt to be compromised. Since there are only three of you, I can get a small chopper in there. It will be a quick and dirty in and out. Easier than the Alpha extraction, more secure than Bravo. How far out are you?"

Eric plugged a bunch of numbers into the device he wore on his wrist. "Forty klicks."

"How long will it take you cross-country?"

In the darkness, Jane could feel Eric's eyes on her. "We're pretty ragged, Nash. Gonna take twenty-four, at least. Especially if we have to avoid military and police presence."

"I hear you. See if you can find a vehicle. I'll do what I can on my end."

"Good deal."

"Ready?" he asked when he'd put the phone away.

"As I'll ever be," she replied. Twenty-four hours of hiking. Would she make it? *Anyone can walk*, Dani had said, but Jane wasn't so certain that was true. Her thighs and the soles of her feet protested

every step.

"Don't worry, we'll take breaks. I promise."

Was she that obvious? "It's okay."

"No, it's not. But it's necessary. I wish it weren't." He took her hand, and once again they moved out. The woods around them stirred with life. Night creatures darted across their path and scurried away as they slid through the jungle. Eric made sure Jane drank frequently from his canteen, and when they came to a small stream, he attached a filter and refilled it and Marco's while she rested and ate another protein bar. If she never saw another piece of prepackaged food in her life, it would be too soon.

The sun rose, and the air heated from tolerable to disgusting as they hiked. Eric kept their pace relatively slow, but after the third or fourth stop, Jane simply couldn't get up.

"Okay," Eric said. "We rest. I'll call Nash."

Jane sat with her back resting against a thick tree trunk as Marco moved away to scout the area for any lurking threats. Eric paced as he talked, his crystalline eyes surveying the area without stopping.

"Nash says Trey and Dani landed safely," Eric said. "They're in Mexico City. Miguel's called in, too. He's going to fly them to Nuevo Laredo, where Nash will have transport waiting to fly Dani to a good hospital. No one is looking for him; they just fired on that plane because they knew it was coming to pick us up."

"Laredo is a fucking pit," Marco's voice echoed in Jane's earpiece.

Eric laughed. "And this isn't? But seriously, Nash and Trey can get her across the border there easily."

Thank God. Dani would be safe.

Eric sat down next to her. "Marco, you good keeping watch?"

"Yep."

"Holler if you see anything." Unceremoniously, he picked Jane up and settled her in his lap. "Sleep," he ordered, his arms closing around her like blankets of pure muscle. She rested her head against his chest and closed her eyes. He stank, but so did she. She didn't care. He felt so damned good. Like security and home and light in the darkness. She buried her head against the peculiarly hard surface of his vest and went to sleep.

CHAPTER 12

Eric rubbed his cheek over the top of Jane's head and tried to come up with a plan beyond "get the fuck out of Mexico." Assuming they could make it to the LZ, and assuming Velasquez didn't blow the fucking helo up the way he had Miguel's plane, he'd take her back to New York. He'd love to lock her in his apartment and keep her there until Velasquez was dead and gone, but she'd never agree. She had a life, and he had to respect that. But he couldn't let her go back to work at AHI, either. Not only would that be the first place Velasquez would look for her, but also he didn't trust Clive Handler further than he could throw him. The man ran the lab where the Warlock research had begun.

Jane believed in him. If she didn't, she wouldn't be able to sleep now, no matter how tired she was. He wasn't about to fail her.

He tightened his grip slightly, and she shifted, cuddling closer. She was a mess. The bandages Trey had put on her feet were filthy and ragged, he could see broken nails on her hands, and a wide variety of bugs had bitten the tender skin of her face and neck.

But she'd soldiered on as well as any man under his command ever had. He'd watched her try to stand twice before she gave up. He could carry her, and he would if he had to, but allowing everyone a breather was a better plan.

"Marco?"

"So far, so good."

Move forward. When you can't think thirty steps ahead, think twenty. When you can't do twenty, do ten. Or five. Or one. First, they had to get out of the jungle. A chopper wouldn't have the gas to get them out of Mexico, but Velasquez didn't control the whole country. Just his little corner of it. They'd make their move stateside into California or Texas, then from there back to New York.

"Yo, boss. We've got movement."

"Fuck." Eric glanced at his watch. Forty minutes. For him, for Marco, forty minutes of sleep would get them through three days, but it wasn't going to help Jane much. "Hey, baby," he whispered into her ear. "Time to wake up."

"Huh?"

"We have to get a move on."

"Oh." Her eyes widened and she struggled to her feet.

"Can you walk? If not, I can carry you."

"No, I'm okay."

"We're moving, Marco. Headed upstream."

"Gotcha."

He waded into the middle of the stream. "We're just going to follow this for a while. You go ahead of me so I can catch you if anything happens."

She picked her way into the water, a muscle jumping in her cheek the only sign that her feet bothered her. She moved forward, each step carefully placed so she didn't fall, but even the muddy water couldn't obscure the blood on her pants from earlier mishaps. He could happily murder both Velasquez and Bryan Axlerod with his bare hands for what they'd done to her.

Thunder rumbled, rolling over them. Just what this clusterfuck needed, a storm. He counted to six before lightning pierced the sky above them. Maybe it would miss them. But with the way things had gone on this mission, it would come down just in time to make landing the helo impossible.

A shot rang out behind them and to the east.

"I'm on the move," Marco said. "Apparently, they're tired of being picked off."

"What can I do?"

"Get out. I can take care of myself. I'll meet you at the LZ if not before."

"Be careful."

A grunt was Marco's only answer.

"Okay, Janie, we're going to have to run for it, which means you get a ride."

"I can go faster if you need me to."

Yeah, he doubted it. Besides, he was built for this kind of life; she wasn't. "Remember what Trey said? I'm the expert. And in my expert opinion, we'll make better time with you on my back."

"Are you sure?"

"Absolutely." He shrugged out of his pack and made her put it on, tightening the straps. Then she climbed onto his back, wrapping her legs around his waist and her arms around his neck as she had leaving the mansion. Had that really been just twenty-four hours before? He abandoned the stream for more secure footing next to it and took off at a steady jog.

Luckily, the stream went in their direction for a good ten kilometers. Before they peeled away from the water, they stopped for a quick drink, refill, and snack. He left Jane with one pistol while he took another and scouted the area. She couldn't hit the broad side of a barn, as he'd seen at the airfield, but maybe she'd scare away anyone who showed up. He didn't see their pursuers anywhere, but he missed the assurance of Marco's eagle-eyed presence. The forest was so thick men could be a hundred yards away—a hundred feet if they were being quiet—and he might miss them.

Once they left the water, their direction took them downhill for a while, so Eric slowed his pace to a quick walk, which meant Jane could keep up with him by herself, though she sometimes had to break into a few jogging steps to do so.

The storm hit midafternoon. Torrents of rain sluiced down like waterfalls off the broad leaves of the trees and created runnels in the dirt. Thick muck clung to Eric's boots, and Jane lost both her shoes when they were sucked right off her feet. He stopped to dig them out of the muck, then lifted Jane and carried her to a spot where the dense cover provided some protection from the downpour.

"I'm going to tape the shoes to your feet over the bandages. You can't afford to lose them. Trey wasn't kidding about the dangers out here, and I don't want you to step on something that might bite or sting without the damned shoes."

"Yeah, okay."

He wrapped layers of duct tape around her feet, trying to leave enough of the rubber soles of the shoes showing to stop her from slipping badly in the mud and wet undergrowth. "Sorry, this won't be comfortable."

When he was done, she flexed her feet a couple of times. "You weren't kidding about uncomfortable. Jeez." But to his surprise she winked at him. "I bet these things would protect me from a freaking piranha-conda."

His heart lightened a little. "At the very least."

"Good. Then I feel much safer. Let's go. I need a shower." She stepped out into the rain, and he joined her, taking her hand.

S HE INSISTED ON walking the rest of the way, refusing to let him carry her as they hiked through the afternoon and into the early evening, and insisting she could go on when he stopped to let her rest. On the third such rest, while she sat atop a tree stump, he heard shouting in the distance. The rain had lightened to a drizzle, but the sun was sinking and visibility was nil.

"Can you climb?" he asked. She nodded. "Up you go, then." He jerked his head at a tall tree. She scrambled up clumsily, the blasted shoes with their layers of padding giving her trouble. When she was settled well above his head in the leafy canopy, he pulled on his NVGs and picked his way through the woods toward the voices.

The men were below them in a small valley that he and Jane would have to pass through to get to the helo landing zone. Three Jeeps, ten men, a whole lot of firepower. The men were dressed in military garb, but in Eric's experience that didn't necessarily mean they were members of Mexico's actual armed forces. Drug lords liked to dress their soldiers as Army to obscure their operations and confuse opposition.

He flattened himself to the ground and belly-crawled toward the group. When he reached the edge of his cover, he stopped and craned his neck forward, hoping to hear the conversation. The men spoke Mexican Spanish, but in the kidnap and ransom business, Eric had picked up more dialects than he could count.

"We should go back," one of the men said. "We'll never find them out here without dogs."

"Shit," said a second, "we don't even know there's anything to find. Some fucking American sets up a fancy lab here because it's cheaper than it is at home, his competitors take him out, and we're expected to clean up the mess? What has he ever done for us?"

"They say the woman stole information. Bigger finder's fee if we can get the thumb drive, or at least its location, before we turn her over."

Information? Thumb drive? That was news.

"We're chasing ghosts," a third chimed in. "She and that fucking thumb drive probably went up in the Bear. We're out here waiting to be picked off by the assassin. We should head back to base."

"We have our orders." The stocky speaker cut the air with his hand, ending the conversation. "If you wish to return to Velasquez and explain that the weather made you turn back, it is, of course, your choice. For myself, I will stay on the ones who did not fly out until I am told otherwise."

Eric wormed his way backward up the trail he'd made, pulling together vines and leaves to hide his passage, though he doubted they'd see it in the increasing darkness. When he got to the tree where Janie hid, he hoisted himself into the branches.

"Did you take any of the research with you when you left the lab?"

She shook her head. "I thought you destroyed it all."

"We destroyed what we could. But according to the soldiers blocking our way down there, someone made off with a thumb drive containing valuable data."

"It wasn't me. Or Dani. She was a prisoner."

"So who was it?"

"The only person who had access was Bryan."

Eric considered that. "Okay, let's say he did. Why blame you?"

"I have no idea. Unless . . . this isn't exactly Bryan's milieu. He might be trying to get out of his relationship with Velasquez. If he says I ran off with the research, he won't have to take the blame for the fact that they never actually made the process work. And if there was research, and he took it himself, he can go somewhere else and sell it to start over. Then he can tell Velasquez it was me who sold it so he doesn't have to spend a lifetime looking over his shoulder."

"So we assume there really is a drive. The existing records show someone downloaded a bunch of data from the Warlock servers before they were destroyed. Velasquez wants you back, but he wants the data, too, and wants to be certain no one else gets their hands on it. That's good. Really good."

"It is?"

"Sure. They know someone escaped in the little plane. Who, they can't be certain. And if you did have this thumb drive, you'd no doubt have sent it along with Dani and Trey. So once we get you back to the States, we can pretend you have the data and use it as a bargaining chip, something to bait a trap for Velasquez with."

"Of course, that means we have to get home."

"We will. You just have to have a little faith."

"In you? I do. In me . . . not so much."

"You're doing great." Although he could no longer hear the soldiers, from his perch in the tree he could see pinpricks of light beginning to spread out, flashlights guiding their way through the dense forest. One man remained behind to guard the vehicles while the others created a starburst search pattern. They beat the bush with scythes and paddles but only rarely looked up. Jane took his hand and squeezed. He squeezed back, sending all his confidence into her through their linked fingers. Two soldiers paused feet away from their tree, examining the ground.

"They came through here!" one shouted to his companions. The others joined him there, and Jane curled into herself, making her body as small as possible.

The leader made a circling motion with his hand, and the men spread out again, eyes on the ground, hunting for a trail.

Eric counted off their distance. Ten yards. Twenty. Fifty. At sixty yards, he slipped down the tree and held out his arms to Jane to help her down, too. Silently, they worked their way toward the valley. When he was within range, Eric pulled a suppressor out of his pack and attached it to his pistol. With a single shot, he put down the truck guard. Soldier or not, the man had become a bounty hunter, and Eric couldn't afford to worry about him. He put bullets through the tires of two of the Jeeps while Jane jumped into the third. He didn't even have to hot-wire the thing, as the keys rested in the ignition. The engine turning over sounded like a call to arms, and he shoved Jane down and out of the way as much as possible while he sped out of the valley, climbing the hill on the opposite side, headed toward their rendezvous with the helo.

Shouting followed them. They'd been discovered. But they were making good time, and while the returning soldiers would no doubt call for backup, if he was lucky, he'd be able to put a good distance between them. Eventually, they'd have to abandon the Jeep—LZ Charlie could be accessed on foot or by air, but the tiny bare spot had been carved out of the thickest part of the jungle specifically to prevent vehicular access.

He aimed the Jeep on a course that would take them along a slope adjacent to the landing zone. With a little luck—not that they'd had much this mission—they'd evade pursuit long enough to get picked up. For the first hour, every muscle tensed in reaction to any breeze, any rustle in the woodlands. They were making much better time, but they were leaving tracks like the fucking dinosaurs and Jeeps weren't built for stealth. If he weren't so anxious to get to the LZ and so worried that Jane's body was giving out, he'd have insisted on walking despite the SUV's availability.

But no shots came, no one blocked their way, and he began to relax.

"Janie, grab my satellite phone out of the bag, okay?"

She found the phone, pulled it out, extended the antenna, and handed it over.

Nash picked up on the first ring. "Where are you?"

"Close. Maybe two hours out. We found a Jeep, but I'm gonna abandon it soon so we don't make the destination more obvious than necessary."

"Do it. Travis already has the helo in place. After Miguel's experience, I didn't want to leave anything to chance. Mac's at the Brownsville property, and Travis snuck the chopper into LZ Charlie this afternoon without a problem. And Marco called in—he shook his tail, and he'll be at the LZ any minute."

Thank God something was going right.

"Ask him about Trey and Dani."

"Good news, bad news," Nash said. "They made it safely over the border. She's in a trauma unit in a Dallas hospital. The bullet caused a fairly severe traumatic brain injury. I'll be happier when we can fly her into New York, but right now they don't want to move her."

"What are the doctors saying? What's the prognosis?" Jane curled her arms around her knees, and Eric wedged the phone between his shoulder and ear so he could reach over to stroke her back.

"According to Trey, they were 'cautiously optimistic.' Which he says is doctor speak for 'covering their asses.' He's pissed off and looking for a fight."

"He feels guilty."

"Indeed. So do me a favor and find out who the damned American is so I can give him an assignment."

"We'll do our best. Heading into the LZ now."

"Talk to you later." Nash signed off and Eric squeezed Jane's shoulder.

"Okay, baby, you ready for a bit more hiking?"

"Sure. I'm much better."

In the dim light of the risen moon, he could see that she had regained some of her natural color, and the lines pain had cut into her cheeks seemed shallower. His tension eased a trifle. "Okay. I'm going to put a hole in the gas tank so they can't use the Jeep and so, if they check, they'll see we have a legit reason for leaving it behind." The sabotage took only a moment, and then they were on their way, forcing through the ever-thickening growth.

The forest ended abruptly, but Eric didn't step into the clearing. The trees had been deliberately cut away, leaving behind a tangle of vines, grass, and brush. In the center of the clearing, moonlight reflected off the shiny black skin of a UH-72 Lakota. Eric would have preferred a Black Hawk for simple firepower, but the Lakota aroused a lot less suspicion. Her rotors were still, but the lights glowed and Marco stood guard on one side. On the other side, Eric could see the legs of a second person. Jane started to step forward, but he held her back.

"Wait." He pulled a small wooden whistle out of his pocket and blew through it, creating the sound of a scissor-tailed flycatcher, then fixed his eyes on Marco as he slid the birdcall back into his pocket. But Marco did not respond. Instead, he checked the clip on his weapon and paced a few steps around the chopper.

Not good.

Voices shouted in the woods behind them.

"Eric?" Jane whispered.

"We need to work our way around to the other side of the clearing so I can get eyes on the pilot." If Travis was okay, they had a chance. Jane crept along behind him, pushing through the dense shrubs and tangled vines as quietly as possible. The hunting party behind them had no such restrictions, and their shouts and crashes came closer by the second. Eric paused as soon as he caught a glimpse of Travis standing outside the chopper. He tried the bird whistle again.

"I'm telling you," Travis said loudly, taking a single step away from the chopper, then turning back, "I was only contracted to pick up Marco here. That's it. They told me he was on the run and needed an evac."

An unintelligible rumble followed, giving Eric the information he needed. The claw was closing. Nash had sent them to Charlie fearing Bravo would be compromised, but clearly all the landing zones were too obvious—the Hijos men must have staked them all out, knowing airlift was the best way to get Jane out of the country. Time to take the fight to them. They'd undoubtedly disabled Marco's weapon and would be holding a gun on Travis from inside the chopper where they were out of his sightline.

"Climb up and stay as quiet as you can," he said, indicating a thickly leaved tree a couple of feet to their left. "Whatever happens, whatever you see or hear, do not come out of hiding." He handed her a gun. "Take this. In case anything goes wrong."

Once she was hidden, he backtracked toward the sounds of pursuit. He ghosted carefully from tree to tree, just another shadow among a hundred.

The first scout went down easily, quietly. A quick, two-handed twist broke his neck before he could warn anyone of Eric's presence. The next four clustered together, how-ever, and Eric had no hope of taking them without alerting the rest of the team. He took down two with bullets, but the angle of the shots gave away his position, and the others fired in his direction. He dodged through the woods, ducking and weaving, keeping tree trunks as protection as he aimed toward the clearing but away from Jane.

⌒

Sweat trickled down Jane's cheeks, creating itchy run-nels. But two men had paused beneath her tree, and she didn't dare move her hand to scratch. The crack and echo of a shot rang out, and one of the men ran toward the sound, but the other remained. He leaned against the tree and lit up a smoke. Why was this guy so casual? She squinted down through the branches to study him.

Bryan. That little shit. Hanging back, waiting to see how the fight turned out, caring only for his own skin.

Eric had said to stay hidden, but Eric hadn't known that Bryan would park himself right under her very tree. Bryan knew the American investor's identity. And he was a wimp. He'd give it up to save his own skin in a flat second.

She considered the figure beneath her for a long moment. Was attacking Bryan a rational decision? Might it be better to wait for Eric? But what if Bryan ran when he realized his side had lost the fight? Or, worse, what if his side didn't lose? Might it not be a good idea to have a prisoner?

She shifted position slightly and retrieved the gun she'd stuffed down her pants to climb the tree. Beneath her, Bryan took a step forward, peering through the trees. *Now or never.*

She launched herself out and flattened him. For a second, she thought she'd knocked him unconscious, but he regained his breath and fought back, hollering for help as he shoved her away.

"Shut up or I'll shoot you!" she shouted, pointing the gun at him. He backed up slightly, then laughed. *Laughed.*

"You wouldn't. Too much respect for human life and all that crap."

"You're not human. You're slime. Worth less than the scum floating on the top of a swimming pool. And I have no problem chlorinating a pool."

"Bull." He sprang toward her, and, indeed, she could not shoot him. But she could whack him upside the head with the gun three times until he stopped trying to fight back and lay still and silent in the dirt. Had she killed him? But no, his chest still rose and fell. She'd aimed for his temple and apparently gotten it, causing him to black out. How long it would last was anyone's guess, but she would take advantage of the time she had.

Quickly, she searched through his pockets, hoping for anything with which to tie him up, but found nothing. Time to get creative. Using the knife he had strapped to one leg—for show, obviously, since he'd not made a single move toward it while she held him at gunpoint—she cut the sleeves off his long-sleeved tee, wrung out the moisture, and used one to tie his arms behind his back. His feet she left alone.

She couldn't carry him, so he needed to be able to walk. But the other sleeve functioned nicely as a gag.

She was looking around for something to use to wake him up when he shook his head and began to struggle. Behind the gag, he shouted, and his eyes cursed her.

"Get up," she ordered.

He lay still, daring her to force him.

"Get up. You may have been right that I was reluctant to kill you, but I think I've proven myself more than happy to hurt you." She brandished the knife in what she hoped was a menacing—and not ridiculous—manner.

Bryan crawled to his feet. "Oo'll ee sowwy," he said around the gag.

Yeah, probably, but not for the reasons Bryan meant. Eric was going to be furious. Now that she had him, she wasn't even sure what to do with him. Keep him here, away from the action? Or force him forward, use him as a bargaining chip? Was he worth anything to Velasquez, or would he get shot the minute they showed themselves? Because that would defeat the purpose of having taken him.

"Who's the American investor?"

He glared at her.

"Look, that's all I want from you. I'll let you go if you tell me who he is and where the data is stored so we can collect it. I know you wouldn't have risked leaving it all on the servers at the lab. It's uploaded somewhere. Just tell me where it is, how to access it, and I'll let you go."

Nothing.

"Fine." She poked him in the back with the gun until he moved toward the clearing. At the edge, she grabbed the back of his shirt and yanked him to a halt. He squealed behind the gag, but the men in the clearing either didn't hear him or didn't care. She pulled him an extra step backward and hid them both behind a tree trunk.

Eric was nowhere to be seen, but Marco's eyes paused on her before passing along in their constant surveillance of the area. Suddenly, a canister rolled and bounced to the center of the clearing, right beneath the helicopter.

Eric. It had to be.

"Grenade!" shouted someone she couldn't see. She pulled Bryan even farther back as a violent explosion of gray smoke erupted from the canister, poisoning the air. The smoke tickled the back of her nose and throat, making her desperate to sneeze, and she squeezed her nose between her fingers to stay quiet.

"Hold your positions, dammit!" shouted a man's voice. "It's nothing but smoke! They won't hurt the chopper!"

A second canister bumped into the clearing, and Jane instinctively closed her eyes. A split second later, an enormous crash shook the earth beneath her feet and the world beyond her eyelids lit up like a carnival. Men were screaming, or so she thought, but her ears didn't seem to be working well.

Over the rumbling echoes of the flashbang, she heard the sharp staccato of shots being fired. Then the engine of the helicopter came to life, and against her sweaty skin she felt the push of air from the rotating blades. She peeked out from behind the tree where she'd hidden and saw the smoke beginning to dissipate. A man lay beneath the helicopter, with another leaning over him, cuffing him. Eric held Eduardo Velasquez at gunpoint, and Marco had two dead men at his feet while a third knelt with hands raised.

"Move," she ordered Bryan. When he refused, she stuck the knife in his back just enough so the point pierced his clothing, and he shuffled forward.

At the edge of the clearing, just as he stepped into it, he shouted behind the gag and stumbled. The thin material of the T-shirt she'd been holding on to tore, and he fell forward, leaving her exposed. All heads swung their way, and the frozen tableau erupted into motion. The man kneeling in front of Marco grabbed a pistol from the waistband of his pants and aimed upward, but before he could get a shot off, Eric's bullet took him out. Eduardo took off running for the edge of the woods. Marco fired a single shot, and Eduardo stumbled forward and fell, head smacking a tree stump with a sound Jane would hear in her dreams for the rest of her life.

The cuffed man remained where he was but twisted to the side so he could watch what was going on.

"What the fuck, Jane? Did I or did I not tell you to stay put?"

"We couldn't afford to risk Bryan getting away! He knows where the data is!" But she couldn't explain further—she had no time. Two men emerged from the forest behind her. One grabbed her, and without thinking, she swung around and put a bullet into his gut. The recoil knocked the gun from her hand, and more men appeared, cutting her off from Eric and Marco.

"Go!" Eric shouted.

Jane ran. She would be caught—there was no question about it—but if enough of Velasquez's men followed her, Eric might have a chance to escape. She crashed along, zigzagging randomly as gunshots echoed behind her. Voices shouting in Spanish bounced off the trees, seeming to come from every direction. How many men had Velasquez sent?

"*Alto!* Stop or I will shoot!"

Yeah, right. Velasquez wanted her alive. She dodged around a thick trunk, only to find herself tackled by two large, sweaty men who forced her to the ground.

"*Aquí! Nosotros la tenemos!*"

GODDAMMIT, THEY WERE so fucking close. What could be so important about Bryan and the damn data that Jane would risk her own life? He picked off two of the men who came through the woods, then shouted for Marco to cover him. Bryan was struggling to his feet, and Eric had no intention of losing him. With Marco's bullets flying by on both sides, he slammed the man into the ground. Bryan squirmed and twisted, trying to get free.

"Give me an excuse. Just one," he growled, and the man stilled.

"Get the fuck in the chopper!" Travis shouted. "Only way out right now is up!"

Eric dragged Bryan over and threw him into the helicopter. Travis was already lifting off when Marco heaved himself inside and began firing down at the men pouring into the clearing.

"This is what happens when you go on a mission without me," Travis grumbled from the pilot's seat. "I have to come in and save your ass."

"Fuck off." The guy was just trying to make him feel better, but it wasn't working. Eric hoped to hell Jane didn't hear the chopper flying off and assume it meant he was giving her up for good. *Hold on, baby. Have a little faith.*

"Goddammit," Travis said. "Someone down there has a MANPAD. Hang on." The chopper dipped and banked sharply to the right, then rose again. "It's gonna get rough." Man-portable air-defense systems were cheap and easy to acquire. Velasquez's men had used one to take out Miguel's plane. If Eric hadn't been so focused on Jane's well-being, he would have warned Travis ahead of time.

"Your friends don't seem overly concerned with your safety," Marco observed to Bryan.

"Hell, killing the guy is probably what they planned all along. If he annoyed them half as much as he does me, they can't have wanted to keep him alive," said Eric.

Over the *whomp-whomp* of the chopper blades, he heard Bryan trying to speak.

"You wanna hear what he has to say?" asked Marco.

"Might as well," Eric replied. Marco removed Bryan's gag. First, he just cursed, but when Marco offered to stuff the sleeve back into his mouth, he held up a hand.

"You want to know who sponsored this? I can tell you, but you'll never catch him at it, and I won't ever testify, so it won't do you a bit of good. I'm guessing you're little Jane's body-guards, which means you work—or at least you worked—for Clive Handler at AHI. I have no idea what you're doing out here, though, since he for sure didn't tell you to come to Mexico. This is his project. Always has been. He recruited me way back when I was . . . released . . . from a lab for run-ning an off-the-books experiment in gene doping on a pair of rhesus monkeys. It didn't work, you understand, but he fig-ured I'd be a good candidate to run the Mexican lab. I watched everything Jane and her pals did, sent word to my guys down here, and eventually when we had a good enough sense of the direction they were going to take, I came to oversee this lab, to start training Velasquez's soldiers.

"So, yeah, you go right ahead and try to catch Clive Handler colluding with the Hijos. Not a chance he keeps anything where you can find it."

"Why did Jane think you were so important? What did she think you knew about the data?"

"How to retrieve it. Clive wouldn't allow Velasquez to keep it somewhere he didn't have access to it. There's a cloud account they can both get to."

"Where? How do you access it?"

"I think I'll keep that information to bargain with someone higher up the food chain than you. They were going to kill me. You were right about that. It was just a matter of time. So I waited for my chance, and you gave it to me. Thanks for saving my life, by the way.

"He's lying. He doesn't know anything useful," Marco said. "Want me to kill him?"

Bryan paled.

Cowardly asshole. "Nah, let Nash at him. There may be more we need. But shut him up, okay?"

Marco stuffed the cloth back into Bryan's protesting mouth, then wrapped duct tape around his head to keep it in place. Eric kept watch out the side of the chopper as they left land for the Gulf, relaxing only when they were over the water, away from land where any of Velasquez's men might fire on them.

"We headed for Brownsville?"

"Safe and close," said Travis. "Easiest place to plan a recovery mission."

Eric climbed into the copilot's seat and radioed Nash.

CHAPTER 13

Tʜᴇ ᴏɴʟʏ ᴛʜɪɴɢ that comforted Jane as two men marched her through the jungle at gunpoint was the sound of helicopter blades overhead fading away. Eric's friends would not desert him. If they were taking off, they were okay, or at least on the way to being okay.

The two men who had first taken her down stuck close to her, one holding a gun in her back, the other using the rope they'd tied around her wrists to drag her along. The other men spread out around them, beating through the woods. To be sure none of her friends survived, most likely.

Jane dragged her feet through the undergrowth and tripped several times—catching herself on her elbows since her bound hands were being used as a leash—to slow down their progress and leave a trail. Not that it would make much difference. Wherever HSE's helicopter had gone, it wouldn't be coming back to this spot. Even she could figure out that Velasquez would leave a contingent in wait.

They walked for hours. In the skimpy light provided by the flashlights of the men around her, vines appeared as snakes and leaves as creatures intent on harm. At last they came out onto a road, where two Jeeps and a covered truck were waiting. One of the men shoved a gun into her back and pushed her into the back of the truck, where she found wooden slatted benches affixed to the sides.

"All the way in," he said. She crawled forward and he followed. The rest of the men piled in, too, a stinking, sweating mass. Not that she figured she smelled like roses, either. How many days had it been since she'd last bathed? Or eaten, for that matter.

"Where are you taking me?"

No answer. The canvas covering of the truck blocked out even the light from the moon, and as they'd turned off their flashlights all she could see was the faint glint from the eyes of the men around her. She could make out no features. Were any of these men she'd met at the compound? Men she'd interviewed? If she could talk to them, could she change their minds?

"Will it take a long time to get there? I really need to pee."

Still no answer.

Jane waited about ten minutes, then began squirming in her seat.

"Sit still," said the man next to her.

"I told you, I have to pee."

"No one is stopping you."

Was he serious? He just expected her to sit there and wet her pants? And the bench on which he himself was sitting? Apparently so, because he leaned forward and spoke rapidly to the man across the way, ignoring her.

The truck clunked through a giant pothole, and Jane's bladder protested. A few minutes later, they came to a stop.

"Now we wait," said the man next to her.

"Can't you let me go out in the woods? I mean, really. What am I going to do? Run away?"

A quick conversation between two of the men, and the one next to her picked up the rope tying her hands.

"Let's go." He walked to the back of the truck, lifted the canvas, and looked around before jumping out and tugging on the rope to pull her along.

They'd stopped on the side of the road by a crossroads of

sorts. The headlights of the truck and SUVs shone down the road, but her captor pulled her off into the darkness.

"Go," he said.

She moved as far away as the rope would allow, behind a bush to give her a modicum of privacy.

All too clear in her mind as she allowed her bladder relief was Velasquez's threat to sell her to the highest bidder to recoup his money. She feared privacy would be in short supply once she was returned to him. But she had escaped him once, with Eric's help, and she would do so again. No matter what else happened. She just had to remember that.

The rumble of engines caught her attention. Would the transfer happen now? Was Velasquez coming to get her? The man who held her tugged on the rope and brought her close to his side just as a box truck pulled up.

The truck's driver stepped down, and she recognized him immediately. He'd been at dinner the night Velasquez brought his entourage.

"Garcia," said her captor.

"*Lo has hecho bien. Usted será recompensado.*"

Okay, she didn't need much Spanish to understand "recompense." The guy was going to get a reward. Bully for him.

"And you, Dr. Evans. You've caused a number of problems. But that's all about to change." Another man came up beside him. Bulky and bald headed, he was one of the experimental subjects. "Juan, put Dr. Evans in the truck."

Juan grabbed the rope and yanked on it, almost pulling Jane's arms from their sockets. "Move."

She followed him to the truck, where he rolled up the back gate. "Climb up."

Not likely. She couldn't fight back, but she didn't have to cooperate, either. She stood where she was.

"Fine." Juan reached into the truck and grabbed a stick. Was he planning on hitting her with it? And then prongs jabbed into the skin of her neck and electricity shot through her in waves of screaming pain. Cattle prod. *Fuck, fuck, fuck.* She crumpled to the ground, and her vision faded into a white blaze speckled with black spots.

From far away, she felt herself being manhandled, lifted, then dropped on the floor of the truck. Hurricanes of blood roared through her, and she couldn't hear what the men said to each other.

When she came back to herself, she was inside a cage. She could feel it around her. Like a crate used for transporting livestock, it had walls composed of metal bars set three or four inches apart. She reached up and felt the top. The whole thing was maybe three feet wide by three feet tall by four feet long.

Oh, Jane, you are in it now.

She felt around the front area, where an animal crate would have a door, and found a padlock. The back gate of the truck was still open, and outside she could see the crowd of men breaking up, heading back to their individual vehicles. Juan jumped up into the back of the truck and began repositioning a bunch of boxes around her crate. From his grunts, they were heavy. More boxes—lighter ones—were laid atop her crate until she was completely surrounded and all the light was blocked.

"If we get stopped," he said, "you will make no noise. If you make a noise, it will result in the death of all those who have stopped us, in the death of your father, and in the death of your friend who is now in the hospital in Dallas. Los Hijos are everywhere. You will obey, or you and everyone you know will suffer. Do you understand?"

She didn't say anything.

"Answer me, Dr. Evans, or I will make certain you understand."

"I understand."

⸺

THE BROWNSVILLE PROPERTY was small and rundown but only a few miles from the airport where the chopper was housed. Eric and Travis did a lot of their work in Mexico out of the property, so they'd fixed it up some, but it was still little more than a flophouse. They'd never brought prisoners to it and had no place to secure Bryan, so Eric took him down to the basement, where they'd set up a minimal gym, and handcuffed him to the power rack.

"I'll make grub," Travis said as he came up the stairs. "Get Nash on the line, and let's see what he can do for us.

Before Eric could even dial, his satellite phone rang. It was Miguel.

"I hear things went to shit."

"Yeah. You know these guys. Where would they take her?"

"Velasquez has a lot of hideouts, a lot of places he stores cargo. I don't know where he'll hold her, but I just received notice that their auction scheduled for three days from now will have additional, special items."

Were they selling us? Dani's question the first night he'd found her and Jane slipped through his memory. The threat had turned him inside out even when it was unlikely. Now it had become a reality.

"You know where that will be?"

"Yeah. I know the auction salon. It's a warehouse in Tenancingo."

"You don't think he'll move it?"

"Honestly? He can run his auctions anywhere." Disgust dripped from Miguel's words. "But if he wants to show that he's still in control, he won't want to admit he has to change from the plan he sent out last week. And there are very good reasons to keep the sale in Tenancingo instead of elsewhere. The police who run the district where the Hijos' auction parlor is located are kept men. They don't touch the auctions. In fact, if they see girls they think would go for good money, they're allowed to break them in themselves and then bring them in."

"Christ."

"It is worth a reminder here that not all of Mexico is like this. My country has a sickness. Yours does, too. The disparity between rich and poor, the lack of resources . . . It is hard to see a way out. Evil breeds evil when there is no hope."

"You're telling me this because . . . ?"

"Because you cannot give up hope. Nash has many resources. We will get your girl back."

"Yes. We will."

He wondered what kept Miguel going, where he found his hope, but didn't ask. The man had lost his family. Maybe cleaning up the worst of the mess was the way he managed.

"You say you were notified of an addition to the auction?"

"Yes. I was told that there would be more openings for bidders than previously expected. I was asked specifically whether I knew anyone outside the country with similar taste to my own who might be in the market."

"They don't want Jane in Mexico."

"No. And between that and the fact that my cover is not a wealthy man, I cannot simply purchase Dr. Evans for you. From the question I was asked, I can tell you that they don't want what is left of her life to be easy. There is a man from Thailand who I suspect will be invited. And one from Belgium. Believe me when I say you do not want either of them to get their hands on Dr. Evans."

"You've actually bought women from Velasquez?" Acid burned at the back of Eric's throat.

"Usually, I am outbid. But yes, this is how one maintains relationships in Tenancingo. You must be a procurer, a sales-man, or a customer. Otherwise, you are looked upon with suspicion. At the auctions, no one wants me to succeed. The women I buy are rarely seen again. I do not put them out on the street to recoup my losses when I tire of them, so the assumption is that they do not survive."

"What really happens?"

"In many ways, they are dead. They are not allowed to contact their families or friends. My housekeeper and I train them as domestics and find them positions outside the coun-try where they will not be recognized. It is not the life many of them hoped for—their dreams of fame and fortune end when they are sold—but they are better lives than they would have elsewhere. But it does not happen often because, as I said, my cover does not have vast sums of money. He goes to the auc-tions, occasionally buys a woman, and sees who else is there. If those men get picked up after the auctions, well, he is grate-ful to live in a country that turns a blind eye to such things."

"How many women are apt to be there? Are we going to be operating around dozens of innocent civilians?"

"No. At most five or six. The great majority of sex slaves are sold in bulk to *padrotes*—pimps—who transport them to houses either across the border or to places here in Mexico where they won't be recognized. Others are kidnapped by special request—a trusted customer requests a blond-haired, green-eyed teenager—and he pays outright. Only those deemed special go to auction. Very young boys or girls who fit a certain profile, those with exotic looks, high-profile victims that some clients will spend good money to own . . . These Velasquez reserves for the auctions he holds three or four times a year."

Hold it together, Eric.

"So if he's collecting these women for weeks or even months before the auctions, he must be keeping them somewhere."

"Believe me, I've looked for them. Two years ago, a friend of my daughter's was taken. I thought I would find her first, buy her if necessary, but I could not find the holding location no matter what I did and she did not turn up at the auction. She had asthma. She may have died before they could sell her."

Jesus. "I'm sorry."

"I am still looking. I can hope that she was taken for other reasons. As long as there is no body, she may be out there, waiting to be saved."

"So five or six innocents." He looked over at Marco, who was standing in the doorway to the kitchen. "I think we can work around that."

"You will have to be quick and quiet. The salon is very secure. I will do my best to protect Dr. Evans, but no weapons are allowed inside the auction area and the minute your attack begins, Velasquez will know exactly who you are there for. I advise you to approach as quietly as possible."

"Yeah, I see your point."

"How do you plan to get here?"

"The quickest way is probably to rent a private plane and fly into Mexico City."

"Yes. You remember the apartment?"

"Of course."

"Go there," said Miguel. "I will call you when I can. Is Trey with you?"

"No. It will be me, Marco, Mac, and Travis unless someone else can get there in time. I can't wait around."

"I will leave a key for you in the boiler room in the basement of the building. It is easy to jimmy that door. The key will be on top of the hot-water heater."

"Great."

"Mac and Travis I do not know. Be sure they do not kill me at the auction."

CHAPTER 14

In the darkness and heat of the truck, memories of Velasquez's threats assailed Jane. He'd been very clear about how he intended to recoup the money he'd spent on the lab if she couldn't provide him with his supersoldier formula. How much angrier would he be now that his nephew had been killed trying to capture her?

The truck jolted to a stop, and she heard voices outside. Damn her lack of fluency.

They started up again without the back opening. This would be one of the stops Juan was worried about. How many men were at these stops? Could Juan really fulfill his promise to kill them all if she made a sound? Could she take that chance? And what did he mean by the Hijos were everywhere? Were there men actually watching Dani in the hospital? Surely Trey would protect her. She had to believe that. Had to believe Dani, at least, was safe.

The ride was endless. The thick, muffling darkness left her with no sense of time. Despite the terror that threatened at the edges of her mind, she dozed, dreaming of faceless men speaking harsh words she could not understand. Strange creatures menaced as well, a thousand giant bees and a giant black panther with the mane of a lion.

When the back of the truck finally did open, sunlight filtered through the boxes, turning her prison a dusty, dusky brown. Voices alerted her to the presence of multiple men.

The light became stronger as they lifted out the boxes until she was completely uncovered.

The truck was backed up to a rundown motel. From her position inside, she could see the "No Vacancy" sign bolted to the roof of the long building and count a dozen rooms.

"Get her out," said a blond man.

Juan and another man climbed in and lifted her crate. They handed it off to two others, who carried it inside one of the rooms. It was accomplished quickly, but not furtively: they didn't care who saw them. They dropped her inside the room on the floor next to one of the two double beds covered with dingy, worn polyester coverlets and slammed the door on the way out.

Dust motes floated through the light coming through the yellowed curtains, and the room smelled not just musty but moldy. *No vacancy my ass.* No one had stayed in this room for a long, long time. She examined the cage, but nothing appeared loose. All the bars were carefully soldered or welded together at the corners, and no rust weakened the individual joints. Experimentally, she crouched in the crate and pressed her back against the top, then attempted to straighten her knees, but the bars at the top dug into her spine and refused to give. The bars weren't particularly thick. How strong could they be? She pressed harder.

Voices outside attracted her attention, and she sat back down. If she'd had any success in weakening her cage, she couldn't afford to have them find out what she was up to. She slumped into the corner of the cage and tried to appear exhausted and harmless. It wasn't as hard as she would have liked.

The door opened and the blond man entered, speaking in Spanish on his cell phone. His eyes flicked over her several times, and he switched to English.

"Yes, she is. And she smells. I will have her ready for you when you get here." He stuffed the phone in his pocket.

"Where is the data drive?"

Screw you. She didn't answer.

"Shall I search you myself?"

Eric had said they could pretend to have it. He'd also said they would assume she'd sent it on the plane.

"It's safely in the States already. You'll never get it."

"Don't be so certain. But we do not need it yet. Velasquez is coming, and he has a job for you. I am going to let you out so you can shower. If you try to escape, you will be punished. Do you understand?"

"Yes." A job? That did *not* sound promising.

He opened the door and called Juan inside. Juan brought the cattle prod in with him and pressed it against her arm as the blond removed the padlock. Only when the gate was open and the blond had stepped away did he withdraw the prod to release her. She crawled forward and out, maintaining a defeated posture and leaning heavily on the crate as she stood.

"Juan is going to make sure you don't run off while you get cleaned up. Clean clothes will be provided, so just give him your old ones." He left and Juan gestured toward the bathroom and followed her inside.

"Take your clothes off and hand them to me," he said. Jane plucked at the bottom of the shirt, watching his face for any reaction, but saw nothing. It should have comforted her, but it didn't. She remembered Juan's chart. He'd never killed anyone. He should have been a prime candidate for her to talk out of playing along with Velasquez, but if they'd destroyed all his emotions, even desire, he might be too far gone for her to reach. Sympathy, empathy — those would be early casualties.

"Move it," he ordered, tossing the cattle prod from hand to hand.

She leaned in and turned on the shower. The water came out lukewarm and showed no sign of heating up no matter how hard she cranked the handle. *Okay, time to get this over with.* She stepped into the shower and, behind the curtain, stripped out of her top and pants and handed the sopping bundle out to Juan. Her bra and panties, she kept. Through the translucent curtain, she saw Juan searching the bundle, presumably for the thumb drive. *Good luck with that.*

As much as she wanted to exit the shower as filthy and smelly as she entered it just to spite Velasquez, she'd face whatever he had planned for her a lot better without the constant crawling sensation on her skin. Her captors had not supplied shampoo, so after loosing her hair from its braid, she scrubbed her head with the sliver of soap in the soap dish.

Gross. Sharing soap with faceless strangers, yet another small cruelty for which Velasquez would pay. Some people might not mind, but she rubbed and rinsed what was left of the bar until it all but disappeared before using it on herself.

"Time to get out," Juan said. He'd left the bathroom briefly with her wet clothes, and she'd had a moment of privacy, but then he'd returned.

"You leave the bathroom, I'll get out."

"You shy or something? Garcia said to be sure you don't get away."

"How am I going to escape? There's not even a window." She thought about his file. "You wouldn't want your sister drying herself off in front of a strange man, would you?"

"I have clothes for you."

"Well, lay them on the vanity and leave. I'm not going any-where."

He grunted and through the curtain she saw him lay a small pile on the vanity before he left. "You have two minutes."

The moment he was gone she hopped out and scrubbed the water off her skin. On the vanity she found a pair of scrubs and a loose-fitting, thin cotton tank top. No bra. No panties. No damned *socks*. She carefully hung the underwear she'd washed out in the shower on the knob. She'd put them on again when they were dry. She leaned on the vanity and faced herself in the spotty, cracked mirror.

"You look like shit, girl." But if Velasquez hoped to grind her down, the shower—however suboptimal—had been a tactical error. Cleanliness might not be next to godliness, but it certainly improved her outlook.

A banging on the door interrupted her self-examination.

"Get out here." *Velasquez.*

She sucked in a long breath and let it out slowly before opening the door.

Velasquez stood just outside the bathroom door, a glower creasing his dark features. "It is time for you to get to work."

"I am not working for you anymore. You have no hold over me."

"No?" He looked her up and down, and she straightened her spine.

"No." He could kill her. But death was preferable, at this point, to creating more broken souls like poor, lost Alvaro and the conscienceless Juan.

"Your choice, of course. But I thought you doctors were compelled to save lives."

"There's no vow, no amount of inducement that would compel me to save your life."

He laughed.

"I would not trust you to. But I am not the one in need

of a doctor, and at the moment you are the only one nearby." He stepped back, and against her own advice she followed, glancing toward the beds when he waved in that direction. And then the world shrank down to a tiny, almost lifeless body lying bundled in a quilt on one of them. She ignored Velasquez and hurried to the child's side. His bright blond hair was matted with dried sweat, and he lay so perfectly still that if his cheeks had not been ruddy with fever she might have thought he was already dead.

"What the hell?" She settled next to him on the bed and put a hand to his forehead, then almost snatched it back from the heat. He couldn't have been more than six or seven, and he hovered on the very edge of life.

"I can't fix this. He needs a hospital. IV fluids, antibiotics . . . What's the matter with him?"

"If we knew that, we would not ask you. And he will not be going to the hospital."

"What's his name?"

Velasquez didn't answer.

"What's his name? I need to be able to talk to him, to reach him. And I can't do that without knowing his name."

"Fritz."

Oh, cripes. Here was a complication she hadn't even considered. "Please tell me he speaks English."

"He does."

"Okay." Her brain whirled. Yes, she had a degree, but she'd never practiced medicine. Any halfway-decent mother would probably be better in this situation than she was. Start with the basics. "We need to get his fever down. And I need something with electrolytes. Pedialyte, Gatorade, anything is better than nothing at this point. You said you can get IV fluids, which is great, but I don't have a lot of experience inserting IVs and this kid is severely dehydrated, which will make finding a vein damned near impossible."

"He wouldn't stop crying." This from another man she hadn't even noticed.

"And whose fault is that?" Was that her? Really? Who knew she had it in her? "His old sweat has baked on to his body, and even with his fever he's completely dry. He's going to die if we don't get some fluids in him."

Juan handed her a bottle of cool water.

"This is fine for mopping his skin, but how the hell do you expect to get it inside him? Osmosis? I need an IV. And water isn't good enough." She thought back to her training. "Fill the bathtub with tepid water. If you stick your hand in, you shouldn't feel anything—it should be the same temperature as your skin. A cooling bath will help a little, but I can't keep this boy alive without antibiotics."

"Medication is on the way, along with the IVs," said Velasquez. He waved the stranger to the door. "Get her the Pedialyte."

Juan stepped into the bathroom to run the bath, and Jane found herself alone with Velasquez.

"Who is he? The kid?" Why hadn't Velasquez wanted her to know his name? Was he important? Being held for ransom?

"This does not concern you. All you need to know is that you must keep him alive, or suffer the consequences."

"Right. So if he lives, I live?"

"There are things worse than death. Only a foolish, privileged girl would believe otherwise."

And that was true, she supposed. But if the old saw about "a fate worse than death" was true, so was the one that went "where there's life, there's hope." And she had hope. Eric and his friends were out there somewhere. All she had to do was keep herself alive. And this child. She had to keep this child alive, too. Because, dammit, for all the evil she'd inadvertently been part of, she was going to do some good.

"Give me a washcloth. And a clean one," she ordered, without even realizing the only person to hear her was Velasquez himself. He didn't move. "You want this kid to live? Get me a fucking washcloth!"

He got her a washcloth, and she poured the bottle of water over it, then pressed it to the child's lips.

"Come on, Fritz. Have a little water. Move your mouth for me, sweetheart." She squeezed the cloth so water dripped on his cracked lips. "Wake up just a tiny bit, Fritzie; it doesn't have to be much. Just a little." The drops rolled to the corners of his lips. She squeezed some more over his eyes and thought she saw them twitch a tiny bit, but his body didn't stir. She brushed the hair away from his forehead and kept up a steady stream of crooned, senseless chatter, using his name along with a host of endearments.

"The bath is ready." Juan's eyes lingered on the child as she lifted him. Maybe there was hope for the guy after all, but for the moment she couldn't worry about it. Especially with Velasquez looking on. She tugged away the quilt and stripped the boy's clothes off, then carried him into the bathroom. She carefully lowered him into the water. When his whole body submerged, she reached for a washcloth. But there were none handy and she couldn't let him go or he would drown. She turned to ask for help and found Juan ready with a cloth.

Velasquez had stayed in the bedroom, so as she used the cloth to gather water and drip it over the boy's head, she addressed Juan in low tones.

"How did you know I would need that?"

He shrugged. His file hadn't mentioned a wife or

children—none of the men Bryan had allowed into the program had family ties like that—but Fritz had shaken him, had broken through his conditioning; she was certain of it.

"Do you have younger brothers or sisters?"

"I am not here to talk to you. I am to assist you." But his eyes didn't leave the boy.

"Well, I am very grateful. Seriously. Fritz here needs all the help he can get. So if you have experience with small children and fevers, I'd appreciate hearing about it, because I don't. I'm a scientist, a researcher, not a practicing physician and certainly not a pediatrician."

He frowned and remained silent for a long moment before allowing himself to speak. "My brother had many fevers when he was small like this. My mother did just as you do now. But . . ."

"But?"

He looked away from Fritz. "We had no money for medicines."

And his brother had died. He didn't have to say the words, and the fact that he couldn't gave her a tiny shred more hope. "I'm so sorry."

She heard a knock at the outside door and quiet voices. Then Velasquez called out that the medicine had arrived. With Juan's help, she lifted Fritz from the tub and dried him off. The terrible stillness had been replaced by a violent quaking that brought tears to her eyes. She held him close to her body as she carried him out to the bedroom and then wrapped him once again in the quilt.

"What have you got?"

"Children's amoxicillin." The driver who'd brought her to the motel held out a small bottle. At least he'd gotten a liquid, but she still had no idea how she'd get it into the child.

"*Dámelo.*" Juan held out his hand to the other man, who passed him the bottle.

Upon closer inspection Jane saw that the nondescript brown bottle had a dropper built into the lid but no instructions on how much or how often she should give it to a child Fritz's weight and age. *Sorry, kid.* She sat on the bed and cuddled his swaddled body close to her own, holding him upright so she could attempt to force the liquid down his throat. But she couldn't hold him and get his mouth open at the same time. Juan leaned over and pried Fritz's jaw open. Mentally crossing her fingers, Jane filled the dropper all the way to the top and slipped it between Fritz's lips.

For a moment, the boy choked, his frail body convulsing, but then he swallowed. His eyelids fluttered, and Jane thought he might wake. She held her breath, but he settled quietly again in her arms.

NASH WORKED HIS usual magic, and within hours, Eric and the rest of the crew were boarding a private jet at Brownsville's small airport. A rental SUV waited at the airport where they landed, and they were at Miguel's apartment by noon. The key was exactly where Miguel had promised, and they let themselves into the first apartment and then headed directly for the secret entrance to the second. The dining-table armory had been refilled—efficiency at its finest—and even included a few grenades. Despite the violence inherent in his line of work, Eric usually tried to minimize loss of life. But people who bought and sold women and children needed to be eradicated. Even if they could be captured, it was likely none would serve time—a man who could afford to buy a woman at auction simply had too much money for the system to combat.

He'd carried his own knives because they were flying private and not landing in a major airport, where their luggage and persons would be checked carefully, but even small airstrips frowned on transporting long guns internationally, and he'd given Jane his Glock. So he selected an HK45, while Marco, Mac, and Travis sorted through the rest of the gear.

"How much firepower are we going to need here?" Mac asked. "This is well outside my usual area of expertise." Mac mostly took the kind of assignments Eric couldn't stand—personal security for the rich and famous. Despite a rather egregious scar that ran diagonally across one cheek, the guy looked totally at home in a tux.

"Whatever you can carry that won't impede your ability to move would be my suggestion," said Travis. "Go military rather than law enforcement." Travis and Mac had served together before Mac went on to become a member of the Atlanta Police Department.

Mac grunted acknowledgement and sighted down the length of a Glock G41 before setting it aside and gathering a couple of loaded magazines. Marco, as usual, went straight for the rifles, nodding in satisfaction when he found his favorite HK417 in the lot. He already carried two pistols of his own, one beneath his shoulder and one at his back.

Eric's phone rang and he moved away from the group to pick it up.

"It's on," said Miguel.

"Where and when?"

"The salon is a warehouse building outside Tlaxcala. No street name. I'll send GPS coordinates to your phone. It will take you a couple of hours to get there. The auction begins at four tomorrow afternoon."

"Tomorrow afternoon?"

"Yes. They added her to the one that was already scheduled. This has several advantages for Velasquez: those invited are people the Hijos have done business with in the past, and there will be no unusual activity to alert anyone who may be watching. Everything will proceed as normal."

"But you have no idea where she is now. Where they'll hold her before the auction. What will happen to her between now and tomorrow afternoon."

"I'm afraid not."

"Okay." Eric rubbed the front of his forehead with two fingers, trying to push away the headache forming there.

"I'm not coming to the apartment. I don't want to take the chance on being seen with you. I'll meet you at the auction. I'm sending the coordinates now. Give yourself a couple of hours to get there."

A second later, Eric's phone beeped. Travis walked over and looked at the coordinates.

"What time do we have to be there?" The others gathered around.

"Tomorrow at four."

"We should scope it first," Marco said.

"Yeah. Grab some food and we'll head out. We probably shouldn't come back here. It's Miguel's hole, and since he's been invited to the auction, he may be being watched. We'll hit a no-tell motel for the night once we've checked out the auction spot."

They gathered gear in silence and left the apartment. Travis led the way. He and Eric had pulled more than their fair share of jobs in and around Mexico City. He drove with easy competence, not too fast, not so slowly that he'd draw attention as a tourist.

Two and a half hours later, they drove past the coordinates Miguel had sent. The building looked like a warehouse from the outside, but it was set so far back from the road that Eric could not make out many details. They'd have to get closer on foot to make a proper assessment. Travis kept moving as Eric and Mac, holding binoculars, called out what they could see to Marco, who wrote it all down.

A couple miles down from the warehouse, they pulled into a seedy motel. Mac, the least likely to be recognized by Velasquez or any of his men, made a three-day reservation. Travis drove around the L shape of the building to park out of sight.

The room was everything the first glimpse of the motel promised. Paint an off shade of yellow meant to look gold covered the stucco walls. The two "queen sized" beds were doubles at best, and a faint scent of marijuana hung in the air. The television got three channels, none of which were in English. Eric turned it on anyway. They were too close to their target to chance being overheard.

"We go in at three in the morning," he said. "It's our best chance of getting a good look at what we're facing. I don't want anyone getting too close, though. Miguel doesn't think the women are held there, so we can't afford to tip our hand early. They can't know we know the location, or they'll move the auction, and that would be disastrous."

"Got it."

"Until then, get some rest, eat, weapons check, whatever you need to do so you're at your best. We'll be hiking in tonight, probably tomorrow, too."

Jane sat on the bed with Fritz, using the dropper that had come with the medicine bottle to drip Pedialyte—also supplied by Garcia, the driver who'd delivered her and brought the amoxicillin along with IV bags, a kit, and a stand—down the child's throat. He was swallowing more easily but showed no sign of actually waking up. Of course, he might just be hiding inside himself. She knew that reaction all too well. She'd spent a shocking number of years doing it herself. Only now, having had the wall of science that separated her from the messy world of human emotions forcibly torn down, did she realize what a disservice she'd done not only to those around her but also to herself.

Just let us get out alive. I'll do better. She cuddled the child to her and rocked him slightly.

Velasquez, Garcia, and Juan were in a heated conversation, but she couldn't understand it. But whatever they were talking about couldn't be good for her, so she interrupted.

"Hey, I need to put Fritz back in the tub, and I can't do it alone. Who's going to help?" She kept her eyes on Garcia, ignoring Juan.

Another heated exchange between Velasquez and Garcia, then Velasquez gestured for Juan to assist her. She tried not to let her relief show. *Another chance to win him over.*

"I'll carry him; you bring the bottles and dropper and stuff. I'll need help holding him up while we keep his head wet, too."

They trooped into the bathroom, and Jane added some more water to the bath, testing the temperature so that it would leach some of the heat from the child's skin without shocking the capillaries into clamping down.

She unwrapped the quilt and handed it to Juan, then lowered Fritz into the water. His leg muscles clenched as she did, but she pretended not to notice. The child would open his eyes when he was ready. Juan had picked up the water bottle and brought it in with him, so she used that to scoop water from the tub and pour it over Fritz's head. Some trickled down his face, and he squinched his eyes shut. Jane dropped the bottle into the tub and smoothed his hair away from his forehead.

"Come on, Fritz, you can open your eyes. You're safe with me. I just want to know you're okay. Come on, sweetie. Show me your eyes."

Again, that little flinch of his eyelids, but then the child's eyes opened. A brilliant, bright blue, they reminded her shockingly of Eric's. This, she suddenly realized, was what Eric's children would look like. Of course, he'd said he didn't want a family, that he couldn't guarantee anything for them, but surely there was more to fatherhood than financial security. And Eric had everything else in spades. Strength, gentleness, a true moral compass. *Please let him be okay.*

"Hi there," she said, shaking off the memories of Eric's grin.

He did not speak, merely regarded her solemnly.

"My name is Jane, and this is Juan."

Juan scowled and Fritz shrank back under the water. For the first time he seemed to realize he was exposed, and his hands went to his groin. Juan reached over and got a hand towel and passed it to him. Fritz snatched it and covered himself.

"You need to tell Velasquez we need some food. Soup would be good for Fritz to start. His stomach won't take much more. Maybe some eggs and dry toast if that's possible, but otherwise soup."

Juan stayed put.

"What, you want me to tell him? Fine. Fritz, can you sit up a little?" She eased her arm out from behind the boy and stood. The front of her tank top was soaking wet, and the cotton clung to her body. *Damn.* Her mind flashed back to Velasquez's perusal in the mansion the night he'd so coldly evaluated her potential for sale, and she shivered. Swallowing her fear and anger, she thrust her shoulders back—let him make of it what he would—and stepped out into the bedroom.

"We need food. Both Fritz and I do."

"It's being handled."

"His has to be easily digestible and nutritious. Not fast food."

Velasquez glared at her. "I said, *it's handled.* It's not your concern. Keep his fever down."

"We will need to keep putting him in the bath on a regular basis. He can't be moved."

"Until?"

"Until he's better." She spat the words. "I'm not a pediatrician or ER specialist. I don't know when that will be."

"He has until one in the morning. No longer."

Jane glanced at the clock on the bedside table. *Eleven hours.* It wouldn't be enough. Who would take care of Fritz if she could not? "What happens at one? What if he's not well yet?"

"He does not have to be well. Just alive. Then you both move on to the next phase of your lives." Velasquez grinned, and it was not a pretty sight.

CHAPTER 15

IN THE THICK, green, predawn darkness Eric, Marco, Mac, and Travis made their way spread out in a ragged line through the woods around the warehouse that Miguel had identified as serving as the auction house. They all wore NVGs and earbuds from the Brownsville house.

"You seeing what I'm seeing?" Marco's voice in his ear made Eric twitch. They were closing in on the warehouse, about a hundred yards out, approaching from the side facing away from the road, where trees provided at least minimal cover.

"Yeah." He peered through his goggles at the men lingering outside the back of the box truck that had just pulled up. Each held an AR-15, and they surveyed the area with far more care than those he'd seen at the lab compound. These men were nervous, alert. Whatever was in that truck was valuable.

The back door to the warehouse opened, and two more men came out. These two carried pistols in shoulder holsters. The driver and passenger from the truck's cab came out and greeted them, and the four spoke for several minutes.

"The driver, that's Fernando Ruiz," said Marco. "He's one of Velasquez's lieutenants. He was in charge of one of the crews that came after us in the jungle."

"You know the others?"

"No."

"I know one of them," said Travis. "The blond. I've seen his file in Nash's office. Gordie Ambler. He's a trafficker, pimp, and all around scumbag. But I didn't realize he was associated with the Hijos. Not sure Nash knows, either."

"All right. You're getting this, Trav?" Travis wore special goggles that included a small video camera. Every mission was recorded for both intel and training purposes. "I want these guys. All of them."

"You know it."

Two of the men climbed into the truck, and a minute later they lifted out a large metal crate and handed it to the two waiting below.

"Fuck," said Travis, "please tell me that's not what I think it is."

Eric looked through his binocs at the green glow of the crate and the person inside it. Was that Jane? No way to tell from this distance. "It's exactly what you think it is."

"Fuck me," said Mac.

The two men carried the crate inside the warehouse, then came out and got another. And another. And another. All in all, seven crates of varying sizes were transferred. One was tiny, and Eric's stomach heaved. Kids. Jesus. Who the hell bought and sold kids young enough to fit in a fucking spaniel-sized dog crate?

"You want to go in ASAP?" Travis asked. "Now that we know they're there?"

Yes. He did. He wanted Jane out of there right fucking now. But Velasquez wasn't there. Or at least they couldn't be sure whether he was.

"Velasquez will be at the sale. He has to save face. If we go in now, we lose him, and I don't want to do that. Much as I hate it, we stick with the original plan."

"We have time," said Mac. "More than twelve hours before the sale begins. You want to involve the federales?"

"No. There are good guys in law enforcement down here. Trav and I have worked with them on kidnap cases. But police forces—all police forces—leak like fucking sieves. We tell them we're going after Velasquez, and even with all the best intentions in the world, he'll find out. We keep this small and private."

Marco didn't answer. He didn't have to. Eric knew that was his preference as well.

The men below finished unloading the truck—some non-human cargo had come in as well—and one drove it around to the back of the warehouse and into a garage. Then all the guards went inside.

"I want to get closer," Eric said. "The rest of you, hang back and cover me."

He slipped through the trees until he saw trip wires, which began some ten yards into the woods and hung about knee-high. He looked up into the trees and saw, closer to the warehouse, that cameras had been set into the branches. Luckily for him, they were all focused toward the open area of the property, not into the forest. Tiny lights blinked at the base of each. Motion sensors. The minute they got in front of those cameras, they'd set off an alarm. If they didn't blow themselves up first.

"Trav, we've got trip wires and motion sensors. Ideas?"

"The trip wires are probably tight as hell out here. You don't want every damned rabbit or coyote setting them off. But the motion sensors—you'd think even birds would drive those mad."

"They don't need them all the time," said Mac. "Maybe they turn off the cameras and alarms until they have something they need to protect."

"Give me a couple minutes," said Marco.

Eric leaned against a tree, a camera pointing over his head, and waited. Ten minutes later, Marco appeared next to him. In his hand, he held an assortment of leaves, twigs, cones, and pebbles.

"Camera?"

Eric pointed up.

Marco passed his rifle to Eric and swiftly climbed the tree.

"Get ready to move if this brings them running." He passed his hand, covered in leaves, in front of the camera. At the first motion, floodlights popped on all around the warehouse. Obviously automated. Two men came outside, but after peering into the darkness beyond the lit plain, they went back in. The lights remained on for a full five minutes.

Once the area went dark once more, Marco passed a twig in front of the camera. Nothing happened. Twice more and still there was no reaction.

"Heat sensor," Eric said.

"Probably a combination. Pass me some tape." Eric took a packet of duct tape out of his pack and ripped off a piece.

Carefully, Marco inched a leaf down in front of the camera and over the small blinking light. Once the sensor was covered, he taped the leaf into place. He waited for a reaction from the warehouse, but nothing happened. Then he took his hand and placed it next to the sensor.

Eric tensed, but once again the lights remained off and the guards inside.

"You think they have visuals inside from these cameras?"

Marco thought about it. "Probably not. There's too much wildlife. They use a combination of motion and heat to trigger the lights, which notifies the guards."

"Good. So we find the sensors and disable them like this. That gives us a chance to get a little closer before the auction."

Finding the cameras and placing leaves took a little over two hours. In the process, they also discovered multiple trip wires and even a few bear traps.

"They aren't kidding around," Travis said as he played a small light across the iron jaw of the bear trap.

"Nope." Eric squatted next to the trap. "And the advantage to traps is that—for the most part—people don't die in them. They get prisoners to question, find out who's gunning for them. I bet these set off some kind of alarm in the warehouse. They don't send men out to check them every day. We'll have to avoid them when we go in because we can't trigger them in advance."

"Also means we can't just let the innocents make a run for it," Travis said. "Which is going to make our lives more difficult."

"When has anything ever made our lives easier?"

"True that."

Jane pressed her back against the top of the cage again, pushing with all the strength in her legs. Again, as they had in the motel, the bars bit into her spine, but this time she did not stop. Was there give? Anywhere? Around her in the utter blackness of the truck, she heard the sounds of other prisoners. They'd stopped twice during their interminable drive, and each time things were loaded into the truck, but she couldn't tell whether guards remained inside the back of the truck with them. Did she dare speak? But then, what difference could it possibly make?

"Hello?"

No one answered. But Fritz, at least, was nearby. She'd seen them load him in, forcing him into a tiny crate the same way they'd shoved her into hers, with the threat of the cattle prod.

"Fritz? Where are you, honey?"

"Fritz?" Another voice from the darkness, this one female. "Fritz? Are you in here?"

"Helene?" A scrambling sound, and then a rattle she imagined was the child shaking at his cage. "Helene!"

"Fritz," Jane said, "who is Helene?"

"My sister."

"Oh my God, Fritzie, they told me you were dead. They told me…" The girl's words ended in a sob. "*Gott sei dank, es dir gut geht. Wo bist du gewesen? Haben sie dich verletzt?*"

"I was sick. Miss Jane helped me."

"Thank you, Miss. Thank you."

"Of course. I didn't do much, really. But I promise, I'll help you guys get home, too."

A bitter laugh came from the back of the truck. "Good luck with that." The woman's English was heavily accented. "Once they sell us, we'll never see each other again unless one man buys us. You have as much chance of helping them get home as you do of getting home yourself. None." Fury vibrated in her voice undiluted by even a hint of defeat.

"There's never no chance."

"American. If you lived here, you'd know hope is a dream, a waste of time." Again the words seemed out of sync with the tone. Who was she trying to convince?

"What's your name?" Jane asked. "Where are you from?"

"Raquel."

"What about faith, Raquel? Could you find any faith, if no hope?"

"God abandoned the poor of Mexico years ago."

"I believe, Miss Jane." Fritz's confidence in her brought tears to Jane's eyes.

"You hang on to that, sweetheart," she said. "I promise, no matter how long it takes, no matter what happens, I won't give up. I won't ever stop trying."

The truck jolted to a halt, and Jane dropped from her cramped crouch back into a seated position. Her legs gave thanks, but she wished she'd had more time to try to break the cage. The tailgate opened, and dim light filtered in. Men clambered aboard and began to lift the crates, handing them to others, who carried them inside a large warehouse.

Now would be an excellent time to show up, Eric.

But he didn't, and Jane found her own pen lifted and passed along. Should she scream? But the moon's pale light shone on a desolate landscape, nothing but the warehouse and parking lot hidden in the midst of a thick forest. Who would hear her? Who would care? And if she screamed and Velasquez or his henchmen punished her, how would she protect Fritz?

Inside the warehouse the cages were assembled into a rough semicircle on a platform of some kind, and Jane saw that there were seven of them in all. A blonde was placed next to Fritz, and the boy reached through the bars of his cage to take her hand. This must be the sister. Helene. Even in the half-light, Jane could see heavy bruises beneath her red, swollen eyes. Like her brother, she was too thin and her long hair was a matted mess.

The other four cages held young women. Two of them were barely teenagers, and rage ate holes in Jane's gut at the sight. Despite the taunt in the darkness, Jane understood that her own hope came from a place of privilege. They had all ended up in this hellhole together, but the two girls next to her would not have had her options even if they hadn't been captured for sale. The two other women, who had been placed farthest from Jane on the other side of Fritz and Helene, looked to be in their late twenties. One appeared to have simply given up. She lay on the bottom of her cage curled into a ball. Her face bore the marks of a hard life, for despite having no wrinkles or spots, her skin had an almost gray tinge. If Jane had to guess, she'd hazard that the woman had worked in a sweatshop or some similar situation. She looked as if she never got out into the sunlight.

The last one was likely the one who'd spoken in the truck. Anger seeped from her pores, and a truculent expression set gorgeous features into severe lines. If Jane could get out, this was the woman she'd free first—she'd never stop fighting. If guards hadn't been hustling to and fro in the warehouse, Jane would have spoken to her, tried to plan.

"How can you be so calm?" The whispered words came from Helene. "Aren't you afraid?"

Jane glanced at the guards around them. Admissions seemed like a bad idea if the men were listening, but they did not appear to be paying the prisoners much heed. Two of them were bringing in heavy, plush chairs of red velvet. Another two were setting crystal glasses on a rolling table. The warehouse was becoming a fancy auction space before her eyes, and the platform on which the crates rested was obviously a stage. She shuddered.

"Terrified. But I learned a trick a long time ago, of putting the terror away. If I focus on planning, on facts and numbers like how many guards there are and where they're standing and what kinds of weapons we have, then I don't think about what might happen. I try not to worry about the future." And once upon a time, when her life had revolved around her mother's illness, she'd thought that was the way to live every day. She hadn't even realized what she was missing. Before Eric, before Fritz, before Dani and poor, lost Varo. She'd lived insulated and isolated. It was surprisingly difficult to pull that shield back around her now, but the tools she'd learned from her childhood kept her stable. Otherwise, she'd likely have curled up into a ball like the woman on the end.

"But we don't have any weapons."

"We always have weapons. Your mind is a weapon. Your hands, your feet, your elbows and teeth. Your heart." She remembered one of her mother's favorite books. "Did you ever read the story of Scheherazade?"

"The Arabian Nights?"

"Yes. Now, there was a woman with no weapons, no options. She saved her own life with nothing but her imagination and her voice. You are never truly powerless. Never."

"But that's just a story."

"Maybe. But the best stories all have kernels of truth. And that's the truth I choose to believe from that tale."

"These men won't listen. They won't want to hear stories."

"No, they won't. But neither are they monsters. They are men. Despite being corrupted, they have minds and hearts, too. Maybe you appeal to greed; maybe you appeal to kindness. You have to be smart. You have to find what they want and use it to get what you want."

She thought about Juan. Would he be there? Could he be counted on to protect Fritz? Over the hours they'd spent at the hotel, he'd softened toward the child, but was it enough?

The auction space took shape around Jane. A fancy Persian rug was rolled out on the cement floor in front of the platform; a dozen of the velvet-upholstered chairs were set onto it, each with a small table next to it; and a bar with a large bookshelf behind it was set up with every kind of alcohol imaginable and a large icemaker that was wheeled in and plugged into the wall. Velvet curtains in a charcoal gray on rolling frames were placed all around the room, and men climbed up into the ceiling and rigged cameras that pointed down at the stage.

The process took hours, and the whole time Jane and her fellow prisoners sat in their cages. There was no way to escape, no chance to get free. The two girls next to Jane cried quietly, and one eventually fell asleep. The girl next to her reached out to check on her, but Jane understood. Sleep was simply an escape. The girl's body needed to shut out reality for a while.

Eventually, when the warehouse had been transformed into an elegant and comfortable space that hid its true purpose, the guards turned toward their charges. Garcia, who had been at the motel with them, picked up the cattle prod that had been left lying at the edge of the stage and approached the angry young woman.

"*Eres la primera, muchacha. Levántate y ven conmigo. No me de un problema, Entiendes?*"

Jane got "primera" and "muchacha." Whatever they had planned, this woman was to be first.

"Fuck off," the woman said. Without hesitation, Garcia shoved the prod through the bars and shocked her. Her whole body convulsed, and Jane's nerves fired in sympathy.

"*Vamonos,*" he ordered the minute he retracted the prod. She spat. He shocked her again, longer this time, and when he let her go she was a shaking mass in the corner of her crate.

"*Vamonos,*" he said again. The woman didn't respond, but neither did she follow his order to leave the cage. "Juan! Gerardo!" he called. When the two men appeared, Garcia shocked the woman again and then had Juan unlock the crate. While she was still shaking and out of control, Juan and Gerardo reached in and pulled her out; then all three of them hustled her away. Another pair of men began bringing chairs up onto the stage. Unlike the fancy seats for the audience, these were tall metal chairs, like barstools with slatted backs.

An eternity later, the men brought the woman back. She'd been bathed and dressed in a nightgown so sheer it left virtually nothing to the imagination. She was handcuffed, and her arms showed numerous burn marks that Jane assumed were from being hit with the prod. A good deal of the fight seemed to have gone out of her, but she dragged her feet and found the strength to push back a bit until Garcia threatened to shock her again. Juan and Gerardo forced her into one of the chairs, sliding her cuffed hands over the back and using a second pair of cuffs to attach them to the rungs.

They repeated the process with the second woman, who let them drag her out of her cage without a fight but would not, or could not, walk. Gerardo lifted her up, and Garcia followed behind, holding the prod against her skin in case she decided to kick up a fuss. Jane doubted she had it in her.

In minutes, they came back with her and—after securing her to a second chair—moved on to Helene. Helene huddled in the corner of her crate and refused to come out.

"You want what she got?" Garcia asked, jerking his head at the first woman. Helene shook her head but didn't leave the corner.

"Let her and Fritz go together," Jane said. "They'll help each other."

Helene turned huge eyes on her, and she nodded with as much encouragement as she could. "This isn't the time to fight. Get clean. Help your brother. Protect each other."

Garcia tilted his head, and for the first time Jane realized he wore an earbud like the one she'd had with Eric. Whoever was on the other end approved of her idea, apparently, because Garcia poked Helene with the prod but didn't shock her.

"Okay, kid, you and your sister go together. You act up, I hurt her. You got it?"

Fritz nodded. Juan leaned down and unlocked his cage, and Fritz crawled out. Jane wanted to tell him to play on Juan's sympathies, to do his best to continue bonding. Luckily, he was a smart kid. He cowered against Juan's side as Gerardo unlocked Helene's cage. The siblings shared a quick embrace before Garcia shoved the prod between Helene's shoulders and told her to get a move on.

They were gone quite a while, and every minute, Jane's blood pressure rose. What was taking so long? Was she wrong to have told Helene to take Fritz with her? But eventually they returned. Helene was carrying Fritz on her hip as one might an infant. They'd dressed him in pajamas, but they were as skimpy and sheer as the women's gowns, and Jane felt a howl of rage and sorrow screaming for escape at the back of her throat.

"He can sit in my lap," Helene was arguing as they approached the chairs.

"He cannot," said Garcia.

"We won't cause a problem if you let us sit together."

"You won't cause a problem no matter what."

Helene turned pleading eyes on Jane.

"Why don't you pull their chairs close together? What could it hurt?" Jane asked. "Let them hold hands."

"This isn't recess at a fucking preschool."

"Do you think I don't know that? Or they don't know that? We get it. Life is going to suck from now on. What purpose does making it worse than it has to be now serve?"

And if they were going to get out of this, Jane needed Helene and Fritz—and the rest of them—as calm as possible.

Garcia studied Helene. "No laps. But I will hook you to his chair. You can hold his hand. It will make a pretty picture for buyers."

He shoved two of the tall metal chairs close together and hoisted Fritz into one while Helene took her time climbing into the other.

"He needs a blanket," Jane said. "He still has a fever, and you're going to get him chilled sitting there wearing so little."

"That's not how it works," Garcia said.

"You want him passing out? Sick like he was when you brought him to me? Put a blanket around him until the auction begins."

Garcia grumbled but ordered one of the men to bring him a blanket, which he wrapped around the boy. Jane saw a tear slip down Helene's cheek. Don't fall apart now. Hold it together. The silent commands were as much for herself as for Helene.

"You're next," Garcia said, banging her cage with the cattle prod. What would they do if she rushed them when Juan unlocked the crate? Was this the right time? As if he could hear her thoughts, Garcia pressed the prod down onto her neck as Gerardo released the padlock.

No, surrounded by men was the wrong time to fight back even though every fiber of her being shouted for her to do so. Garcia behind her with the prod against her skin, she followed Juan down from the stage to an office at the back of the building.

"Bathroom's through there," Garcia said. "Gown's on the vanity. Shower and get dressed by yourself, or do it with help. Your decision."

"Yeah, yeah, I hear you." Jane walked into the bathroom and turned to shut the door, only to realize there wasn't one. Garcia laughed. She gritted her teeth. *You're going to get out of this. You've survived worse.* But the pep talk wasn't helping much.

Once again she climbed into the shower fully dressed. Both the water pressure and the heat were better here than at the motel. All the comforts of home. Through the flimsy shower curtain, she saw Garcia, Gerardo, and Juan deep in discussion. She washed her hair and used the conditioning shampoo sitting in a small bottle in the corner. The last thing she did was take off her clothes and leave them in a soaking pile in the shower before grabbing a towel from the pile on the vanity and wrapping it around her. Another towel she used to dry her hair before attacking it with the wide-toothed comb next to the sink. She went as slowly as she could—not difficult considering how snarled and matted her hair had become. The towel, while small, covered her better than the little negligee would, so she kept it wrapped tightly around her as she combed out her hair.

"Get a move on," Garcia ordered after a couple of minutes.

Jane didn't answer but gritted her teeth and pulled the little nightie over her head. God, it was worse than walking out there naked. Which she supposed was the point. A little tease, a hint of covering that did nothing to hide her nudity. The men hadn't seemed to care with the other women, however. They were cattle, widgets, totally interchangeable products for sale, which provided an obscure kind of comfort. *It's just a body. It's not really you.*

After a long breath for courage and calm, she stepped out of the bathroom, passed the three men, and walked back to the stage without pausing. She settled herself on one of the high chairs, pressing her thighs together to maintain a sliver of privacy. The metal of the cuffs was cold as Gerardo snapped them to her wrists, and she twitched.

The process went on until all seven of them had been washed, dressed, and seated for display. Jane's heart skipped beats, sped up despite almost constant self-admonishments to remain calm, to watch for the right time to fight back.

Screens were brought in, and the cameras that had been set up earlier were focused, tested. Jane saw herself appear at least ten feet tall on giant screens on either side of the stage. Well, hell. No hiding from that. Several of the women were openly crying now, and their sobs called to her soul, bringing a lump to her throat and tears to her eyes, but she blinked rapidly, refusing to let them fall.

The lights in the warehouse, with the exception of the spotlights pointed at the stage, went out. Jane squinted and thought she might see flashlights moving about, but the stage lights were too bright to make out any details. Over the crying of the women, she heard shuffling and low voices. Near as she could guess, they sat there for about half an hour while sweat gathered on her skin from the lights and dripped down her back. Fritz, who seemed to be cried out because he'd not made a single sound since they'd brought him back from the bathroom, shrugged off his blanket.

Then out of the darkness, Velasquez's voice came over a speaker.

"Welcome, my friends," he said. To Jane's surprise, he spoke in English. Perhaps it was easier for his buyers. "I am aware that you may have heard rumors about difficulties the Hijos have been having. I am here to assure you that those rumors are, if not entirely untrue, at least greatly exaggerated. As you can see, we are still in business, still providing you with the highest quality merchandise. It is true that we had hoped by this time to have a new kind of weapon to offer you, but that particular program is taking longer than we anticipated."

A new kind of weapon. That would be men like Juan. Men she'd helped create. Jane's stomach muscles clenched, and bile rose in the back of her throat.

"I won't say more than that we have had breakthroughs in that arena as well, and at our next meeting I anticipate being able to offer at least a few trained soldiers. For that, I will contact interested parties individually."

A murmur arose from the darkness.

"But this afternoon, we have an excellent array of merchandise for you to choose from. As is our usual practice, I will begin with the items I think will bring the highest prices, so you don't have to worry about saving your money for them and then missing out."

Jane swallowed the vomit coming up in the back of her throat.

"The first piece comes with a stipulation. She must be removed from Mexico and North America. If you cannot assure that, don't bother bidding. If I find out she has remained here or returned to the United States or Canada, I will take it as an insult to the Hijos as an organization, and the purchaser will be punished accordingly."

The screens at the side of the stage blinked, and Jane's face came up on them. Then the camera panned down her body.

"This is Dr. Jane Evans. She's about to become famous. She's also a raging bitch." Glee colored the words, and Jane couldn't help remembering his comments about buyers liking to tame women. "Get her up, Gerardo."

Gerardo came over and released Jane's hands from the back of the chair but left her wrists cuffed together behind her back.

"Spread your legs," he said. "Give the men a show."

"Fuck you."

Gerardo looked off into the darkness, then smacked Jane across the face so hard he knocked her down. With her arms cuffed behind her, she couldn't catch herself and landed hard on her shoulder. He was hauling her to her feet again when doors slamming and the sound of gunshots exploded through the warehouse.

Eric. She could feel it, feel him. Her hands reached behind her for the leg of the chair, and she tipped it over, then held on tight as she swung her whole body in a circle. Halfway around, the chair was ripped from her hands as it connected with Gerardo's body. He crashed to the floor behind her, and she tried to twist, but he grabbed her hair and yanked her in front of him and stood, using her as a shield. She'd just gotten her balance when he stumbled back, almost pulling her down with him. Jane scrambled away on her knees, sure he would grab her again at any second, but he didn't. She reached Fritz's side and pushed to her feet. She looked for Gerardo, but he lay still, a massive blood pool spilling out around the back of his head. The bullet must have passed damned close to her face.

Thank you, Marco.

A minute later, a blond stranger was beside her with a pair of bolt cutters in hand.

"Friend," he said when Jane jumped between him and Fritz, shielding the child. "I'm Travis. Turn around and give me your wrists."

Christ, she didn't want to turn her back on this man. On any man. But he looked like one of HSE's guys, dressed in black with that same hard, battle-worn appearance Eric, Marco, and Trey all shared.

"Free Fritz first."

"Yes, ma'am." He went around the back of the child's chair and snipped the chain of the cuffs, then moved down the row. The minute Helene was free, she grabbed her brother and lifted him onto her hip. He clung to her but turned his head to look at Jane.

"You didn't lie."

"We're not safe yet."

As if to prove the statement, a bullet whizzed by. Helene screamed, chaos erupted on the stage, and Travis slammed Jane to the floor, covering her with his body. "Everybody down!" he shouted.

At the edge of the platform, a dark-haired, dark-eyed man in a business suit was urging the nearby women to come with him. A buyer? Why wouldn't he have run when the shooting started? Raquel held the others back, unconvinced by whatever he was saying. Smart woman.

Travis fired a volley of shots out into the audience area. His weight, combined with sheer terror, was squeezing the air out of Jane's lungs, and she tried to wiggle out from beneath him, but he told her to stay put.

"And tell the girls to go with Miguel."

"The guy in the suit? He's with you?"

"Yes. He has a vehicle. He can get them out."

"Raquel!" she called. "He's a friend! Go with him."

The woman raised her eyebrows, but another series of shots decided her. She and the other three Hispanic women crawled across the stage, keeping low, and slipped off the side with Miguel. Helene and Fritz, however, stayed close to Jane.

"Okay," said Travis. "On the count of three, we're out. Everyone ready? One… two…"

On "three," they all jumped and ran for the side of the

stage. They were almost there when Fritz tripped and went down. Jane and Helene turned back, but Travis almost threw them off the stage.

"Stay!" He tossed Jane a gun and grabbed another from his boot, but by the time he went back for the boy, Juan had clambered onto the stage and had him in a choke hold.

"Give me the kid," Travis said. Juan shook his head.

Helene tried to climb back onto the stage, but Jane held her down. "Don't distract them."

"He can't protect you. You know that," Travis said.

Juan clung to Fritz. "The boy needs to come with me. I need him."

Oh, hell. The training. "You don't need him," Jane said. "Look at him. He's just a sick little kid like your brother. He can't keep the Black away."

Juan backed up a couple of steps.

"Look at him, Juan. What good is he to you? Velasquez is gone. Hurting Fritzie won't help you. Velasquez deserted you because he was a coward. He couldn't protect you, either. You need to face this yourself. Decide whether you want to live in the light or let yourself go into the dark. It's a choice. Your choice, no one else's. You can fight the Black. But not by hurting a child."

Juan looked down at Fritz. As he did, more shots sounded, one hitting him in the shoulder. He curled over, and first Jane thought he was trying to use the child as a shield, but then she realized he was pushing the boy toward the edge of the stage. Helene reached up, and Juan dropped Fritz into her arms just as bullets tore through him, knocking him backward. Helene screamed again, and Travis dropped off the stage next to them and hustled them down a narrow corridor.

"Moving, boss," he said.

"What?" asked Helene.

"He's talking to friends," Jane explained. "He's got an ear-piece."

They came to a door, and Travis told them to wait, pushing all three of them against the wall while he poked his head outside.

"We're clear out back. Gonna make a run for it." He listened for a second, then nodded. "Got it."

They dashed out into the afternoon's fading sunlight. Dust rose around their feet, choking Jane, and she saw that they were in an unpaved parking area behind the warehouse.

"Head for the forest," Travis instructed, "but don't go in. They booby-trapped a lot of spots, and we're not sure we disabled them all."

"Just fucking great," Jane said.

"Welcome to life with HSE."

They ran for the trees at the edge of the woods.

CHAPTER 16

THE HECTIC PACE of the firefight did not give Eric much chance to find Velasquez. Inside, they encountered far more guards than expected. Eric had gone through the front and was dealing with two determined opponents when Mac's voice in his headset alerted him to the fact that he'd had to back out the side door to escape a three-man shooting team.

"Stay out. If the concentration's that high in that direction, that's probably where Velasquez is. Or plans to be."

Fuck, fuck, fuck. He worked his way over to the side, knocking over the tables that had been set up for buyers and using them as cover. Up on the stage, one of the men had grabbed Jane and pulled her up in front of him. A second later, a bullet put a nice, neat hole in the front of his head. *Thanks, Marco.* On cue, Travis jumped onto the stage. Which was all Eric had time to see before a guard required his attention. He slipped around the side of the table protecting him and fired off a few rounds as he dashed toward the next table. The man popped up, looking for him, and Eric put a bullet through his chest.

One down. Now where the hell had Velasquez got to?

He spotted the three shooters who had converged on Mac. Unfortunately, they saw him, too, and bullets shredded the oaken table he'd hidden behind, sending splinters in every direction. For a moment, he thought a hunk of wood had embedded itself in his left biceps, but as the burn set in he realized it was a bullet.

"Now, Mac!" he shouted as he returned fire. The side door

slammed open, and the men were caught in the crossfire. Two went down immediately. The third scuttled away and took shelter behind a stack of amplifiers brought in for the auction.

"Where's Velasquez?"

"He didn't come by me." Mac shook his head. "I vote we get jerk-off to tell us." He aimed at the stack of amps.

"Nothing back here," Marco said into his earpiece.

"I want this asshole."

Mac climbed on the bottom amp, then put his shoulder to the next one, sending the stack tumbling over. As their quarry struggled beneath the weight of the heavy cases, Eric stood over him with a pistol. Mac dragged the man from his hiding spot.

"Where's your boss?"

The man shook his head.

"You have no idea how badly I want to kill you right now," Eric said in Spanish, just in case the guy hadn't understood him. "Give me one reason not to."

"My soul is safe," replied the man in English.

"What the fuck?" said Mac. "Listen, asshole, if I were you, I'd worry a bit more about my body. You want me to shoot you? Because I'd be happy to do that. Somewhere it hurts but won't kill you. At least for a while."

"My soul is safe."

Mac ground his pistol into the guy's shoulder.

"Hold up," said Eric, watching the man's impassive face.

"Trav, you got Jane?"

"Yeah, we're at the rendezvous. Where are you?"

"Give us a few. Stay hidden. Put Jane on, will you?" He heard Travis pass over the earbud.

"Eric?"

It was so damned good to hear her voice, even shaky and

distanced by the earbuds. But he didn't have time to tell her. He'd make time for that later.

"Janie, I think we're facing one of Bryan's subjects. I need him to tell me where Velasquez is, but the usual tactics aren't going to fly. What do I do to turn off the programming?"

"I don't know. I'm not sure you can." Her voice cracked, and guilt bled through.

"Just give me anything. All we need to do is throw him off a little bit."

"Tell me what he looks like. Any significant features? Any scars or tats?"

"Big fucking snake up the left arm."

"Okay." She breathed deeply, and he wished he could reach out and hold her. "That's Arturo. He has a twelve-year-old sister, Maria Guadeloupe. You need to make him understand that Velasquez is not who he thinks. Give me a second to think about how."

Jane gave him the words and Eric repeated them, though they made no sense to him. How Velasquez could not protect Arturo because he had become infected by the Black. How the Black devouring Velasquez led him to sell girls no different from Maria Guadeloupe to men who would abuse them physically and sexually. How if Arturo stuck by Velasquez he, too, would be swallowed up by the Black and no one would be left to defend his family against the encroaching evil.

"How do you know these things?" Arturo asked.

"Tell him you've been fighting the Black for years. Tell him you need to know where Velasquez is so you can save him before he is swallowed up completely. He won't feel as if he's betraying Velasquez so much that way."

As she predicted, the man noticeably relaxed when he heard they were battling the Black.

"We were to prevent any invasion," he said. "Those were our orders. Protect the merchandise and do not let anyone see where Velasquez went. He has tunnels, but I have never been in them."

Well, fuck. Of course he had tunnels. The cartels loved tunnels. Hundreds of varying sizes and complexity riddled the soil beneath the US-Mexico border.

"We should head for the rendezvous," Marco said. "Cops will be here soon enough despite any protection they've paid. We've made too much noise. Plus, you need to get patched up."

Eric looked down at his biceps, where the stream of blood had slowed to a sluggish ooze. "I'll be fine."

"But Jane won't," said Mac. "C'mon, man. You don't want to leave her alone with Travis, now do you? God knows, I won't leave Callie with him until I get a ring on her finger… and maybe not even then."

"I hear you." He heard the subtext, too. They could always come back for Velasquez—and they would.

"Janie, put Travis back on," he said.

"What's up?" Travis asked.

"Keep sharp. We've lost Velasquez. But we're coming out. See you in five."

"Ten-four."

⌒

"The guys are on their way, so we'll be heading out soon," Travis said. "But those virginal outfits are going to show like neon in the moonlight. Grab some dirt and muddy yourselves up a bit."

Jane started to lean over and then realized that would

bring the short nighty right up over her ass, so she squatted instead, grabbed a handful of dirt and dead leaves, and began to rub them over both the gown and her pale skin. Helene and Fritz followed suit. Then they helped each other, dirtying up the backs of the outfits. Jane was just rubbing filthy fingers over her face when a prickle at the back of her neck alerted her to Eric's presence.

He swept her up into a bear hug, and she clung to him, burying her face in his neck. Tears sprouted behind her eyes, and she squeezed them away. His rough hand cradled the side of her face and tilted it up to look at him.

"You okay?" His blue eyes blazed, gas flames in the gathering darkness.

"I am now." But she didn't let go. His body, her bulwark against all evil in the world. She wanted so desperately to beg him never to go again, but instead she straightened her spine and stepped away from him.

"What do we do now?"

"We have a car hidden on the other side of this stand of trees. We'll go get it, then drive to our hotel. Tomorrow, Nash has arranged an appointment for us at the US embassy in Mexico City."

"But we are not Americans," said Helene.

"Doesn't make any difference. At the hotel, I'll get all your information, send it to Nash, and he'll fix it with the embassy folks. He's good at that."

Helene looked to Jane for reassurance, and Jane squeezed her hand. "He is. He'll get you home. I promise."

"And the others? The ones who went with the buyer from the auction."

"He wasn't a buyer," said Eric. "Not really. His name is Miguel, and although he does live here in Mexico and participate in…shall we say shady practices in order to keep his hand in with the Hijos, he will protect those girls. He won't let them get hurt."

They trudged through the woods, always alert for followers, but the Hijos seemed to have given up on them—at least for the moment. They arrived at a ratty-looking van, which Marco and Eric checked comprehensively before allowing them inside. The drive was relatively short, and when the back doors opened, Jane almost cried because the motel and parking lot were so similar to the one where they'd been held before the auction. The only real difference she could see was the fact that the "Vacancy" on the roof was blinking out a red neon calling sign to anyone who might pass by.

Eric hustled her inside while Travis and Marco took charge of Helene and Fritz. Mac pulled the van up closer to the front of the hotel and went inside to ask—as a tourist might—where he could find a bite to eat.

"He's checking out the area," Eric explained. "He's the one who took the room, and they think he's alone. It's best that way. Tomorrow, we drive to Mexico City. It's a couple hours away."

Travis was working at the door to the next room with a lock pick, and a few seconds later he had the door open. "Bingo. A veritable suite."

"What if they rent that room to someone else?" asked Helene.

"This shithole? Sorry. This place isn't going to rent out more rooms tonight. Trust me. And we'll leave some extra cash for the maids. But we didn't expect to be bringing more people along." He dug through a duffel and pulled out two shirts. "Here. Take your brother in, shower off, and put these on. They'll cover you better." He looked at his fellow operatives. "Anyone got sweats? All I brought is shirts."

Both Eric and Marco found sweatpants, but Fritz was so small he would just have to wear the T-shirt like a dress, with a pair of boxer-briefs like pants beneath it. Helene and Fritz disappeared into the bathroom.

"Marco and I will stick it out in here," Travis said. "You take the doc and get her cleaned up in the other room." He practically shoved Eric toward the door, and Jane felt a blush rising along the back of her neck.

Eric grabbed the sweats and T-shirt he'd dug out of his duffel and carried them in with him.

"Go ahead and shower. I bet you can't wait to be clean again."

That was true, but she wasn't ready to let him out of her sight. "Can't we share?" *Oh, hell. That came out totally wrong.* "Not—I didn't mean—"

"I know what you didn't mean." He pushed her hair away from her face. "Trust me."

"I do." She leaned against him and wrapped her arms around his waist. He held her close, stroking her hair.

"It's going to be okay, Janie."

She nodded against him. She was so tired. "Don't leave me alone."

"I won't. Leave the door open. I just need to make a quick call; then I will be in. Okay?"

"Okay."

In the bathroom, she stripped off her filthy, see-through nighty and stuffed it in the trash container under the sink. Then she turned the shower on hot, fully expecting the tepid, foul-smelling water from the other motel. But this came out nearly scalding and perfectly clear. *Bliss. Absolute bliss.* She closed her eyes, letting the hot water cascade over her. It smelled fresh and clean and fabulous, and her muscles slowly began to unknot.

How long she'd been standing there before Eric stepped into the bathroom, she had no idea.

"Right here," he said, and when she peeked out she saw him settling himself, fully dressed, on the vanity counter, prepared to keep her company. But it wasn't enough. He was hidden out there, behind the curtain. She slipped her arm through the curtain and beckoned him to join her.

Nothing happened.

She peered out again and met his serious, crystal blue gaze. He waited a long moment but finally nodded. She ducked back into the shower, and a second later he slipped inside. His big body crowded hers and suddenly the space shrank. He reached past her for the soap, still in its wrapper, with one hand while his other arm came around her waist and drew her back against him.

"How you doing?"

"Better." She leaned into him, letting his broad chest take her weight.

"Good." He held her in place while he unwrapped the soap and smoothed the bar over the front of her body, then rubbed it between his hands before putting it back. "Let's have a look."

She turned around and he examined her critically. "You're a mess." He slicked his soapy hands over each arm, kneading her sore muscles as he did, then up her neck, into her hair. "Rinse." He reached for the soap again and, dropping to his knees in the small space, repeated the process with her legs.

The muscles in her thighs went loose and loopy, and it wasn't from relaxation. How did he manage to do this to her, even now? She steadied herself with her hands on his wide shoulders. He looked up at her and winked before sliding soapy fingers between her legs.

"Oh my God. Eric."

He just smiled and continued his ministrations. She was shaking by the time he decided she was sufficiently clean and turned her around to start all over again on her back. With his hands on her shoulders, he pressed his thumbs to the base of her neck, releasing the tension collected there. He poured shampoo into his hand and massaged it into her head, easing through the tangles and carefully teasing out the knots that had formed despite her braid.

"I love this."

"I'll tell my hairdresser you said so."

"I wasn't talking about the color. Or at least, not just about the color. It's the wildness, the texture. It's so untamed. Like a hidden part of you no one sees behind all those lab coats." He let the strands trail over his hand as he rinsed out the shampoo.

The words cut through her, cut down to a truth that hurt: she wasn't what he thought she was. She wasn't wild. She didn't do casual sex, regardless of what she'd told him a hundred years ago back in his apartment. There was nothing in the least casual about her feelings for him.

But she couldn't let him know that. To tell him that was to lose him immediately. He'd warned her as much. So it was time to turn the tables before she fell apart on him.

"Whereas you wear your wildness right up front." She poured shampoo into her palm and faced him. "I like you better as a blond, though. Especially now that your beard is coming back in."

"Yeah." He rubbed a hand over his chin. "Don't worry, the dye doesn't last more than a few weeks. Looks like crap when it fades, though."

She reached up and rubbed the shampoo into his scalp, enjoying the sensation of his silky hair sliding through her fingers and the freedom of touching him. If only they could stay like this forever, hidden away inside this shower, with the rest of the world held at a distance. Of course, it was an impossible dream, but oh, how she wished it were not.

When she went to soap down his body, however, her fingers rubbing across his arms disturbed a healing wound, and blood flowed, tinting the water.

"Eric! You've been shot."

"It was nothing. Just a graze. I promise. It was already healing."

"But you were *shot*."

"Janie, it's okay. I swear to you." Eric bent his head to rinse out the shampoo, taking the opportunity to brush his lips lightly across hers. He growled, startling a laugh out of her.

"Enough playing around." He grabbed the soap and scrubbed himself down, then flicked off the shower, stepped out, and toweled off. "C'mon."

Jane took the hand he held out to her and allowed him to wrap her in one of the towels next to the sink. He dried her far more gently than he had himself, then shocked her by lifting her into his arms to carry her out of the bathroom.

"Eric?"

"You know what my favorite part of this entire mission has been?"

"Getting out alive?"

His body shook with laughter as he stripped away the shiny yellow coverlet and laid her on the bed, then slid down beside her. "Well, that, too. But I was going to say having you on my back. Feeling your arms and legs around me."

Oh God, he was trying to kill her. Tears clogged the back of her throat, and she blinked them back. She needed to shut him up or she'd fall apart. She propped herself up on one elbow and ran her hand down his chest where droplets of water still clung to the sprinkle of golden hairs after his hasty drying job. "Enough playing around, buster." She licked one of the droplets away and felt as much as heard his sharp intake of breath.

"Don't start what you can't finish."

Her hand found his cock and she stroked it lightly. "Who says I can't finish?"

"I thought you were exhausted." He swallowed and she watched his Adam's apple bob.

"Second wind. Or third. Or something." She felt his pulse throb beneath her hand. Who needed sleep? She kissed her way down his body, sipping the water that had collected out of the tiny knot of his belly button. When she replaced her hand with her mouth, his whole body arched up off the bed and his hands fisted in her hair.

"Jesus, Janie."

He tasted so good. This was the one thing he hadn't let her do when they'd spent the night in his apartment. But oh, how she'd wanted to. And she hadn't wanted to with anyone else. It was so intimate. Far more so than sex. Although she was atop him, he set the pace with his hands and his body, and the power of it made her crazy. She could feel her own release closing in on her.

At the last moment, when she could taste his pre-come in her mouth, he pulled her away from him and flipped her to her back.

"Please, baby, not like this. Not now. I want to be inside you."

She didn't even hesitate, didn't think, just pulled him down over her and wrapped her legs around his waist and urged him on. He thrust into her, slamming her down into the cushy bed, but the violence didn't bother her. If anything, she wished they were on the floor. She needed purchase she couldn't get, and she tried to push herself upward to meet him. And then she flew into a million pieces and every muscle convulsed. She might have screamed. She had no idea. Heat flooded her body, both from his orgasm and from hers.

⁓

JANE HAD TWO thoughts simultaneously when she came back down to earth: First, there was no way the others hadn't heard her. Which was absolutely mortifying. The second was that they hadn't used a condom.

Eric seemed to realize it at the same time she did. "Janie—"

"No, don't. It's okay."

"No, it's not."

"Eric, look at me."

He did, his flame-blue eyes dark and serious.

"It's okay. I promise."

He was clean. She had no doubts on that score. And if she got pregnant, well, that was okay, too. She had a good job, a good life. She could have a child. A towheaded little boy with bright blue eyes? A girl with Eric's shaggy blond mane? She'd never imagined herself a mother, but she could do it. She would love a child, and that's what mattered. Not that a single act of unprotected sex would result in a child, but if it did…

She leaned up and kissed away Eric's frown. "Don't worry."

"I swear to you, Jane, that's the first time in my life I've ever forgotten protection."

"I believe you."

He launched himself from the bed. "I can't believe you're so calm about this. Are you on the pill?"

"No."

"Then why aren't you freaking out?"

"Because…" She couldn't very well tell him the truth. *Because it's you. Because I love you.* Hell, that realization freaked her out far more than the idea of a baby that might or might not be on the way. How had she fallen in love with Eric Sorensen? But she had… She could feel the truth of it in her bones. He made sense of all the madness in her world. "Because the idea of having a child doesn't scare me. I don't lead a wild life, despite my hair."

"Janie…" He sat on the edge of the bed and dropped his head into his hands. "You would be an amazing mother. But look at this from my point of view. My life is crazy. Most of time, I work with Travis in some hellhole outside of the US. It's no kind of life to bring a kid into."

"I wouldn't ask you to do anything you didn't want to, Eric."

"But if I had a kid—if we had a kid—I would want to do everything. I'd push you in ways you can't even imagine now."

"I think you've pushed me quite a bit already, and I haven't complained."

"You don't understand. I'd never let my child be raised by someone else. If you have my kid, you have me. And no sane woman wants that." He laughed, but it was a harsh, hollow sound.

"I do."

He stared at her. "You do what?"

"Want you. Of course, I may not be sane, so maybe you're right on that score."

He took a breath, started to speak, stopped.

"I want you, Eric." She ran a finger down his cheek. "I know you think it's just adrenaline, or gratitude, or something like that. And I can't prove any different until our lives get back to normal, but you have to trust me. I couldn't wait to go out to dinner with you on our first real date forever ago, and I'm still hoping to get a chance to do that. In the extremely unlikely event that I get pregnant, it won't be me who has to change."

"You really mean that."

"Absolutely." It was as close as she could get to admitting the truth.

"And what if I got hurt, like my father? What if I couldn't provide for you? For the baby? I'd feel like utter shit."

"Your father wasn't a soldier. What happened to him could happen to anyone. And if you were injured…" She ran a finger over the wound. "If it were so serious that you couldn't work for HSE, you'd find something else to do. It's like a mission. If your first plan fails, you go to a second. You're not your father, and I'm not your mother. Or *my* mother, for that matter. I have a good job. I can support myself, a baby, even *you* if it came to that."

"Oh, hell." He scrubbed a hand over his face. Beneath the brown dye, the true gold of his beard was beginning to show.

"What?"

"You don't have a job. The inside man? The American investor? It was Clive Handler. Bryan gave him up. We got it confirmed last night while we were watching for you. Dani's in the hospital in New York, so Trey took it upon himself to pay Clive a little visit. He had one foot out the door, passport in hand."

"Clive?" She barely managed to force the word out.

"I know it's hard to believe, baby, but he was ready to run when Trey caught him. One-way ticket to Cuba. Who knows where he planned to go from there. But it's a damned good place to disappear right now. Trey…persuaded him to admit everything. The Department of Justice is going to have a few words with him, and then I imagine Homeland Security will have their say as well."

"And Ruth? Please tell me Ruth wasn't part of this."

"We're not sure. She's certainly been helping him for a very long time, and it's hard to see how she couldn't have at least had an idea. She controlled all the finances, including the money that was coming in and going out from the Warlock project.

"But Janie, none of this is on you. AHI will be dissolved, but you'll find another job in no time."

"What do you mean it's not on me? AHI was my first job out of grad school. It's the only job I've ever had. Who will hire me now, tainted by this?"

"It will sort itself out, I promise. People will realize that Clive was operating on his own. The qualifications that made him hire you in the first place still stand. You're still a great scientist and a great teacher. You developed that schizophrenia medication — that alone will make people sit up and take notice."

"And what about Dani? AHI was her internship. An internship is supposed to get you a job, not turn you into a pariah."

Eric was silent for a long time. Too long.

"You said she was okay. That she was in the hospital." Jane looked up at him. "What haven't you told me?"

"I was on the phone with Nash while you were in the shower. He says she's suffering from amnesia. It's the brain injury. She remembers that she used to work at a lab, but she doesn't remember her exact position. She doesn't remember the kidnapping or her brother's death. Her parents had to tell her he had died, but the doctors didn't want her to hear any details, so they just told her that both she and Alvaro had been in an accident. She's having some trouble speaking, too."

"Am I… Will they let me see her?"

Eric pulled her into his arms and settled her against his chest. "Right now, they are saying it's a bad idea for anyone from that time to see her. That's why they kicked Trey out. Jake's with her, protecting her, because she never met him. They want to give her a few weeks before she starts seeing you guys again to let her mind clear up."

"What will she do if she can't remember? All that studying. All that school."

"If she never remembers her academics, she'll turn out to be brilliant at something else. She may have lost her knowledge, but not her capacity for learning and growing. You just finished telling me that if I couldn't work for HSE I'd find other work. Have the same faith in her."

"I do." She sucked in a breath. "I do."

He stroked her hair. "It really wouldn't bother you? Being pregnant?"

Where to even start? She gathered the sheet around her and curled her knees up beneath her chin. "When I was twenty, I went to an ob-gyn and asked for a hysterectomy. I was old enough to vote, old enough to smoke; I figured I was old enough to know I didn't want children."

Eric pulled her tighter into the heat of his body. "Oh, sweetheart. That must have been so damned hard."

"It doesn't horrify you?"

"Baby, you're the most relentlessly logical person I've ever met. My guess is you figured the chances of having a schizophrenic child were better than average and you didn't want a child to suffer the way your mom did."

He understood. Of course he did. It made her tear up. Damn, emotions were a pain in the ass.

"The doctor disagreed. He said if I didn't want to have a

kid, I could use the same methods as other women. I resented him for a while, but it turned out not to be a big deal. I wasn't all that active, sexually speaking."

"But you're not afraid now?"

"No. I'm almost past the usual age for schizophrenia onset. My child would still be more likely to have the disorder than a child whose family had never been touched by mental illness, but not so high as if I had it myself. And I think—I hope—that changes in society at large as well as in the medical community mean that life would be easier today than it was for my mom."

She could feel him behind her, gearing up to make a point, and she tensed.

"Janie, I know you're logical—"

"So are you, Mr. 'memorize the opposing team's statistics.'"

"Well, yeah. Okay. But I am being serious here. This isn't logic. It's more like faith. I need you to believe me even though it doesn't make sense."

She twisted slightly so she could look up into his face. "What is it?"

"I—"

A banging on the connecting door interrupted him, and it popped open to reveal Travis. "We're found. Time to hit it."

"Shit." Eric was out of the bed in a shot and pulling on his clothes. He tossed Jane a shirt and sweats but urged her down to the floor next to the bed before she could get them on. Her legs tangled in the sweats, and she peered up anxiously over the edge of the bed as she tried to pull them on.

Glass broke in the other room, and bullets pinged and crashed. Travis hustled Helene and Fritz into Jane's room, and they huddled together. "Travis, stay with them," Eric said. "Marco, try to get a viable position." Eric bolted to the doorway between the two rooms, using the frame for protection, minimal though it was. He fired a few shots through the window of the other room.

"How the hell did they find us?"

"Whole fucking country's controlled by the cartels," Travis said. "You know it as well as I do."

"Yeah, I had just hoped we'd have a few hours of peace."

A second later, Mac shouted from the other room. "Fuck! Grenade! Get 'em down!"

Travis landed hard on all of them, and an enormous blast echoed through the room. The wall between the two rooms listed to the side, and chunks of ceiling rained down while dust choked the air.

"Mac! Mac! You okay?"

"We gotta get the fuck out. This place is a death trap." Mac ushered Helene and Fritz through a hole in the ruined wall.

"Agreed. Travis, grab the axe. Take them through to the next room. We don't want to come out the door of this one, either—they're bound to guess we're in here."

"No shit." Mac urged the kids down behind a bed for safety.

"I'll take point once we're outside," said Eric. "Jane, you follow me. Travis, bring the crew out next, and Marco, keep them off our six. Low and tight, everyone. There's a line of cars to the left, around the corner of the building. That's where we're going. We get a reasonable distance out, Mac, you fall back, and Marco, take to the roof."

"Got it." Travis hauled the duffel Jane hadn't even noticed him bringing into the room close to them and then, with a curt order to stay covered, pulled out an axe and began hacking a hole in the wall next to the bed. In no time, he'd cut a small crawlway into the next room. Helene's eyes went wide when the axe head slammed through the cheap wallboard.

"That's why you don't stay in fancy places when you're gonna have to go for the quick out," Travis teased. "They have things like firewalls and insulation." He went through and held out a hand. "C'mon, let's go."

Helene and Fritz went first, followed by Mac. Jane was halfway through the hole, her head in the second room, when she heard another enormous explosion.

"Fuck, fuck, fuck," said Eric behind her. "Go!"

Jane squeezed through, tearing open the scabs over the wounds on her feet in the process. Eric followed immediately.

"Marco's already out and on the roof for cover," Mac said. "Let's hope they don't notice us. Bathroom window?"

"On it," said Travis, swinging the axe as he ran for the bathroom. Helene and Fritz followed, but Eric swung Jane up into his arms when she tried to stand.

"What was that?"

"Second grenade. We thought you were through already. I'm sorry, Janie. I'll get you out of this, I swear."

"I know you will." She meant every word. Eric would get her out or die trying.

"I swear."

"No, really, I know it." And he deserved to know why. "I love you."

THE WORDS HIT him in the solar plexus. Would she never stop surprising him?

"Helluva time to tell me." He took a deep breath and pressed a kiss to her lips. "But in case you hadn't figured it out, I love you, too. And if you try to tell me it's not logical,

I'll tell you it's a whole hell of a lot more logical than you even noticing me."

"No—"

Gunfire from the next room stopped her from speaking. "We are not having this argument right now," Eric said, but he could feel a laugh bubbling up despite the danger. Inside the bathroom, Travis had hacked the window frame out and enlarged the space. A steady stream of gunfire sounded all around them—Mac and Marco at work, keeping their enemies busy.

Travis went through the hole first. Then Helene lifted Fritz out to him, and she herself followed.

Eric boosted Jane to the window, and she crawled through. On the other side, Travis helped her down and she knelt in the dirt. Why did she always end up barefoot at the worst times? Eric dropped to

the ground beside her, lifted her into his arms again, and jerked his head at Travis. The small group ran as quietly as possible along the side of the building toward the front, and the parking lot.

At the corner, Travis held up a hand for them to stay. He popped his head out, took in the situation, glanced back at Eric, and then dashed out toward the SUV parked next to the manager's office.

Travis got the vehicle started, but that drew the attention of the attackers. They turned their guns on him as he ducked and put the car in gear. As Eric watched, three bullets hit the side of the SUV, but the change of focus left the gunmen vulnerable and four of them went down almost immediately under fire from Mac and Marco.

That left, as far as Eric could see, two. Good odds.

"Let's go!" Travis shouted, slewing the SUV around so that

the side doors faced their little crew of refugees. As the two gunmen jumped into a Jeep driven by a third, Mac, Helene, and Fritz stuffed themselves into the backseat. Marco was already in the process of stealing a second vehicle, into which Eric tossed Jane. After firing off a volley of shots at the Jeep, he swung himself into the car, and Marco took off, following Travis.

"Where are we going?" Jane asked.

"Mexico City. To the embassy. We'll be ahead of schedule, but nothing to be done for that right now. It's still our best bet."

"Split," Marco said, peeling off from behind Travis. The Jeep stayed on their tail.

"Tell Travis to get his ass to Mexico City. We can handle these guys."

Marco relayed the message. Eric checked the magazine in his pistol. "What else do we have?"

"Not a lot. But neither do they. You want to try to outrun them, or take them down here?"

"Here. If we damage the car, we're in worse shape. Find a choice position."

"Will do."

A few minutes later, Marco pulled off the road at the top of a hill into a small copse of trees. "This is as good as it's gonna get."

"Right. Jane, stay down."

The Jeep had been on their tail for most of the trip, but it had dropped back slightly after its occupants had failed to shoot out their tires. Eric couldn't see it, and that made him damned nervous. Where the hell were they? What was taking them so long?

Just as he was about to venture out of their cover, he heard it. He steadied his pistol on the trunk of the car and waited for them to come into view. Marco had already taken his rifle and climbed a tree, settling himself in for a long shot. The Jeep had been in view for less than a second when one of Marco's bullets took out the engine. A second went through the windshield, and it was dead in the road. Eric signaled for Marco to stay in the tree and approached the Jeep. Inside, he found the driver dead and one man with his arms out the window.

"Open the door using the outside handle and get out," he ordered. The man obeyed. "Where's your fucking boss? Where's Velasquez?"

The man looked past Eric and smiled. "Where's your girlfriend?"

Eric whipped around to see Velasquez holding a pistol pressed against Jane's temple. No wonder the Jeep had taken so long—they'd stopped to let him out. And while both Eric and Marco had been focused on the Jeep, he'd snuck up on Jane.

"Say good-bye, asshole," Velasquez said.

"You know the minute you hurt her, you're dead."

"I'm dead anyway after this clusterfuck. So—"

Jane dropped to the ground, pulling him off balance, and Eric and Marco fired in unison. Velasquez's head exploded, blood and bone and brain matter flying everywhere.

"If I were you," Marco called from his perch to the surviving gunman, "I'd stay very fucking still."

Eric was beside Jane in an instant. She was shaking, covered in the muck of death, but alive. Alive and relatively uninjured. He gathered her to him. "My God, Janie. Why didn't you call out?"

"I didn't know he was there. By the time I saw him, he had the gun. I just kept hoping he would let me out of the car so I could kick him or headbutt him or something. I figured he would want to show off a little. And I knew if he would do that, you'd be able to kill him."

"I'm so sorry. So sorry it had to come to this. I wanted to take him back to the States for you and throw him in jail. I know that's your kind of justice."

And yet again, she surprised him. "Prison will do for Clive. In fact, I can't wait to see him put on trial. But Velasquez . . . I'd never have felt truly safe, even if he were locked away. He'd forever be the monster in the closet, waiting to get out."

He dropped his forehead to hers. "My bloodthirsty little love."

She grinned and his whole body lightened. "Don't you forget it."

EPILOGUE

Jane looked up from the papers in her lap when she heard the key in the lock. Quibble, the patchwork cat she and Eric had adopted the month before, leaped from her perch on the back of the sofa and headed for the front door. A moment later, Eric appeared, Quibble riding on his shoulder.

"Working again?" he asked, bending down to kiss her. The cat scrambled away, affronted at the lack of attention, and Eric's laugh rumbled against Jane's lips. "You work too hard," he said. He lifted the papers from her lap and set them down on the coffee table, then settled next to her.

"You're a fine one to talk." She ran a hand through his hair, and damp strands clung to her fingers. "You even showered at headquarters."

"Yeah, I had time before Nash could see me for a debrief anyway." He took her hand, playing with her fingers. "I ran into Trey."

"How's he doing?"

"He says he's fine."

"But you don't believe him."

He gave her a half smile. "He's wrapped almost as tight as you used to be. Bringing the kid's body back was good, but I don't know that he'll ever forgive himself for the shooting." It had taken nearly a month to straighten out all the jurisdictional and logistical issues with the Mexican government. When Alvaro's body had at last been released, Trey had insisted on being the one to go get him. He'd accompanied the body back to the United States and had helped the Peraltas make arrangements to take their son home to Argentina for burial. He would also, no doubt, have confessed his role in the boy's death had not the terms of HSE's agreement with Homeland Security forbidden it.

Everyone involved in Jane's rescue, the destruction of the lab in Mexico, or the attempted recovery of the data from Bryan's experiments was expressly forbidden from revealing any of the details of their mission. As for the data itself, Bryan's thumb drive had been accidentally crushed in transit when Nash's men had brought him back from Texas, and the cloud servers were mysteriously erased, leaving no way for anyone to replicate the work. A number of officials were less than happy about that, but Jane had thanked Nash profusely enough that he became visibly uncomfortable and claimed no knowledge of how either of those events had occurred.

Although Nash's agreement with Homeland Security held no power over Jane, she had no desire to talk about that period of her life. And Dani could not. Even now, three months out of the hospital, she still suffered the effects of her injury. She had chosen to stay in New York rather than returning to Argentina with her parents, but she had no recollection of her life as a scientist, and even before her scar had healed she had gone back to modeling. She had trouble speaking, and the doctors were fiddling with the cocktail of drugs she took to control her anxiety and occasional seizures.

It had taken some time, but Jane had slowly become friends with the new Dani, as had Eric. Trey, on the other hand, had never even visited her. He claimed not to want to traumatize her, but Jane was pretty sure it was guilt.

"He feels responsible for Dani, too, don't you think?"

"I do. He won't visit her, but LeRon says she's flagged and anything that shows up about her goes straight to Trey."

Of course, Jane shared that responsibility. The job she had taken paid significantly less than others in her field, but she was working with a lab trying to develop drugs and practices for PTSD. In her spare time, she spent hours researching traumatic brain injuries, how they happened, their effects, and therapies.

To the people in her new lab, she was just another scientist. They knew — everyone knew, after Clive and Bryan had been sent to prison at ADX Florence in Colorado for kidnapping and providing aid to a terrorist organization — that she had been through some tough events. They assumed, however, that her life before the kidnapping was very similar to her current one.

It was not. As she rested her head on Eric's shoulder and his strong fingers massaged her neck, she thought about how fundamentally she had changed. No, she hadn't gotten pregnant in Mexico, but Eric had moved in with her the day they returned, and shortly afterward they had adopted Quibble. Jane was pretty sure he was working his way up to a proposal, though she couldn't figure out why he was waiting. It wasn't as if she was going to say no. But Eric liked to do things at his own pace, so she was content to wait as long as he came home to her after every mission.

Here, finally, were all the pieces she had never even known the puzzle of her life was missing. With Eric's arms around her and Quibble mewing for dinner — the cat had come by her name honestly, since there was not a single thing she did not opine on loudly — Jane was happy. She tilted her head and pressed a kiss into Eric's neck.

"Thank you for loving me."

A laugh rumbled under her ear. "Easiest mission ever."

ACKNOWLEDGMENTS

THIS BOOK WAS written at an especially difficult time in my life, so first I'd like to say thank you to everyone I know for putting up with me while it was going on. But in particular, I owe both my editor, Leis Pederson, for fixing all the things I messed up, and to my agent, Jessica Faust, for riding herd on everything I couldn't.

When you're writing a book about drugs and their development, it's handy to have a friend in the business. Mine asked not to be named, so I'll just say she's awesome and leave it at that. Any mistakes or liberties taken with how labs work and how drugs are developed are mine. When you're writing about Mexican drugs, it's also handy to have a copy editor who has a friend in Mexico City to check on the language for you. All copy editors deserve awards, but this was above and beyond!

And of course, many, many thanks to those of you who have read my books, liked my books, reviewed my books, and stuck around to find out more about the people who live in my head. Without you, there would be no books at all.

And last (but never least), my deepest thanks go to my husband. He knows why.

ABOUT THE AUTHOR

LAURA K. CURTIS gave up a life writing dry academic papers for writing decidedly less dry short crime stories and novel-length romantic suspense and contemporary romance. A member of RWA, MWA, ITW, and Sisters in Crime, she has trouble settling into one genre. She has published four romantic suspense novels (*Twisted*, 2013; *Lost*, 2014; *Echoes*, 2015; and *Mind Games*, 2015), two contemporary romance novels (*Toying With His Affections*, 2014; *Gaming the System*, 2015), and a host of short stories, many with a supernatural bent.

www.ingramcontent.com/pod-product-compliance
Lightning Source LLC
Chambersburg PA
CBHW051645180726
48284CB00006B/1866